Prai... JOANNE PENCE's

ANGIE AMALFI MYSTERIES

"Joanne Pence provides laughter, love, and cold chills."
Carolyn Hart

"If you love books by Diane Mott Davidson or Denise Dietz, you will love this series. It's as refreshing as lemon sherbet and just as delicious."
Under the Covers

"A rollicking good time . . . murder, mayhem, food, and fashion . . . Joanne Pence serves it all up."
Butler County Post

"A winner . . . Angie is a character unlike any other found in the genre."
Santa Rosa Press Democrat

"[A] great series . . . [Pence] titillates the senses, provides a satisfying read."
Crescent Blues Reviews

"Joanne Pence just gets better and better."
Mystery News

Angie Amalfi Mysteries by
Joanne Pence

Red Hot Murder
Courting Disaster
Two Cooks A-Killing
If Cooks Could Kill
Bell, Cook, and Candle
To Catch a Cook
A Cook in Time
Cooks Overboard
Cook's Night Out
Cooking Most Deadly
Cooking Up Trouble
Too Many Cooks
Something's Cooking

COOK'S NIGHT OUT

AN ANGIE AMALFI MYSTERY

JOANNE PENCE

AVON BOOKS

An Imprint of HarperCollinsPublishers

This is a work of fiction. Names, characters, places, and incidents are products of the author's imagination or are used fictitiously and are not to be construed as real. Any resemblance to actual events, locales, organizations, or persons, living or dead, is entirely coincidental.

AVON BOOKS
An Imprint of HarperCollins*Publishers*
10 East 53rd Street
New York, New York 10022-5299

Copyright © 1997 by Joanne Pence
ISBN-13: 978-0-06-104396-3
ISBN-10: 0-06-104396-6
www.avonbooks.com

First Avon Books paperback printing: March 2006
First HarperPaperbacks printing: January 1998

Avon Trademark Reg. U.S. Pat. Off. and in Other Countries, Marca Registrada, Hecho en U.S.A.
HarperCollins® is a registered trademark of HarperCollins Publishers Inc.

Printed in the U.S.A.

20 19 18 17 16 15 14 13 12 11 10 9 8 7

To Lewis and Loretta, with love

ACKNOWLEDGMENTS

My sincere thanks for technical assistance to Sgt. Michael J. Seligsohn of the San Francisco Community College District Police Department, gaming expert witness John Campbell, and attorney Frank Snyder; to Kate Moore for information on chocolate making; and to Ed Moose for one of North Beach's finest restaurants.

My apologies for any errors, omissions, or license taken with the facts for purposes of the story.

COOK'S
NIGHT OUT

PROLOGUE

Not even muggers went to San Francisco's Ocean Beach late at night. A ribbon of dark, grainy sand edged by a cement wall, it boasted a frigid wind and a treacherous undertow known to snatch those who wandered too near the water's edge, suck them out to sea, and keep them churning beneath the surface until they could hold their breath no longer.

It was definitely not your basic fun-in-the-sun type of California beach.

That was why Homicide Inspector Luis Calderon, an eighteen-year veteran of the force, had been surprised to be awakened in the middle of the night and told that a body had been found out there. Calderon and his partner, Bo Benson, were the on-call inspectors that week.

On the beach, two patrol officers huddled together, their flashlights jerking in time with the stamping of their feet against the cold. A short distance away the victim's body lay sprawled on the sand, face turned up to the moonless night.

As Calderon slogged toward them, one of the policemen moved forward to meet him. "Officer Kellogg, sir. Richmond station."

"Calderon, Homicide. You touch anything?"

"No, sir."

Calderon walked past him without another word. He stopped about six feet from the victim and took a quick inventory. White male, early sixties, balding, overweight. Gunshot wound to the chest.

"Did you walk around here much?" Calderon asked, searching the sand for signs of a fight or scuffle.

"We did not, sir," the other patrolman answered. "I'm Officer Rosenberg. We were careful to disturb as little as possible, sir."

Calderon looked up in surprise at the second "sir." The young patrolman stood with his chin up, shoulders square, hat and uniform starched and spotless as the day he got out of the police academy. His partner was the same. Must be a new breed of cop, Calderon thought. He couldn't keep up with the changes anymore. Casual, formal; liberal, conservative; melting pot, diversity. Up was down and down was up. Hell, he was too old for all that. He turned back to the body.

Inspector Bo Benson, Calderon's younger partner, had checked out the area quickly before joining them. "Nothing out of the ordinary," he said.

"Out here, who can tell?" Calderon muttered. "I hate the beach. Hate all this sand. Looks like cat litter."

He glanced at Kellogg. "So who called in the report to the station?"

"No one, sir. We heard there was a gang of kids causing trouble out here, so we came by to investigate. When we arrived, they were gone. That's when we discovered the body."

Calderon grunted, his most common form of communication.

"Did you look for identification?" Benson asked.

"We touched him just enough to know that he was cold."

Calderon put on his latex gloves, then grimaced as he stooped to go through the jacket pockets. The outside ones were empty, but the inside breast pocket held three sheets of paper. "I'll be damned," he said, then handed the papers to Benson, who had also put on gloves. "I haven't seen any of these in years."

Benson studied the columns of numbers. "Tally sheets. Who bet what, and when, and the numbers bet on. Luis, my man, I'd say we got us a dead numbers runner." He put the sheets in a small plastic bag.

Calderon had to strain to lift the dead man's hip high enough to work his hand under it and reach the back pocket. When his hand appeared again, he held a wallet. He slowly stood up, his knees protesting loudly.

The wallet was thick with cash, over six hundred dollars, but there was no driver license, no credit cards, no ID. "So much for robbery as a motive," Calderon said, as much to himself as anyone else, since the truth of his statement was obvious.

"Luis." Benson's voice had a strange edge to it. Calderon looked up sharply.

"Look at his mouth. What's that?"

When Calderon had jostled the body to pull out the wallet, the victim's head flopped to one side and his lips parted. There was something yellow in his mouth. "Go ahead," Calderon said, giving the okay to the younger man to bend over and push down the victim's lower lip.

Kellogg and Rosenberg also moved in closer.

"It's paper," Benson said. "Yellow notepaper with green lines." Using two fingers, he reached into the mouth, took hold of one end of a folded-up strip of paper, and pulled it out. It was soggy with saliva and postmortem fluids that had bubbled up.

Benson carefully unwadded it. One side was blank. He turned it over. "Looks like a telephone number," he said. Then he brought his flashlight in closer. "Damn, but it looks familiar for some reason."

Calderon took the paper, peered at it, then stepped away from the two patrolmen. Benson followed. Calderon stared out at the waves lightly lapping the shore, listening to the faint whistle of the wind. "It's familiar, all right," he said quietly.

Benson waited.

"Can't you place it yet?" Calderon asked. "We've called it enough times over the years."

A slight tightening of Benson's lips betrayed his tension. "Someone in Homicide?"

Calderon carefully bagged the evidence, keeping his expression completely neutral. "It's Paavo Smith's home phone number."

CHAPTER

ONE

Angelina Amalfi flung open the window over the kitchen sink. After two days of cooking with chocolate, the mouthwatering, luscious, inviting smell of it made her sick.

That was the price one must pay, she supposed, to become a famous chocolatier.

She found an old fan in the closet, put it on the kitchen table, and turned the dial to high. The comforting aroma of home cooking wafting out from a kitchen was one thing, but the smell of Willy Wonka's chocolate factory was quite another.

She'd been trying out intricate, elegant recipes for chocolate candies, searching for the perfect confection on which to build a business to call her own. Her kitchen was filled with truffles, nut bouchées, exotic fudges, and butter creams.

So far, she'd divulged her business plans only to Paavo, the man for whom she had plans of a very different nature. She was going to have to let someone else know soon, though, or she wouldn't have any room left in the kitchen to cook. She didn't want to start eating the calorie-oozing, waistline-expanding chocolates out of sheer enjoyment—her taste tests were another thing altogether and totally justifiable, she reasoned—and throwing the chocolates away had to be sinful.

She'd think of something to do with them soon.

Right now, though, she had to air out the apartment. She didn't want Paavo distracted by the heavy, cloyingly sweet odor.

Leaving the gale-force breeze whipping through the kitchen, she went off to shower and dress for his visit. He was working late at the Homicide Bureau but had promised he'd stop by.

After a liberal splash of Fleur, she wriggled into a slinky purple silk jumpsuit. *Ah, Inspector,* she thought, taking a look in the mirror, *tonight we do some serious soul-searching.*

Along with whatever else they might decide to search.

She combed and fluffed her hair, then put on long, dangling amethyst earrings. Recently, she'd spent nearly two weeks living at Paavo's house trying to get over a truly frightening experience. Since coming back to her own apartment, she often thought of that time with him and how wonderful having him come home to her each night had been. The possibility of a permanent arrangement along those lines was exciting. It was getting-down-to-business time about their relationship and their future.

Paavo's loud rap sounded at the door.

She smoothed the jumpsuit over her hips. No time like the present.

With a big smile, she swung open the door. One look at him, though, and her smile vanished.

Usually, Paavo was a man adept at not showing his

emotions. He was tall—at six-two almost a foot taller than she was in her bare feet. Of course, she was rarely barefoot, since she loved shoes, especially those with high heels and platform soles. He was broad-shouldered, narrow-hipped, and high-cheekboned, and he had the lightest, most beautiful blue eyes she'd ever seen on a man. To her amazement, most people looked at him and saw a tough cop. She suspected that perception had more to do with their guilty consciences than with his looks.

At the moment, though, the cop was frowning fiercely. Even as he stepped into the apartment, shut the door, and kissed her, she knew all was not well. "What's wrong, Paavo?"

"Nothing worth talking about." His gaze might have been admiring her jumpsuit and all it covered, but his mind was clearly elsewhere. "It's been a long, ugly day."

"Come and sit." She led him to the sofa. "Have you eaten?"

"I'm not hungry. Just some coffee would be fine."

She knew him better than that. He was the type to become so engrossed in his work he would forget to eat. If she were that way, she wouldn't have to be perpetually watching her diet. Her philosophy was that food helped make big troubles into little ones—and she did all she could to avoid big troubles.

She prepared a sandwich for him of ham, turkey, Sonoma jack, and avocado overflowing on thickly sliced sourdough French bread, with a glass of Dos Equis amber beer. When they first met, she never bought beer. But then she learned that sipping a glass of chardonnay or pink zinfandel wasn't exactly his cup of tea. Now she always kept a six-pack in the refrigerator.

She poured herself some coffee and sat in the

antique yellow Hepplewhite chair beside the sofa. After he took a couple of bites, she could almost see him realize how hungry he was. Maybe all he needed to put aside thoughts of the bad day he'd had was a little food in his stomach. She was anxious, after all, to begin talking about their living arrangements . . . and then some.

"Better?" she asked, eying the almost demolished sandwich.

He finished the last bite, then nodded. "Much better."

"That's good." She smiled. "You looked so upset when you first arrived, I thought something really troubling had happened at work."

He took a long swallow of the beer. "It did."

That was *not* good news. "It did?"

"I can hardly believe it." He leaned back against the sofa. "You might remember a few weeks ago I arrested a guy, Peewee Clayton, for the murder of his girlfriend. Nice guy . . . if you like the type who gambles, does drugs, and kills women with beer bottles."

"That horrible little man! Of course I remember him." She shuddered at the memory of lurid newspaper articles about the murder. "You tracked him down fast. It was an open-and-shut case, as I recall."

"Everything but an eyewitness," Paavo said. "We had good evidence. Great evidence, in fact. Until today. Today was the preliminary hearing. All I had to do was swear to the fact that the blouse the victim was wearing—the one stained with both her blood and Peewee's—plus the beer bottle that he'd used to kill her were found and tagged by me at the crime scene."

"That's normal procedure, right?" Angie asked, propping her chin on her hand.

"Right." He reached for the Dos Equis and emptied it into his glass, as if stalling would cause his next words to make more sense to him. "The trouble was, when

Hanover Judd, the assistant DA on the case, held up the victim's blouse, it wasn't the right one."

"What?" The disbelief in Angie's voice echoed his own. And he'd been in court to witness the fiasco.

"The blouse had been switched. Same with the beer bottle."

"What do you mean, switched?" she asked.

"They weren't the ones at the murder scene, the ones with Peewee's fingerprints and Sarah Ann's hair, skin, and blood all over them."

"I've never heard of such a thing. I thought trial evidence was locked up tight," Angie said.

"It is, and every time it moves, a property tag is signed." He rubbed his brow in frustration.

"So how did it get switched?"

He lifted weary eyes to her. "I spent the afternoon trying to answer that question. No one could figure it out." He stopped speaking as his mind replayed the ugly accusations that had been hurled back and forth between the DA, the assistant DA, the crime scene investigators, the Property Control Section officers, the laboratory, and Homicide. "Of course, the press showed up." Disgust and bafflement filled his voice. "It'll be front page news tomorrow. And some prisoners' rights group is demanding that every case that's been tried in the past year in the city be tossed out on the grounds that no one can trust the evidence presented by the DA's office."

She had rarely seen him so troubled by the internal machinations of his job. He bent forward, elbows on knees, hands clasped, his shoulders hunched and tense.

This wasn't the best time to bring up the possibility of permanent changes in their relationship. Instead, she moved from the chair to sit beside him on the sofa and began massaging his neck and shoulders. "I think I've got the picture," she said softly, soothingly.

"I don't think anyone will go so far as to throw out any old cases." He stared at the far wall as if it might offer some solution. "But any hint of evidence tampering is extremely serious. As far as the criminal justice system goes, this is every DA and homicide inspector's worst nightmare."

"And I can feel every bit of that nightmare in the knots in your neck and shoulders," Angie said, massaging them more forcefully.

"You know what the worst part was?" Paavo said, looking over his shoulder at her.

"What?"

"The smirk on Clayton's face." He faced forward again. "Clayton knew he was going to get off. With no evidence, the judge threw out the case."

"You think this was an inside job?" She spoke the words almost in a whisper.

"That's what everyone's afraid of," he said. "That a cop's gone bad."

She stopped rubbing his shoulders, and he could feel the cold shudder that rippled through her. She understood, he knew, that a cop gone bad put everyone else in danger. Sometimes on purpose.

"Tell me about your day," he said quickly, to change the subject. Having Angie worry about any of this was the last thing he wanted to do. "How's the candy-making business?"

"Not good."

"Oh?" He glanced at her. Angie rarely sounded downhearted.

"In order to compete in a very full market, I've got to develop a new confection that's different, yet appealing enough that people will be clamoring for it. I haven't come up with anything like that yet."

"You'll find something. Give yourself time."

"When I do, I'll write magazine and newspaper articles

about it, making my candy wonderfully popular." Her hands slowed and became languorous as she dreamed. "Maybe I'll even convince Oprah that it's the one thing worth breaking a diet for."

He heard the wistfulness in her voice. He'd heard it before when Angie had come up with other great adventures on the road to fame and fortune. "Great disasters" was more descriptive of the results, unfortunately. But there was no way he'd ever try to discourage her. After all, people had once laughed at Bill Gates and his Windows.

As she continued with the shoulder massage, he realized the tension was draining away from his neck muscles. He also realized that as she took his mind off the ugliness at work, a whole new kind of tension was building up within him.

"There's one thing, though," she said, "that troubles me very much."

"Troubles you? We can't have that, Miss Amalfi." He turned around and faced her. "What is it?"

"I haven't figured out what to call my creation," she cried.

"Ah, nameless chocolates." He drew her into his arms. "Most trying."

"The name needs to make my chocolates sound special, classy, inviting . . . ," she began.

He eased her closer.

". . . and delicious." She gave up trying, or wanting, to talk about candy and wrapped her arms around his neck.

He kissed her. "I've got it."

"Oh, my, but you certainly do, Inspector," she murmured, her fingers raking his hair as she snuggled closer.

"Call your candy the *angelina*."

CHAPTER

TWO

The taxicab swung into the red no-parking zone and braked hard. Angie lurched forward in the seat, her arms tightening around the boxes of chocolates on her lap. The top box began to slide, but she managed to stop it before it hit the floor.

"That's the place, lady," the driver said, pointing at a two-story building that looked as though it had been standing since before the big 1906 earthquake. It had probably once been a small hotel or, considering that this area used to be the roughest part of San Francisco's Barbary Coast waterfront, a brothel.

The front of the building was pale gray, with the gingerbread trim along the roof and over the doors and windows painted a deep red and navy blue. Six evenly spaced windows paraded across the second story. A bold navy and gray striped awning shaded the first story, which housed the Senseless Beauty Café and Pâtisserie, on one side, and the Random Acts of Kindness Mission, on the other. The names reminded her of a saying she'd seen on bumper stickers and coffee mugs.

"I never imagined a rescue mission would look like that," Angie said, juggling the boxes and her purse while trying to pull up on the door handle. The cab driver frowned, got out and opened the passenger door, then took the stack of candy boxes from her.

"Isn't the mission lovely?" she said, climbing out of the cab.

"If that's a rescue mission, my taxi's a Rolls-Royce," the cabbie murmured.

Angie fished through her purse for her money. "I hope Reverend Hodge is in this afternoon," she said as she counted out the fare plus a tip. "I do so want to meet him."

"Gee. This might be your lucky day." Angie thought he sounded a little sarcastic, but then, since he didn't know about the Random Acts of Kindness Mission, he probably didn't know Reverend Hodge, either. She lifted a box from the top of the stack he still held.

"For you, if you like homemade chocolates," she said, tucking it under his arm.

"Oh . . . hey, that's real nice, lady. Thanks a lot." She took the remaining boxes from him.

As she walked toward the mission he called, "Hope you find your reverend, and he's able to give you what you're looking for." With that, he hopped into his cab and started the engine.

"What I'm . . . ?" Angie was puzzled. "I'm not looking for anything." But the cab was already pulling out into traffic.

Angie was on the Embarcadero, the street skimming the waterfront from the northeastern edge of the city southward. On the east side were the piers that jutted out to the bay; on the west, a hodgepodge of construction that ranged from exclusive apartments and condominiums to factories and empty lots. The mission was located to the south of Market Street, in an area once filled with warehouses, canneries, factories, and cheap housing for the workers. It was undergoing a massive redevelopment, with newly built or renovated apartments, shops, and boutiques. Even the new Giants baseball stadium was expected to be built along the waterfront there, with a ferry dock just past the outfield fence.

Angie pushed open the mission's door, then stopped. It was like walking into a lavish bed-and-breakfast. The parlorlike entry hall had a sofa and elegant armchairs in a cozy seating arrangement. To the right were stairs to the second floor; straight ahead was an office. A short, older woman, her hair in a perfectly coiffed and lacquered French roll, wearing a pale pink Chanel suit and bone-colored Ferragamo high heels, stood up from the small cherrywood secretary in the office and walked toward her. "Hello. I'm Mrs. Sheila Chatsworth," she said, extending her hand to Angie. "May I help you?" Her voice was cultured and reserved.

"I'd like to meet Reverend Hodge," Angie said, unsuccessfully trying to balance the boxes to shake hands. She gave up before dropping them all.

Mrs. Chatsworth frowned and pulled back her hand, but then she made her eyes go soft and friendly once again. "Do you have an appointment, dear?"

"Well, no, I . . ." Out of the corner of her eye, Angie noticed that beyond the French doors to the left was a dining room. She turned her head and stared in amazement. The room was quite large—the building must have once housed a restaurant. But instead of the crowded cafeterialike setting she had expected, there were only a few tables, each set with a rose-colored tablecloth and napkins, white china, silverware, and glass goblets.

Forcing her attention back to the woman, Angie said, "I, uh, I brought a donation."

"Yes, I see," Mrs. Chatsworth replied, her smile rapidly growing more strained and forced. "You're here to practice a random act of kindness."

"You could say that, I guess." The chocolates grew heavier with each passing minute.

"Let me see if Reverend Hodge is free. Wait right there, please." Mrs. Chatsworth disappeared down the long hallway that ran between the front office and the dining room.

Shifting the boxes slightly, Angie stepped closer to the dining room and peeked inside. In a corner she saw two younger women at a table, talking and laughing. Dressed in DKNY and Ann Taylor clothes, they surely weren't here for assistance. Where were the people who needed help?

She inched closer to the kitchen doors at the back of the room. There were no sounds and, more important, no smells of food being cooked or prepared.

Something didn't seem right here, but then she'd never been inside a rescue mission before. She went back out to the entry hall.

Minutes passed. The two young women got up and left, carefully eying her new emerald Anne Klein silk suit as they walked out the door. The boxes of chocolates grew even heavier, but she didn't want to put them down because it was so difficult to lift them all up again—they had a tendency to slide. Where was Reverend Hodge?

Almost daily a story ran in the San Francisco press about him. The leader of the mission was the new darling of the city's top politicians. The enormous charity auction he was planning, to be held in about two weeks at the Palace of the Legion of Honor, had turned him into an overnight sensation.

According to the press, no one was sure where Hodge had come from, but the mystery surrounding him only added to his charisma. He often said he hadn't chosen this city, this city had chosen him, that it was a city ripe for giving, for practicing random acts of kindness on a daily basis. "Acts of loving-giving heal the world and make the loving-giver whole," he'd said on a local radio station just a few days ago. His guest appearance had sparked a flood of phone calls from people eager to become "loving-givers."

There were even rumors that Hodge had dipped into his own money—something practically unheard of—to establish his mission. His bigheartedness and pure goodness were the reasons Angie had chosen to offer his mission her donation of chocolates.

He was her kind of guy.

Her thoughts were cut short by the appearance of a nervous-looking little man creeping out of the kitchen. He was poorly dressed in ill-fitting gray slacks and a baggy black turtleneck, and he looked as though he were walking on eggs. His hair was brown and wispy, thin at the crown, and he wore thick, black-rimmed glasses that looked about three sizes too big for his small, impish face.

He must be one of the unfortunate people who come here seeking help from the mission, Angie decided. She wondered if he'd been scrounging food in the kitchen. The man was so thin, she feared he might be near starvation.

He shouldn't act so frightened, she thought. Surely, no one here would do anything to harm a hungry man.

As he started across the dining room he glanced toward the entry hall and saw Angie smiling at him. He stopped short.

"Oh! You frightened me," he said. His voice was high-pitched and nasal. "I thought I was alone."

"I'm sorry." She kept smiling. "I'm here to make a donation."

"That's nice," he said, looking as if he was thinking about heading back into the kitchen.

"These are chocolates," she added quickly. "You can take a box if you'd like."

"Chocolates?" His expression was a mixture of wariness and surprise—as if he might not have heard her right.

"I wish to practice a random act of kindness," she explained, repeating the older woman's words. "Also, I'm working on starting my own business with chocolates."

"Chocolates?" he repeated.

She wondered if he was hearing-impaired. Poor man. "That's right." She spoke much louder. "I like to think I'm going to become the Lady Godiva—Godiva chocolates, that is—of the twenty-first century." She waited for a laugh, or at least a smile. He looked at her blankly. "That's just a joke," she said, enunciating carefully.

"It is? And why are you shouting?" he asked, also raising his voice.

This wasn't working out. "I have some rejects in these boxes." She dropped her tone back to normal. "I mean, it's good candy, but it's not quite what I had in mind for my business. I'm in for a long, tedious search, I'm afraid."

"Is that why you're donating it?"

"My friends and relatives have received more than enough, so I've decided to give them to a good cause. I know the mission might have some concern about accepting homemade food—the Board of Health's regulations and all that," she added. "But I believe I could set Reverend Hodge's mind at ease."

"You could?" His dark eyebrows rose.

"Yes, when he shows up. I can't wait to meet him."

She smiled and gave a small sigh. "I understand he's simply wonderful."

"Oh . . . well . . ." The little man seemed at a loss for words.

"I've heard so much about him," Angie gushed. "The thought of meeting him gives me goose bumps."

"I'm afraid, Miss—?"

"Amalfi."

"What's that?"

"Miss Amalfi. Angelina Amalfi."

"Oh. That's a nice name."

"Thanks." She searched the back hall, where Sheila Chatsworth had gone. Where was the reverend?

"But as I was saying, Miss Amalfi, I'm afraid . . . *I'm* T. Simon Hodge," he said.

Her head swiveled back to him and she looked at him with suspicion. She'd heard that at times people who don't have much pretend they're someone great. Look at how many go around swearing they're Abe Lincoln. And these days, twentieth-century reincarnations of Julius Caesar were a dime a dozen. "You're the Reverend Mr. Hodge?" she asked.

"Um—"

Ah! He's ready to admit his lie. "The Reverend *T. Simon* Hodge?" Sometimes a swift kick toward reality was the best medicine.

He looked down at himself. "Well . . . yes. I'd say so."

"I'm sorry," Angie said. "I heard Reverend Hodge on the radio, and you are simply not—"

"Ah, Reverend Hodge!" Sheila Chatsworth hustled across the room. "You naughty boy! You weren't in your office. I've been searching all over for you. This young lady wants to give you a donation. Shall I handle it for you?"

"No need, Mrs. Chatsworth, I'll take care of it."

Angie's eyes widened as she looked from the arrogant Sheila Chatsworth, now simpering and sweet, to the wimpy, nasal-voiced man before her claiming to be the charismatic Reverend Hodge.

"But surely, Reverend Hodge"—Mrs. Chatsworth's voice rose and swooped like a contralto's—"you don't have time—"

"No, Mrs. C.—you're the one who doesn't have time." He patted her arm and turned her toward the front office. "I need you right here keeping an eye on the entryway, making sure that only people who are supposed to come in here are admitted. It's a very important job, Mrs. C. I need you doing it."

"Oh." She giggled. "Thank you, Reverend." She headed toward the office, blushing and twittering like a teenager with hormone overload.

"Now." He turned back to Angie. "All those boxes couldn't possibly be filled with candy, could they?" He lifted the boxes from her arms.

"They could be, and are," she said, eying him incredulously. "You know, I heard Reverend Hodge on the radio. He didn't sound anything like you."

"I studied radio broadcasting years ago. Nothing came of it, though. They teach everybody to talk the same way. 'AND NOW, A WORD FROM OUR SPONSOR.' See what I mean?"

"You're right," she said. It was creepy, seeing such a big voice booming out of such a little man. "That was the voice I heard."

"I couldn't go around talking like that all the time. All that deep breathing from the diaphragm, I'd probably faint."

Faint? Right voice or not, this could not be the famous reverend.

"These chocolates are heavy," he said. "You must have spent days making them."

Since he now held the chocolates, her mood about him improved immensely. "I might have gone a bit overboard testing recipes. Sometimes I get a little carried away, I suppose."

"Why don't we step into my office, where I can put this down before I get a hernia?" Hodge said. "You can tell me all about candy making."

They went past the front office down a long hall. The first door had a big sign over it that said Auction Central. Inside a large room filled with papers and boxes were three people, all on telephones. The hall turned, and they passed several more offices until they reached Hodge's, the last one in the long hallway.

The office was plain, with a wooden desk, three chairs, and a small bookcase. The only ornamentation was a small old wooden statue of an angel on the top of the bookcase. Hodge put the chocolates on his desk, took one box, and opened it. His pixieish face lit up. "Beautiful! I can't believe you made these. They're better-looking than store-bought."

Her cheeks warmed from his praise. "I must admit, I was a little hesitant about bringing them to you."

"Hesitant?" His eyes, magnified by the glasses, showed bewilderment. "Why?" Even here in his office, he fairly pulsated with nervous energy.

"Chocolates are . . . well, a bit frivolous," she admitted.

He was counting the boxes now. "If these are as delicious as I imagine them to be, we'll give them—most of them—to the Senseless Beauty Café, right next door."

The café's name was jarring—very mellow California. She wondered if Visualize Whirled Peas was on the menu.

"Many top chefs and bakers in the city donate food to the café," Hodge continued, shaking one of the boxes as if to see how tightly packed it was. "It's sold at high prices, which gives us money to support the needy."

"Oh, really? That's a wonderful idea," Angie said.

"It makes everyone happy. We even put a sign up over the sweets—CHARITY HAS NO CALORIES. We make a lot more sales that way."

She laughed. "I like it. Is that where you feed the poor?"

"Ah, Miss Amalfi. You're very practical." As she watched his face, it reshaped as if made out of Silly Putty. Suddenly, he was sad and downcast. "We don't have the money yet to feed anyone. You have to fertilize the soil before you can plant a garden, you know."

"You have to what?"

"We need money before we can begin to feed the poor," he said. "That's why we're holding the auction. It's a lot of work. We need many, many volunteers. I'd be honored to have you join us. We need someone like you."

His words caught her completely by surprise. "Me? I really don't think—"

"Say you'll give us a try. Just a day or two?" he urged. "If you don't like this type of volunteer work, you don't have to come back."

Although she was sure his brown eyes were quite common and uninspiring, and in fact were rather shrewd, suddenly they seemed to sparkle. His flyaway wispy hair, the dark eyebrows pointing upward in the center, the thick glasses, and the sorrowful little-boy demeanor all added up to someone she couldn't say no to.

"You've convinced me, Reverend Hodge," Angie said, completely baffled by her reaction to the man, "I'll be here."

CHAPTER

THREE

Paavo sat at his desk in Homicide, staring out the soot-dappled window to the freeway that rose like a two-headed snake from the seedy center of the city to carry cars south to the peninsula or east across the Bay Bridge. Right now, a part of him would have liked nothing more than to be on that freeway heading far, far away. But another part knew he'd have no peace until he figured out what had happened yesterday morning in court.

His partner, Toshiro Yoshiwara, had been horrified when he learned that their carefully documented investigation had been thrown out of court. Yoshiwara, whom everyone called Yosh, had been Paavo's partner for a few months now, since transferring down to San Francisco from the Seattle area. Talkative, outgoing, and amazingly jovial for someone who dealt with homicide day in and day out, he was a tall man, solidly built, with a broad chest and shoulders. His hair was clipped in a short buzz, making his head look almost too small for his bulky body. Yosh had been with Paavo at the crime scene and later assisted with the arrest. He hadn't bothered going to the preliminary hearing because they believed he wouldn't be needed. They were right, but not for the reasons they'd imagined.

That morning, Paavo had left Angie's place about four A.M. after lying awake most of the night. He'd arrived at work so early he was able to talk to the night security force and the janitorial staff.

The bulk of the morning had been spent learning all he could about the care and maintenance of courtroom evidence. He'd visited the Property Control Section and reviewed the property request forms and the court logbook for every piece of evidence connected with the murder of Peewee Clayton's girlfriend, Sarah Ann Cribbs. Each piece of property in the section was numbered, identified, and controlled on the computer system. Each time any piece moved, someone had to sign it out with their name, star number, and destination.

Given all that, having the know-how, let alone the chutzpah, to switch evidence meant it had to be an inside job.

"Paavo."

Startled out of his thoughts, Paavo looked up to see Luis Calderon standing in the doorway. His eyes were bloodshot, and his unruly black hair, usually heavily pomaded, was all askew. Paavo figured he must have been working all night.

"Hello to you, too," Homicide Inspector Rebecca Mayfield called from her desk.

"Yeah, right," Calderon grumbled. "Can you join me, Paav? Me and Benson got to talk to you about a case."

"Sure." Paavo tossed aside his pencil and followed Calderon past the inspectors' desks overflowing with papers and folders, into the hallway to the bank of elevators.

"What's up?" Paavo asked.

"I'll explain," Calderon replied. "Let's get some coffee first."

They met Bo Benson in the Hall's cafeteria. He looked every bit as tired as Calderon. His dark skin had taken on an ash gray cast, and lines of weariness across his brow made him look older than his thirty-eight years. He tilted back in his chair, the two front legs lifting off the floor as his gaze darted between Calderon and Paavo.

Paavo knew something strange was going on by the way the two men were acting. They'd worked together too many years for them to put anything over on him. Gone was Bo's lighthearted banter, and gone too—surprisingly—was Calderon's excessive grumpiness. Instead, they both looked subdued and troubled.

"Last night," Calderon began, "Benson and I were called to a homicide out at Ocean Beach, a murder. A big guy, garish dresser. We ID'd him this morning. His name was Patrick Devlin. You know him?"

Paavo was surprised by the question. "No."

"Ever heard of him?" Benson asked.

"Should I?"

Calderon continued. "He ran a small numbers operation with drop sites in a few bars and restaurants out in the Richmond and Sunset districts."

"Numbers? I didn't think we had numbers in this city," Paavo said.

"According to the guys in Vice, it's hardly big enough to pay attention to. They hope it stays that way."

None of this told Paavo why these two were talking to him. "Okay, so how does this involve me? Did you find a connection with one of my cases or something?"

Calderon's hard black gaze fixed on Paavo. "We found something on the body. A phone number. It'd been stuffed in his mouth, like maybe he was trying to hide it from someone. Maybe he was shot before he had a chance to swallow—who knows? Why he wanted to hide the number, though, we can only guess."

"A phone number?" Paavo studied them, trying to read what was going on behind their words. "Did you call the number to find out who it belonged to?"

"No need, Paavo. We already knew." Calderon's eyes were penetrating, wary. "That's why we wanted to talk to you. We didn't want you to feel we'd gone behind your back. Also, we wanted to give you a chance to explain it all to us."

"Explain? Explain what?"

"He had your home number, Paav," Calderon said softly. "Not the pager number that the dispatchers and everybody has these days. Your unlisted home number."

Paavo looked at the two of them as if they were crazy, and then as if they were joking. They weren't. "Are you sure it was mine?"

Benson pulled out his notebook and flipped through a few pages. "Three seven one five five four six."

They hadn't made a mistake. The thought of some dead gambler having his home phone number was chilling. His mind leafed through the gamblers and racketeers who'd crossed his path over the years. There were plenty. "Do you have a mug shot on this guy?" Paavo asked.

"Here you go." Calderon handed Paavo a four-year-old booking photo, plus four-hour-old morgue shots.

Paavo studied Patrick Devlin's pictures a long while. "I've never seen him before," he said quietly. When he lifted his gaze to them, though, he felt as if ice water had been poured through his veins. "You two think I have something to hide?"

"No!" Calderon said. "That's why we're here with you instead of giving this to the chief. The only problem is that this is coming up right after the court fiasco with Clayton. And everyone knows Clayton's involved in all kinds of gambling. It doesn't look good."

"Thanks for the vote of confidence," Paavo said wearily.

"How many people know your home phone?" Calderon asked.

"How many ... What are you getting at?" Paavo didn't like this one bit. They didn't need to question him like some suspect. "To hell with your questions!"

"Relax, Paavo," Benson said, gripping his shoulder. "We're just trying to help you out here."

"Give us names, Paavo," Calderon said. "Your father, your rich girlfriend. Who else?"

Paavo shrugged off Benson's hand. "Angie's mother knows it as well." His voice was clipped and icy. "But she doesn't make it a habit to consort with numbers runners."

"Look." Calderon paused, his gaze locking with Paavo's before he quietly continued. "We could lose the note we found. No one else knows about it but a couple of patrol cops—and they don't know what it means. It's obvious that you're not the type to get mixed up with this kind of skank."

"Take it to Lieutenant Hollins," Paavo said. He didn't have to think about the choice before him. Although he was touched by the support and solidarity Calderon's words revealed, it wasn't the right choice— not the one he would make. "I've got nothing to hide."

"What if IA gets involved?" Benson asked. "It won't take Internal Affairs long to learn that this guy worked the Richmond and Sunset, and that you live in the Richmond. After the Clayton mess, they'll be all over you like locusts."

"They won't get involved," Calderon said. "Paavo hasn't—"

"I don't want this buried," Paavo interrupted.

The two looked at him curiously.

"I don't know how this guy Devlin got my number, and I don't really care," Paavo said. "But I *do* want to know what he planned to do with it."

CHAPTER

FOUR

The next morning, Angie once again took a cab to the Random Acts of Kindness Mission. She wasn't quite sure, though, why she felt drawn there, and from the time she'd gotten out of bed she had argued with herself about returning. Even now, standing on the Embarcadero, she was hesitant about going back in. The Reverend Hodge, after all, wasn't anything like she'd expected him to be. Nor, for that matter, was the mission itself.

She'd have to think about this, and doing so over a cup of coffee seemed like a good plan. She turned on her heel and went to the Senseless Beauty Café and Pâtisserie.

It was small but charming, with five small round tables, two chairs at each, and a large glass display case filled with pastries, croissants, and muffins. A green chalkboard listed the soups and sandwiches of the day, and behind the counter were a variety of coffee-making machines.

She was the only customer at the moment. A woman with straight blond hair, wearing a plum and white Senseless Beauty Café smock, took her order.

"Do you know the people over at the Random Acts of Kindness Mission?" Angie asked as the woman made her a double latte.

"Very well." The woman's smile was open and guileless. "Are you a volunteer there?"

"I'm thinking about it," Angie confessed.

"You couldn't find a better person than Reverend Hodge," she said earnestly. "He helped me start this café. My name's Rainbow—Rainbow Grchek."

The conservative-looking café owner didn't appear to be a "Rainbow" at all, but Angie didn't comment. Anyway, she was sure Rainbow had already heard all the comments that could be made.

"He did? How nice," Angie murmured. Being helped by a man of the cloth was one means of getting a job she hadn't considered yet. A source of constant interest and wonder for her was that so many people managed to find, and keep, jobs they seemed to enjoy. It was a skill she hadn't mastered yet. But if her angelinas became a success, she wouldn't have to worry about it any longer.

Rainbow carried the latte to a table for her.

"I'd love to hear how he helped you," Angie said, "if you've got a moment."

"Oh, sure." Rainbow sat at the table. "I think you'll find it an interesting story. You see, Reverend Hodge found me standing on the Golden Gate Bridge. Actually, he found me sitting on the rail of the bridge, ready to jump."

"You're kidding me." The idea of the woman before her, who had such a pleasant smile and seemed so happy, being suicidal was hard to imagine.

"It's true," Rainbow said. "I thought my life was

over. The man I loved had left me for someone else. I waited until the middle of the night. No one else was anywhere near. Or so I thought. I sat on the rail and then—this is strange—I thought I had let go of the railing. I even had the sensation that I was falling, but instead I heard a voice saying, 'He's not worth it.' To my surprise, I was still holding the rail. I turned to see where the voice had come from, and there was this little man looking at me with sad brown eyes. 'I promise you,' he said, 'that if you talk to me tonight, when you see the sun rise your pain will be gone. If it isn't, then you can jump, and I won't try to stop you.'"

"He was there?" Angie asked. "In the middle of the night?"

"It was like a miracle for me," Rainbow said, her large gray eyes capturing Angie's.

"What did you do?"

"Well, first of all, I didn't believe him one little bit. 'Trust me,' he said. 'You'll be dead for all eternity, so what difference can a few more hours of life make?'"

"That's chilling." Angie shuddered.

"It was. Maybe that was why I sat there on the rail and cried and talked to him. I told him about my life, the bad parts, my disappointments, my son-of-a-bitch cheating lover. Then, when I'd gotten through with my tears, he asked me if there had ever been anything at all that went right for me in life. Had there ever been a moment that I had enjoyed? Well, of course there had been. I told him about those, and as I did, I remembered more of them.

"Then the sun cast a golden glow over the city and the bay, over Alcatraz and Angel Island—even over Oakland. I realized that if I jumped, I'd never see that sight again. I thought of all the other things I'd never see—simple things, flowers, raindrops . . . a rainbow.

For the first time, I even understood my name, what my parents had been trying to say to me.

"That was when I realized that his first words to me were true—Bill wasn't worth it. I got off the rail, followed Reverend Hodge here, and have been with him ever since. I think of him as my angel. My guardian angel. That's the only way I can explain it."

"That's a wonderful story," Angie said.

"Reverend Hodge is a wonderful guy," Rainbow added.

"Hello, Reverend Hodge." The door to his office stood open, and Angie stuck her head in.

Papers were scattered over his desk. He'd been scribbling a note but looked up, startled, when he heard a voice. Behind the oversized glasses, his surprisingly young face spread into a wide grin. "I've been waiting for you, Miss Amalfi," he said.

"You were that certain I'd return?" she asked, stepping into the room. She found herself staring at him. He just didn't seem to be the guardian angel type, despite Rainbow's heartfelt words. What was she missing?

"Here, please, let me find you a chair." He darted to the corner and pulled a chair to the middle of the room near his desk. "Those with a good heart always return to where they're needed."

"Fools also return to their folly," she said, taking the offered seat.

"One man's folly is another man's fortune," he countered.

"Well, who can argue with that?" she asked with a laugh. "I just met Rainbow Grchek, by the way. She spoke very highly of you."

His small mouth turned up with delight. "She's very kind."

"Have you been a minister long?" she asked.

He pushed aside his many papers and folded his hands on his desk, looking as if he had all the time in the world for her. "Oh, yes. A long time."

"Where were you before you came to San Francisco?"

"Here and there. Minnesota. Just outside Minneapolis."

"Really? I spent a month there with a cousin one summer. Where—"

"Your chocolates were extraordinarily delicious, Miss Amalfi. Tell me about your candy-making business."

She wondered why he didn't want to talk about Minnesota, but since his change of subject was to one dear to her heart, she went along. "Not so good, I'm afraid. I can't seem to find the right confection. I want my angelina—which is what I'll call it—to be something special."

"Ah!" He nodded sagely, then his brow wrinkled in confusion. "But why?"

"So that people will notice. So that my business will be unique and valued."

He studied her. "What does the young man in your life think about all this? I'm assuming there is one."

"There is. He's a homicide inspector for the city." She couldn't say Paavo was bursting with enthusiasm over her idea, but he didn't criticize it, either. "He said if it's what I want, I should go for it."

"A homicide inspector?" His dark eyebrows rose at the news of Paavo's job, and she doubted he'd heard anything else she said. "I would have thought a business executive or corporate lawyer was more your type."

"You should meet my father." She couldn't stop a grimace as she thought of the arguments she'd had with her father over her relationship with Paavo.

"That explains a lot," he murmured, then leaned

toward her, capturing her gaze in a way that was almost mesmerizing. "When things get tough, Miss Amalfi, you be sure to come and talk to me. It's not the first time I've heard of the incompatibility between being rational and being in love."

His words, his voice, his demeanor were so filled with empathy and understanding that suddenly she saw another side of Reverend Hodge, a side that people responded to, a side that caused them to give him their money and their time.

"Thank you so much," she said, a little breathless and yet a little perplexed at that observation.

"Now," he said, giving her his most impish grin, "let me tell you all about my plans for the auction."

CHAPTER

FIVE

Paavo and Yosh headed for the apartment building in which Peewee Clayton had murdered Sarah Ann Cribbs. Even if the state hadn't officially declared that to be the case, Paavo knew it was true. Yosh drove, which was good because Paavo's mind was light-years away from San Francisco traffic conditions.

In fact, for the first time in his career, conducting a homicide investigation wasn't his primary concern. Instead, it was to find out why a dead numbers runner had his phone number. Even bigger was the second issue: the care and maintenance of courtroom evidence. Specifically, who had handled the two pieces of missing evidence that were causing him and Yosh to reopen the case?

He had learned that Sarah Ann's blouse had been cut off during the autopsy and sent directly to the crime lab for testing. The beer bottle fragments had been dusted for prints at the scene, then bagged and also sent to the lab for blood and hair identification.

Blood, hair, and prints all matched Peewee Clayton's, leaving no doubt that the crime lab had had the true evidence at one point and had run tests on it. That meant the blouse and beer bottle must have been switched after the lab tests were made.

Paavo had interviewed crime scene investigators, criminalists, criminologists, other homicide inspectors, secretaries, typists, janitors, air-conditioning repairmen, telephone repairmen, even the people who supplied the jars and labels for specimen maintenance. He wanted to know who had access to the Property Control Section, who guarded it, and what happened during breaks, lunches, and shift changes. He asked about the procedure for placing new evidence into Property Control, the procedure when old evidence was removed, and whether any of the officers involved had happened to see or hear anything strange over the last three weeks since the crime lab had finished its preliminary study of the blouse.

He had talked to everyone he could find who had worked recently in the vicinity of the Property Control Section. The only ones he had missed were a secretary on maternity leave and an air-conditioning repairman who'd been fired.

But no matter how many people he questioned or how many questions he asked, nothing specific turned up. No one had seen anything out of the ordinary. It came clear, though, that there were times when the on-duty person who checked evidence in and out might have left the station for a moment. Since the department was shorthanded, he could have been called away briefly to another task. Or he simply could have taken a bathroom break. No one purposefully left the evidence room unwatched, but since there had never been a problem in connection with the evidence before, security had simply become lax.

Paavo could have gone to the district attorney, Lloyd Fletcher, with his findings, but that might have resulted in some firings and nothing would have been solved. In fact, it only would have made it harder for him to get anyone to talk to him in the future.

Besides, Lloyd Fletcher was far from being one of his favorite people. They'd had problems in the past. Despite years as an assistant DA, once Fletcher had been voted into office on the heels of an unpopular district attorney, he turned into a pure politician.

His main political pitch was that cops should overwhelm criminals with love and tender care in the hope that they might reform. It was a very San Francisco philosophy and, from the police department's point of view, dead wrong. The latest civil grand jury report showed that of the fifty-five thousand felony arrests by the police last year, the DA's office had fewer than two thousand cases going to court. It was all but open warfare between the two departments.

Given that, there was no way Paavo would do anything to make a cop look bad in the eyes of this DA—unless he clearly deserved it.

There was another aspect of the switch, though, that Paavo wasn't about to discuss with anyone.

It was the fact that Peewee Clayton was a nobody—a bad egg who pulled petty thefts and beat up women, old men, and kids. Probably kicked his dog, too, if a creep like that even had a dog. So how would a nobody find anyone powerful enough or clever enough to go into the heart of the Hall of Justice and switch evidence? Even if he did happen to know someone so clever or powerful, why would such a guy bother to help a small-time operator like Peewee?

There was more to this than met the eye. A lot more. Paavo never liked coincidence. Didn't believe in it, in fact. So how could he explain the coincidence of his case being blown in court at the same time as his phone number was found in a numbers runner's mouth?

Or was he just being paranoid?

They arrived at the apartment building and rang the bell to the manager's apartment. A tall woman with short hair, red at the tips and white at the roots, opened the door. A yellow kimonolike house jacket was wrapped tightly around her waist and a cigarette was wedged in the corner of her lips. As soon as she saw the two inspectors her eyes narrowed and she removed the cigarette. "You two. I heard you let that Peewee off. I thought you were better at your job than that. Sarah was a good girl. Rotten taste in men, but a good girl. She didn't deserve this."

"That's why we're here, Mrs. Simmons," Paavo said. "We're picking up the investigation again. We'd like to ask you a few more questions, and also ask you to continue to hold Sarah Ann's apartment just the way you found it. Don't disturb anything."

She took a long drag on her cigarette, then tilted her head back and blew the smoke toward the ceiling. "You're late, boys."

The two cops exchanged glances, and Paavo said slowly, "You might recall that we asked you to—"

"I know what you asked," she said. "I also know that I got a call a couple days ago giving me the okay to rent the apartment. I had a cleaning service come through, and today my new tenants are moving in."

"The whole idea of a random act of kindness is that it's random," Reverend Hodge cried petulantly. They stood at the counter at the Senseless Beauty Café. Hodge had decided to buy some coffee and breakfast pastries for his volunteers. Angie had returned to the café the following morning after her talk with Rainbow and met him as he was going inside. She offered to help carry the goodies. "Auctions aren't random—they're planned. Well planned. Look at all the planning going into this one! What if nobody comes?"

"There's nothing to worry about," Angie insisted. She was surprised at how depressed and upset the reverend seemed about the whole affair. "Publicity is getting out. People will come—especially if they think they'll be getting a good deal."

"With an auction, who can tell? It depends on the other buyers." His shoulders slumped. "I don't know what I'm doing. Maybe I should just stick with random kindnesses and forget all this other stuff."

"It's not that hard to pull off, Reverend Hodge."

Hodge turned his small, flat, but effectively hangdog eyes on her. "Easy for you to stand there and criticize!"

"I'm not!"

"She's not," Rainbow said, giving him a cardboard holder with four cups of coffee. Angie took the box of jelly doughnuts and cinnamon rolls.

As they left the café Hodge continued his complaining. "Explain this one. I hired a catering company, but the owner keeps calling and asking me what I want him to serve. How should I know? Who am I—Betty Crocker?"

They walked along the sidewalk to the mission, the morning sun warm, a crisp breeze coming off the bay just beyond the piers across the wide boulevard. "Did you ask the caterer for suggestions?"

His eyebrows nearly touched his wispy hairline. "Could I do that?"

Was he being purposely obtuse? she wondered. "I can talk to him on the phone if you'd like."

"Do you know much about food? Besides chocolate, I mean."

"I know a bit," she replied. "I studied at the Cordon

Bleu in Paris, and I've worked with a number of restaurants and as a restaurant critic."

"I knew it!" he cried, jostling the coffee in his excitement. "You're just what I've been looking for ... no, praying for. In my profession, I always hope that when I pray I'll get a little special attention. Maybe this time I did."

"I don't think I'm heaven-sent, Reverend Hodge."

"I can't imagine you were sent by the *other* place, Miss Amalfi."

That stopped her.

He pushed open the mission door. "Let's sit here a moment so I can give you some details," he said, plopping himself down on the edge of the sofa in the entry hall. She took the chair beside him. "We'll have about fifteen hundred people, each paying two hundred dollars to get in, so that's three hundred thousand dollars. . . . I guess fifty or sixty thousand would be okay to spend on a few hors d'oeuvres and wine." He gazed innocently at her. "Is that enough?"

Angie couldn't answer for a moment. She had no idea of the magnitude of this event. Her only experience working on a large catered affair was the wedding of her fourth sister. Francesca's marriage to Seth Levine had been a major social event on the San Francisco peninsula. Four hundred people attended, and Angie had thought she'd be worn to a frazzle before it was over. But that was a dinner. This was only hors d'oeuvres. Fifty or sixty thousand dollars? No problem. "I think we can come up with something very nice for that amount of money."

"The Palace of the Legion of Honor is shaped like a U." He gestured with his hands, building a picture as he spoke, his nervous energy practically lifting him off his chair. "There's a large hall on one arm of the building. It'll be set up for food and drinks, and people will mingle with each other. That's where the preauction welcome speeches will be given—and that's also where I hope I can persuade people to give generously for the benefit of the mission. The auction will be held across the courtyard, on the other arm of the U."

Suddenly, for all Hodge's complaints about planning, she got the vague idea that she'd just been had. He certainly sounded very "planned" now. "Sounds very nice," she said. The Legion of Honor building, on a hilltop overlooking the Pacific Ocean, housed a museum and a large meeting hall.

"The people attending—most of them—will know good food and wine." He clasped his hands tightly. "We've *got* to impress them."

"Of course."

"Plus, I want a centerpiece that fits the theme of the auction: doing good works for people. Something lofty. Something inspired." He stood, his arms outstretched. "Something . . . global."

"Wonderful!" Angie cried, picking up his enthusiasm. "What will it be?"

"I don't know." He sat and looked woeful again. "I've thought and thought, but I can't come up with anything. I should cancel the whole thing!" He put his head in his hands. "I would, too, but the mission's benefactor—a virtuous, generous man—has already given the mission a lot of money. He rented this building, bought new furniture and rugs for it, even paid for the auction's publicity. How could I let it all die?"

"You can't!" she insisted. "Everything will be all right."

"But it's all beyond me. I can't handle it. I'm such a loser. Why am I even trying?"

She walked to his side and touched his shoulder. "Reverend Hodge, how can you talk this way? Everyone

in the city thinks . . . knows . . . what a wonderful, generous man you are."

He looked up at her. "Do you have a paper bag with
you? I feel a panic attack coming on."

"Stop worrying, right now!" She put her hands on
her hips. "I'll take care of the food for you. I'll work
with the other volunteers. That's what you have volunteers for. We'll all pitch in and do our part. It'll come
together."

"Do you really think so?"

"I know so! Please, Reverend, relax."

"Okay. I'm feeling a little better already." He
pressed his hands against his chest and took deep
breaths. "As soon as I can walk I'll introduce you to
Mary Ellen Hitchcock. She's in charge of most of the
details of the auction. You two can work together."

"Is she in Auction Central, down the hall?" Angie
stood and picked up the coffee and pastries. "If so, I
can find her. I'll take the volunteers their coffee before
it gets any colder."

"Miss Amalfi, you are such a gem."

T. Simon Hodge went into his office to be alone.
Angie Amalfi was a wise addition to his cadre—she
had the right connections and knew food besides. She
fit in with the other women like peas in a pod.
They were giving him a headache, though, with their
enthusiastic good cheer. One could take only so
much of that.

Right now, he had other problems to worry about,
like where to store some of the goods collected for the
auction.

The door to his office opened. He looked up, covering his notes and paperwork with his arms.

"Oh, hello," he said, shifting back in the chair. He

didn't have to hide anything from this visitor. "Is anything wrong?"

The man opened the box of chocolates that Hodge had kept for himself and spent a moment deciding which to eat first.

"We have a new volunteer," Hodge said. "One who knows about gourmet food. She made those."

"I saw her." He chose a cherry cordial and bit into it. Some of the syrup oozed out of the candy and rolled onto his fingers. "She'll be working with us a while, I hope."

"Yes, of course. I didn't realize you took an interest in our volunteers."

The visitor ate the rest of the chocolate, then licked his fingertips. "Did she mention that her boyfriend's a cop?"

Alarms went off in Hodge's head. "You know her?"

"I met her once. She probably doesn't remember me, but I'm glad she'll be around. She might come in handy."

"Handy?" Hodge felt his mouth go dry. "Yes, I'm sure she will."

"More than she ever imagined. Be nice to her, Hodge." He took another chocolate, then left the room.

Hodge waited until he was alone. Only then could he relax enough to take a piece of candy for himself.

CHAPTER

SIX

Angie was not pleased. Paavo wasn't even on call this week, yet he was ignoring her. If he was on call—which meant that he had to investigate any homicide that took place during his shift, either weekdays from Monday to Friday morning, or weekends from Friday to Monday morning—he scarcely had time to go home, and sometimes slept at the Hall of Justice.

On off weeks, like this one, he was supposed to put in a nine-to-five—or six or seven or eight—shift, and afterward spend some time with her.

But his being incommunicado for four days in a row was too much to put up with. She hadn't seen him since the evening he'd come to her house upset about the bizarre evidence switch in court. Evidence switching might be a problem at the moment, but she needed to talk about the future—about them. Her career, his career, and their life together. She had arranged a lovely, romantic evening for the two of them to share, and now she had to get Paavo to agree to spend it with her. Of course, if he said he was too busy to go with her, he'd find out that little Italian-American women in a bad mood were *not* to be trifled with.

She roared into one of the twenty-minute parking spaces outside the Hall of Justice, marched through the metal detectors, and rode the elevator to the fourth floor. Her peach-colored Carole Little suit with its short straight skirt, fitted jacket, linen shell top with a low scoop neck, and matching high-heeled pumps caused heads to turn. She hoped she'd get that kind of reaction from Paavo.

Room 450 was quiet. The secretary had left for the day, and most of the homicide inspectors had either gone home or were out on a case. Past the reception area the room was cluttered with computer terminals, books and papers all askew atop desks, bookcases, and file cabinets. At a far desk, near windows facing inner-city blight, sat Paavo, so lost in his papers he hadn't even heard her come in.

She'd only taken one step into the room, though, when he looked up. The top button of his pale blue shirt was unfastened, his tie was loose, and his sleeves were rolled up to the elbow. Beneath his large blue eyes were shadows of weariness; his face looked drawn and his dark brown hair was mussed as if he'd been running his fingers through it. Her anger evaporated as she wondered how he was feeling, if he'd eaten today, and when he'd last had a good night's sleep.

"Angie," he said, surprised.

"Grab your coat, Inspector. I'm springing you from this joint." She forced a cheerful note into her voice.

"I'd like to, but I've got a lot to do—"

"Are you and Yosh on call tonight?" she asked, her arms folded.

"No, but—"

"No buts. You've worked hard enough, long enough.

A movie, then dinner. I'm going to get you to relax if it kills me."

"Angie, I don't have time for a movie."

"Look around, Paavo." She gave him a moment to do as she asked. "The place is empty. It means other people have things to do besides sit here and work. You can leave for a little while. It won't fall apart without you."

She walked up to him, moved to the side the papers he'd been working on, then sat down on top of his desk blotter. He eased back in his chair, his lips twitching slightly at her audacity. Ignoring his expression, she lifted his pen from his fingers, put its cap on, then tossed it to a corner of the desk. "It's a short movie. A classic. Cocteau's *Beauty and the Beast*. I couldn't get dinner reservations until nine anyway."

"I already know how *Beauty and the Beast* ends," he said.

He could be maddeningly practical. "That's not the point, Inspector."

"The point is the time."

"One evening won't matter."

"Angie . . ." He sounded exasperated.

"Paavo . . . ," she mocked, imitating his tone.

He stared at her, then shook his head. Slowly his mouth spread into a grin. "Maybe you're right," he murmured. Relief washed over her.

He placed his hands on her knees, his fingers stroking her sheer silk hose. His touch made her toes curl.

"So, Miss Amalfi, you've come to rescue me, have you?" His voice took on a deep huskiness.

"That's right. I'll drag you out of here kicking and screaming if I have to."

"Is that so?" He slowly rose out of his chair and, leaning forward, moved his hands to either side of her thighs, his large, square-shouldered body towering over her. The absurdity of trying to force this big man to do anything he didn't want to do wasn't lost on her. So she kissed him.

His arms circled her, and as their kiss deepened he pulled her hard against him. She slid off the desk, taking the blotter with her and causing papers, pens, and notebooks to tumble to the floor.

"Oops," she said.

He let her go and gathered up his materials. "I give up. Let's get out of here."

By the time the movie was over, Paavo had visibly relaxed. To Angie's pleasure and relief, he'd found the film intriguing and enchanting—her words, not his. Only a few times did he seem to slip into thought.

She had made reservations at Moose's on Washington Square, near her church and only a couple of blocks from a small café owned by three friends of hers. She had deliberately chosen not to go to their place. Tonight she wanted to eat a special meal and didn't want to be interrupted by well-meaning friends while she tried to help Paavo forget, for a while at least, his sticky cases.

Their appetizer of hickory-smoked salmon with a warm cheese blintz, baby lolla rosa, and red-onion-and-caper relish arrived as they talked about the movie. "Here's to fairy tales and mythology," Angie said, raising her glass of sauvignon blanc. "May they always point out the truths of life."

Paavo touched his glass to hers, then held her with his gaze. "And may beauty always love her savage beast."

"She does and she will," Angie replied softly.

Percatelli pasta with fennel and spring onion marmellata was served next.

"You were right about coming here this evening,

Angie," Paavo said between mouthfuls of food. "It's a lot better than brooding over a dead numbers runner."

"Numbers? That's gambling, right?"

"An illegal lottery," he explained.

"Why would anyone bother? There's a legitimate state lottery every week."

"For one thing, the odds of winning are much better. Fewer players, fewer numbers. You need to guess only a couple of numbers right to win something in most games. Also, whatever you win, you keep. Tax free."

She ate some pasta, nicely al dente, as she pondered his explanation. "Tax free? No wonder it's popular. But what does that have to do with you?"

"My phone number was found on a piece of paper in the mouth of a dead numbers runner."

She was stunned. "You can't have said what I thought you did."

"I said it, but I can't explain it." His lips tightened. "Calderon and Benson found it. We went to the chief together."

"So why did the dead man have your number?"

"That's what they asked me."

"They can't possibly think you're involved with someone like that." She was scarcely able to believe he'd have been questioned by men he had worked with for so many years.

He was silent for a moment. "It's the kind of incident that makes some cops real nervous."

"Then they're fools," she said bluntly.

It was his turn to look surprised, then he grinned. "Wouldn't be the first time."

The main course, grilled five-pepper beef filet and portabello mushrooms, was served next.

"Everyone really enjoyed the chocolates you sent, Angie," Paavo said, cutting a bite of meat. "All three boxes went fast. Have you found your angelina yet?"

"Not even close," she said with a sigh.

"No?" He chewed ecstatically. She enjoyed a man who appreciated good food.

"I've been experimenting like mad, but all I've ended up with are pounds and pounds of good, but not very special, chocolate candy."

"I'm sure your friends appreciate it." He poured more wine.

"To a point." She sipped her wine, then ran a finger lightly around the rim. "But since it looks like my experimenting will continue for a while, I decided to find some worthy cause—some really *good* people—to donate the chocolates to."

"That sounds like a good idea."

"I settled on the Random Acts of Kindness Mission."

His fork, with a tender morsel of filet, froze in midair. "That's the new rescue mission, isn't it?"

She heard the uneasiness in his voice and suddenly felt defensive. "Yes, it is."

Paavo was silent for a moment. "I remember a couple of guys at the Hall of Justice talking about the place—saying it's billed as a soup kitchen but looks like a private club. They found it fishy."

"That's only because it's just getting started," she explained quickly. "But Reverend Hodge has plans to turn it into a very nice rescue mission once he has enough money. 'You can't plant until you own the land,' or something like that, is how the reverend puts it."

"You can't what?"

"You need to come and see it." Angie desperately wanted Paavo to understand her feelings, even though she had trouble understanding them herself. "Meet Reverend Hodge. He's a good man. Many fine people—some very wealthy women, as a matter of fact—work as volunteers for him, and he needs my help with the food for the auction."

"What auction?"

"There's going to be a lavish charity auction fund-raiser. All the best society people will attend. That's where the money will come from . . . the money for the seed to plant the mission."

Paavo's brows drew together. "Tell me about this Reverend Hodge," he said. "Where is he from? What's his church affiliation? What did he do before coming here?"

"Honestly, Paavo," she exclaimed. "He's not a murderer, he's a reverend. I didn't put him through the third degree. I don't know the answers to those questions, but I'm sure none of them are secret."

For dessert, the waiter brought Paavo a vanilla bean crème brûlée, and for Angie, a passion fruit cheesecake with mango sauce, both served with strong espresso.

"Let me get this straight, Angie," Paavo said. "This mission is in a nice building, comfortably furnished, with lots of wealthy people around it, and the reverend is going to hold a high-society auction in order to raise money to turn said nice, comfortable building into a soup kitchen. Right?"

"Exactly." She beamed, glad she'd finally gotten him to see the picture.

"Sounds like a setup for a scam of some sort."

"A scam? No way! These people are good. And the reverend is simply wonderful. A little nervous, a little unsure of himself, but other than that, he's delightful." She decided to leave out mention of his manipulative trait.

"Let me see what I can find out about the place," Paavo said. His expression made it clear her defense had no effect on him. "In the meantime, it would be safest if you forget about it awhile."

Her back stiffened. "I will *not* forget it. I promised Reverend Hodge I'd go back and help, especially with his auction."

Paavo reached for her hand. "Angie, because of what happened to you not long ago, I know it's important for you to restore your trust in people. But I'm not sure that's the place to do it."

He was referring to a man who had tried to kill her. The experience had left her shaken and fearful. Finding truly *good* people—people such as the reverend and his volunteers—was the perfect medicine for the mistrust she had developed. "Don't worry about me, Paavo. The Random Acts of Kindness Mission is a fine place. As Reverend Hodge says, 'The loving-giver lovingly gives.'"

"Is that a joke, Angie?"

She stared at him, suddenly furious at his crossed brows, his downturned lips. "Paavo, I don't think I like your attitude."

CHAPTER

SEVEN

Paavo took the call from Inspector Rebecca Mayfield that caused him and Yosh to jump back into their unmarked—as if that fooled anyone—police-issue Chevy Cavalier and drive to Sunset Liquors on Taraval and Thirty-eighth Avenue. The Sunset district was a neighborhood of tiny, middle-class homes in the area unaffectionately referred to as the "county" of San Francisco. The charm, hills, cable cars, restaurants, ethnic sights and smells, tourists, and street musicians found elsewhere in the city were conspicuously absent from the Sunset.

As Paavo got out of the car he saw Rebecca Mayfield, the detail's newest and only female homicide inspector, standing in the liquor store, talking to men from the coroner's team. Her partner, Bill Never-Take-a-Chance Sutter, was out on the street, hands in pockets, acting as if he was doing nothing more than passing the time of day with one of the patrol cops. Back at the office, everyone said he spent far more time thinking about retirement than about his most recent cases.

Paavo stopped at the store's entrance. Rebecca saw him and walked over, wearing a smile that the other fellows in Homicide said she reserved for him alone. "Glad you could make it, Paavo."

He nodded and glanced over the crime scene. Only the closed cash register drawer made this scene different from the other hundred-plus armed robberies that went awry each year and ended up with a death. The dead man was the owner, Haram Sayir.

"What've you got for me?" Paavo asked.

"Come this way," Rebecca said. "I've got something I want you to see."

He followed her to the office. They went in and she pointed to a file cabinet with two six-packs of beer on the floor beside it. "The beer was on top of the file cabinet. When I moved it, I found this notebook underneath." A five-by-eight blue spiral notebook lay atop the file cabinet. Wearing latex gloves, she didn't hesitate to pick it up and open it. Inside were columns of numbers.

"Numbers running," Paavo said softly. "What the hell's going on in this city?"

"The numbers are dated, too," Rebecca said. "The dates end five days ago."

"Five?" Patrick Devlin had been killed five days ago.

She nodded. "Going back, I found that at the end of each day a line had been drawn and two letters placed beside it. The letters might be initials. Especially since for the last few weeks, the initials are *PD*. I don't think it means 'police department' . . . or 'paid.' And then the numbers stop altogether."

PD . . . Patrick Devlin? Paavo's gaze gripped hers. "You think this guy was part of Devlin's numbers racket?"

"I sure do." Her words were emphatic.

He nodded grimly, then went back to studying the notebook. "It looks like he took a few more numbers after the prior day's payoff. Maybe word hadn't yet reached him that Devlin had been killed."

"That's what I figured. Then, for some reason, he stopped altogether."

"There's something ugly coming down here involving numbers," Paavo said. "I hope there aren't too many more guys around like Haram Sayir. Messing with racketeers is a no-win, and everybody should know it."

"Despite that," Rebecca said softly, taking in the liquor store that the dead man had owned and worked hard to keep, "I can't help feeling sorry for him."

A tray of marzipan-coated chocolate truffles had been pushed to the back of the countertop to the left of Angie's kitchen sink. On the right side, another tray filled with chocolate-ripple divinity was precariously perched on the dish-draining rack. And scattered about the counter between the refrigerator and the cooktop, stacked atop the microwave, and balanced on the toaster were assorted plates of chocolate-walnut crunch, chocolate-honey nougats, chocolate-covered mini montblancs, chocolate florentines, and chocolate-coconut fudge cups.

Connie Rogers dropped into a kitchen chair and let her head hit the tabletop with a thunk. She and Angie had met in the course of the investigation of the murder of Connie's younger sister and, although opposite in almost every way, had become close friends. Where Angie was slim, dark-haired, and single, Connie was a little overweight, blond, and divorced. Angie had a college degree, traveled widely, and was well versed in art and literature. Connie had graduated from high school only and had never left the United States. Also, Connie owned a small gift shop called Everyone's Fancy, and Angie hadn't yet found the job of her dreams. "Take a break, Angie," Connie said. "You're wearing me out."

"I'm all right." Angie stood in front of the stove, where she was tempering the latest batch of bittersweet chocolate. She was glad there was no mirror nearby. Her complexion had to be nearly as green as Connie's. "Anyway, I'd rather keep busy. When I stop, I begin thinking about Paavo."

Connie gazed over the candy-filled kitchen. "Then you sure don't want to think about him much," she said, propping her head up with her arm. "What's happening that's got you so upset?"

"He's troubled by some strange goings-on at work, and he hasn't quite been himself. I simply tried to tell him about the Random Acts of Kindness Mission, and he made it sound like the place is a front for the mob or something," Angie confessed. "I don't know what to do."

"Do you think it is?" Connie dragged herself from the table to take over the stirring.

"I have no reason to doubt Reverend Hodge," Angie said, grateful to sit for a moment. "I trust him."

"Then don't worry, Angie. What does a homicide inspector know about rescue missions and reverends, anyway?"

"Maybe you're right. I shouldn't let it bother me." She reached for a chocolate-honey nougat and popped it in her mouth.

"I swear," Connie said, "a man can drive a good woman crazy faster than bees make honey."

Angie grimaced. "Tell me about it."

"I've given up on them. All the satisfaction in my life comes from just one thing." She pointed to the pot she was stirring. "Chocolate."

Angie chuckled, which wasn't easy to do when nauseated by the smell and taste of bittersweet, semisweet, milk, and white chocolate. Not to mention the nougat she had just swallowed.

"It's true! I even gave up sex for chocolate," Connie said.

"I don't believe it."

"Why not? Good chocolate, at least, is easy to get."

Angie laughed. "You're right—and you can have it anytime you want. Even in the middle of your gift shop."

"Exactly. And when you say the word *commitment*," Connie added emphatically, "you don't see chocolate pick itself up and go running down the street."

"Like my cousin Buddy?" Angie asked, a bit cautious about this, a sensitive subject. On the other hand, Angie was dying to know what had gone wrong with Connie and Buddy's relationship.

"Exactly!"

Angie sighed. "I understand." She got up and checked the candy thermometer. "Ah! The chocolate's just about the right temperature. Time to start again."

For this latest attempt in the search for the perfect angelina, they had melted chocolate and caramel, and Angie had pitted a bunch of dates while Connie had cracked and shelled pecans, then quartered them lengthwise. Those that shattered were chopped extra fine.

The recipe called for them to pour a smidgen of melted caramel into each date's cavity, then quickly, before the caramel thickened, to shove in a quartered pecan, dip the date into the chocolate, and roll it in the minced pecan.

Connie turned the chocolate over to Angie and began stirring the caramel. "If I didn't love chocolate so much," Connie said, "I'd swear the smell is making me sick."

"Stir, Connie. Be strong. And remember that whatever we have left over will be donated to the Random Acts of Kindness Mission. So all this work is for a good cause."

"I'm stirring, I'm stirring."

Angie picked up a date, opened it without tearing it, and then, holding it with thin tongs, dripped hot caramel into it with a small spoon. "Let's pray that these are the angelinas we're looking for." She handed the tongs to Connie and took over stirring the caramel.

"That's what you said about the last three recipes." Connie shoved a pecan into the date and, still using the tongs, dipped the date into the chocolate. She passed the tongs back to Angie. "Maybe this perfect confection you're looking for just doesn't exist. Why are you doing this? Use something already popular. Does the world need angelinas?"

"I'm not one to jump on someone else's bandwagon," Angie said. "I like the idea of angelinas. Besides, if I called them amalfis, people might think they were shoes."

"Har, har."

The number of candies cooling and hardening slowly began to grow.

"About the mission," Angie began, using her arm to brush her hair back off her forehead. Without thinking about it, she drizzled some chocolate into the date and handed it to Connie.

"Yes?" Connie asked as she too became turned around and shoved the pecan into the chocolate and then dipped the date into the caramel to coat it.

"Why don't you come with me sometime? You can judge it for yourself."

"Just what I need, another place to do volunteer

work. Between my business, my house, visiting my mom, who still hasn't gotten over my sister's death, and my on-again, off-again relationship with your cousin—"

"So it's not completely over?"

"Who knows? Anyway, I'd like to see this fancy mission, but I won't have much time." Connie handed Angie a pecan with caramel smeared over it. Angie rolled it in crushed pecan, then reached for a date to start the next one.

"No problem," Angie said. "It's for charity. Any amount of time you can give will be gladly received." With her head swimming and the smell of the chocolate growing ever stronger, Angie looked down to see that she was trying to shove a date into a pecan. "You know, Connie, even if this *was* the perfect angelina, I'd go nuts making these things all day long. Let's finish this up fast."

"Good idea, but how? Look at all those dates."

"No problem." As Connie watched in amazement, Angie spread the chocolate on cookie sheets, ran the dates and pecans through her Cuisinart, tossed them into the caramel, and stirred. She spread the mixture over the chocolate, then topped it with another, thinner layer of chocolate. Before it hardened, she cut it into half-inch squares.

"You know, Connie"—Angie looked down at the chocolate and cocoa powder that covered her from head to toe. She was exhausted and completely sick of the smell, taste, and sight of candy—"you almost had me convinced about the wisdom of giving up sex for chocolate, but now I'm not so sure."

"Why's that?"

"I've never heard anyone complain about having too much sex."

CHAPTER

E I G H T

"We've gone through every piece of evidence in the Hall," Paavo said to Yosh as they rode down Harrison. "We couldn't find the blouse and beer bottle from the crime scene. Whoever made the switch got rid of them."

"It was worth checking," Yosh said. "We'd have looked like a pair of jerks if the evidence to nail Peewee Clayton was sitting in some locker all the time."

"Right. Even more foolish than we do now." And that was plenty foolish. As much as Paavo was checking out others, the other cops were giving him plenty of odd looks in return.

"I wouldn't take anything for granted around here," Yosh said. "Hey, you got to remember, this is the city where a piece of valuable jewelry placed in evidence was left unattended in a jury room. Then it disappeared. We can't prove a juror snatched it, but we aren't taking any bets that they're innocent."

"Don't remind me of that." Paavo shook his head at

the memory of one of the city's more bizarre courtroom incidents. "This fiasco is bad enough."

"I wonder if you should have tried to bluff your way through the prelim," Yosh mused. "What if you had simply lied and said it *was* the blouse and beer bottle from the scene? I mean, you had lab tests to back you up."

Paavo shook his head. "I saw Clayton's eyes. He knew. His attorney would have asked for an evidentiary hearing. It would have taken a little longer, but the result would have been the same. Clayton would have walked."

They parked the car in the middle of Valencia Street and got out. The buildings on the street were old Victorian flats, most covered with peeling, chalky white paint that obliterated the elegant woodwork on the gables and around the doors and windows. Gentrification hadn't yet reached this neighborhood.

Paavo rang the bell to the walk-up flat. The door buzzed, and he pushed it open—a relic of older times when city dwellers opened their doors without first knowing who was outside them.

"Who is it?" an elderly voice called down.

"Mrs. Clayton?" he called back. He couldn't see her at the top of the stairs. "Police Inspectors Smith and Yoshiwara. We're here to speak with your son."

"He's sleeping. Leave him alone."

"It's important, Mrs. Clayton. We need to talk to him." He waited for her reply.

There was a moment's silence. Then he heard the old woman grumble, "Well, just a minute, then."

He and Yosh waited a good ten minutes before she called them to come upstairs and led them into her small living room. They sat down on a rust-colored sofa, and she settled into a brown lounge chair. She was a barrel-shaped woman with a flat, round, reddish face and spidery tufts of gray hair. Turning her head, she shouted into a hallway behind her, "Peewee, hurry up."

In a few minutes, Peewee came in wearing pajama bottoms and an unbuttoned, mismatched pajama top. His dark brown hair stood on end, his eyes were heavy with sleep, and he needed a shave. A cigarette dangled out of his mouth. Peewee wasn't an especially small man, which led to a lot of speculation as to why he'd been given that particular nickname. But he was a mean SOB, so no one asked. The reality was probably a lot less humorous than the jokes the possibilities gave rise to, anyway.

He was skinny, with small, piglike eyes, a slash of a mouth, and tiny ears resembling corkscrews in the sides of his head. "Ma, get me a beer."

Mrs. Clayton shuffled off to the kitchen.

"I thought I was through with you guys," he said as he flopped onto a window seat.

"You're never through with us, Peewee," Paavo said coldly. "Not when you've killed someone."

"That's harassment," Peewee snarled. "You guys can't pull that one on me. I know my rights."

"Peewee, how can you say that to us?" Yosh said, feigning hurt. "We're your buddies. We want to know how you're getting along, that's all."

Peewee's mother handed him a beer bottle, the cap already removed.

"Is this what you got me out of bed for?" Peewee asked.

"You don't seem too broken up over Sarah Ann's death," Paavo said. "I thought she was your girlfriend."

"So?"

Heartfelt compassion, that was Peewee Clayton.

"Actually," Yosh said, "we want to ask you about your pal Patrick Devlin."

"Who?"

"You knew him, Clayton," Paavo said. "And you probably know he's dead."

"I don't know who you're talking about." Clayton was now just mouthing the words. To the cops' experienced eyes, the initial swagger and bravado were disappearing fast.

"No games, Peewee." Paavo waited a moment for his words to sink in. "When did you last see Devlin?"

"I told you, I don't know the guy."

"What were you doing Wednesday night?"

Peewee took a long swallow of his beer, burped loudly, then said, "I was here with my mother."

Paavo would have loved to ram the beer bottle down the murdering bastard's throat. He tamped down his anger, his tone chilling. "Word on the street is you and Devlin ran numbers together. Now he's dead, just like another numbers runner—Haram Sayir. Two dead men. That should worry you, Peewee."

Peewee's piggy eyes twitched at the news about Sayir. "Nothing worries me. I don't give a damn."

"Others saw you and Devlin together, Peewee," Yosh persisted. "Lying about it makes you look like you're guilty of something."

"Anybody said I was with that guy is wrong." Clayton sounded mealymouthed. "Or trying to set me up."

"Set you up for what?" Paavo prodded.

"I don't know, but it's gotta be something bad or you guys wouldn't be lookin' so happy."

"We're just happy to be here sharing your company, Peewee," Yosh said.

"Screw you, man." Peewee slammed the beer bottle on the coffee table and stood up. He turned his back to the cops, his chest rising and falling with his deep breaths.

Paavo waited, then broke the silence. "Tell us about your numbers-running gigs, Peewee."

Peewee spun around. For a second, his expression gave him away; then his tiny eyes became hooded once more. "I don't play the numbers."

"We heard you do."

"Numbers is for suckers!" His cheek twitched. "It's small-time except for the banker. The banker pulls in money big-time, but everybody else is just a patsy. The runner takes the chances and gets no payoff. That's not for me. I'm nobody's patsy."

"Was Devlin a banker?"

"I told you, I don't know him. But if I did, I'd say he was no banker. He was just a small fish."

"Where were you Wednesday night?" Paavo asked again.

"I already told you." Peewee somehow reined himself in. "I was here, with my mother."

"Friday?"

"Same thing." Peewee turned to face the window, as if suddenly interested in what was going on in the street. "You want anything else, you talk to my lawyer."

Paavo stood. "I don't think I'll waste my breath."

Tall glasses of ice water, open windows, and a long rest in the living room helped ease Angie's chocolate overdose.

Connie took another sip of water and walked over to the view of San Francisco Bay and the Golden Gate Bridge. "I don't get it," she said after a while.

Angie gave her a quizzical look.

"Here you've got all this—great apartment, a killer car, money, good looks—and you want to knock yourself out making chocolates. It doesn't make sense."

Angie pushed her hair off her face, then leaned back in the chair. "Lately, I've felt like the Jonah of the business world. Every job I've had, something has gone wrong and I've ended up out of work. So this time, I decided to become my own boss."

Just then, a peppy shave-and-a-haircut knock on the door interrupted their discussion.

"Oh, no," Angie groaned. She went to the door and looked through the peephole to confirm her worst suspicion. It was confirmed.

"Hi, Stan," she said, opening the door a little way. "I've got company."

"Oh, the cop?" Stan, a tall young man in white jogging shorts and a T-shirt with a Hard Rock Cafe logo, peered over Angie's head into the room. When he saw that the company wasn't Paavo, he smiled broadly. "The more the merrier, I always say." He scooted his lanky body around Angie and stepped into the apartment, giving a quick toss of his head to flick back his silky brown hair. The Hugh Grant look, he called it.

He stopped halfway into the living room and gave Connie an appreciative smile. "Hello there."

Angie shut the door and followed him. "Connie, this is my neighbor from across the hall, Stanfield Bonnette. Stan, meet Connie Rogers."

"Hi, Stanfield." Connie held out her hand.

He pumped it hard. "Call me Stan. Angie's mentioned you to me. I'm always pleased to meet one of Angie's friends." He sat next to her on the sofa, too close. "I work for a major bank in the city. I'm one of those hotshot young executives. Rising fast. Of course, I haven't been able to work since I was horribly attacked a while ago. Life grows more hazardous every day."

"It does. Are you going to be able to go back to work?" Connie asked, concern heavy in her voice.

"Oh, sure. But I'll milk it for all it's worth. Play the system," he added with a knowing nod. "That's me, just a concerned, caring, nineties kind of guy."

Connie eased back from him. "You're amazing."

"I know." He smiled proudly, then turned to Angie. "I couldn't help but notice the wonderful smells coming from this apartment, Angie. It's like walking by a See's candy store. Excuse me a minute," he said to Connie as he got up and headed for the kitchen. "Wow! It *is* a candy store!"

"Help yourself," Angie called out drily.

In a moment he was back with a plate of chocolates. "I've died and gone to heaven," he enthused, finishing one piece and starting a second as he walked into the living room. Draping himself over an antique Hepplewhite chair, he turned to Connie again.

"So," he said, licking his finger, then taking a moment to decide which piece to try next, "you're one of Angie's friends. Are you . . . uh . . . also a cook?"

"No," Connie said, "I run my own business. A gift shop. Everyone's Fancy."

"Aaaaahhhhhh, one of those filthy rich self-employed people." He laughed uproariously, as if it was a joke. Neither woman joined him. His laugh died and he bit into another piece of candy. "You know, Angie, all the candy is good, but these little squares with the chopped dates and nuts and caramel, why, they're simply outstanding."

Angie and Connie both stared at him as if he were crazy.

"Well," he said, standing up, a chocolate melting over his thumb and forefinger, "I guess I'll leave you two alone. Mind if I grab another couple of chocolates, Angie?" He was already halfway into the kitchen when he asked.

When he came back out, his plate was overflowing.

"You're going to be sick, Stan," Angie said. "How can you eat so many?"

"What can I say?" he said. Then his smile vanished and he gave a soulful sigh as he glanced furtively at

Connie. "My love life hasn't been the greatest lately. Not bad, but just not as outstandingly terrific as it usually is." He turned his gaze toward the plate of candy. "At least chocolate never complains when I leave the toilet seat up."

Angie and Connie glanced at each other, then burst out laughing.

CHAPTER

N I N E

"All I want to do is talk to him about our future." Angie sat in the Senseless Beauty Café having a caffè latte with the Reverend Hodge. They had decided to take a break from working out new ways to publicize the auction, and she somehow found herself talking about Paavo. "But his cases keep getting in the way. And now, people he works with seem to be suspicious that he's involved with things he shouldn't be. They're making him feel awful. The whole situation is terrible, Reverend Hodge. Just terrible."

"What was it you wanted to say about your future?" The way Hodge asked made her feel he was truly interested. She'd seen him do that with others, too. "Are you thinking of getting married? Living together? What?"

"I don't think he's quite ready to discuss marriage yet," Angie confessed. "Although he's getting close, I'm sure. Or at least I hope. I've thought about living together, but my father already doesn't much care for Paavo. That would make it worse. My father's the old-fashioned type. But then, I guess most fathers are, aren't they?"

Hodge chuckled. "How do *you* feel about living with him?"

She lightly stirred her latte a moment, then ate a spoonful of cream off the top. "Being very practical," she began, "if we were to live together, I don't know where we'd live."

Hodge's eyebrows rose. "What do you mean?"

"Well, I can't see Paavo being comfortable moving into my apartment. He owns his own home—and his cat would hate it even more than he does."

"Ah, being practical ... oh, yes, that's so *very* like you," he exclaimed. She was surprised he'd said that— not many people recognized her practical side. "So it seems"—he gave a clap of his hands—"that you need to move into his house."

"I couldn't!" she blurted. "I mean, he's got only one closet. No dining room, and a kitchen badly in need of remodeling. Reverend Hodge, I don't know what to do. I don't *fit* in his house."

"Ah! Well," Hodge said after studying her awhile, "that takes care of that. Whether your father approves or not, you don't fit. Case closed."

"Isn't it awful?"

"Sounds like the only answer is marriage and a new home."

Her eyes widened. "Really?"

"Really."

She felt curiously relaxed. "Well, if you say so. Now I just have to hope that someday Paavo sees things as clearly as you do. I'm starting to doubt he ever will, though."

"Don't give up so easily, Miss Amalfi." He waggled a finger at her.

"Why not? Whenever I try to bring the subject up, I

may as well be speaking in tongues for all the good it does me."

She expected him to laugh, but instead he answered with intensity and emotion. "You and your cop friend will get married someday, if you both want it enough and if you, Miss Amalfi, have patience. Right now, he's got to resolve whatever these problems are with his job. He sounds like a man who needs peace in his soul—the peace you can give him—before he can think clearly about the state of his heart. You need patience if you're going to see this through with him. It'll be worth it, though, and in the end, when you're together, it'll seem that all this time actually went by quick as a wink."

"Quick?"

"As a wink."

"No way!"

He shook his head and sat back, suddenly looking as deflated as a punctured tire. "That's the way it often is, Miss Amalfi. At the time, especially when you're young, it seems you wait and wait for things to happen. But in later years, when you look back, it seems it all went by quick as a wink. Life's that way. It's all amazingly short. Too short, I think."

"You sound as if you're ancient," she said. "But you look like a fairly young man. How old are you?"

His eyes twinkled. "Age, my dear, is a matter of mind."

"I'm serious. Forty? You couldn't be much older than that. You're not fifty yet, right?"

"Ah, youthful curiosity—and impatience. God love it. But patience is rewarded. Things will work out for you and your cop friend. Just don't give up."

"I sure hope you're right, Reverend Hodge." She was suddenly too weary to try to get any answers out of him.

"I am. Just remember what I said." Then he winked.

• • •

Angie left the mission that afternoon feeling much better after her talk with Reverend Hodge. He was a curious little man, but despite herself, she was coming to like and enjoy his company.

She opened up her Ferrari as she drove down Highway 280 to Hillsborough, an exclusive community on the peninsula, where her parents lived.

Now, sitting in the library of her parents' somewhat modest mansion, she took in her mother's troubled expression. "Is anything wrong, Mamma?"

Serefina Amalfi heaved a sigh. Angie's mother was a little over five feet tall, a couple of inches shorter than her youngest daughter, and many inches wider. Her hair, jet black with only a little assistance from her hairdresser, was pulled into a tight bun. "A man your father scarcely knew years ago, Frankie Tagliaro, showed up yesterday. I never liked Frankie back then. I like him even less now."

"Why was he here?"

"To make trouble. That's all he was ever good for. Him and his cousin Trecuppa." She leaned close to Angie. "They liked to gamble. Ran around with bad people. If I'd known he was here, I'd have thrown him out. But your father, he's too nice. He invites him in. *Sciocco!* Heaven only knows what your father would do if I didn't watch him every minute!"

"What did the guy want?" Angie asked.

"I don't know. Your father wouldn't tell me, can you imagine? But he was upset after Frankie left, and last night I heard him pacing the floor all night. I couldn't even sleep."

"Would you like me to try talking to him?"

"You?" Serefina looked at her as if she'd lost her mind. "If I can't get it out of him, nobody can."

That put Angie in her place. "Fine, then," she murmured.

The housekeeper came in carrying a tray with a snifter of sherry for each of them and a plate of biscotti. "Anyway, Angelina," Serefina said after a sip of her drink, "what have you been doing? You haven't called me for days."

Angie held the globe of sherry in her hand. It was time to begin to break the news about her business plans to her parents. "I'm sorry. I've been busy. I'm close to figuring out what I want to do with my life."

"*Congratulazione!* So, Paavo finally proposed?"

"No, Mamma. I mean my business life. My career."

"Ah. Your cousin Gina sent me these biscotti. She made them from scratch." Serefina took one. "Pretty good. Not as light as mine, but she'll get better. That's what married life does for you."

Angie drank some sherry, then put the glass down. "I already know how to make biscotti. I'm learning something new. I've decided to go into business for myself."

"Your own business?"

"I want to become a chocolatier."

Serefina's brows crossed. "I've never heard of such a thing."

"It's someone who makes chocolates," Angie said, a little too firmly. "That's what I want my business to be."

"Chocolates? My daughter, a chocolate maker?" Serefina pressed her hands to her chest. "*Dio!* You should be making babies—you and Paavo."

"I'm working on it."

"*Madonna mia!*" Serefina jumped up. "Is that the kind of thing to tell your mother? I raised you to be a good girl, to save yourself for marriage, and now you tell me—"

"Mamma, wait!" Angie flung her arms outward. "I meant that I'm working on us getting married."

"Oh," Serefina sat. "You nearly gave me a heart

attack! You have to get married in white, you know. Otherwise, what will my friends say?"

"I'll get married in white ... someday. Right now, I'm working on my career, on something to do with my life."

"First you get married." Serefina jabbed the tabletop with her finger. "Later you worry about careers. That's what I did."

Angie gulped more sherry. "You helped Papa with his store. I can't help Paavo be a homicide inspector. I need my own career."

"It seems you get involved in his work too much already. You need to settle down. You're not going to find what it means to be a wife and mother by making a chocolate mint patty!" Serefina folded her arms. "The world doesn't need any more chocolates, anyway. We're already too fat."

That does it! Angie stood. "I really don't want to discuss this, Mamma. I'm going home. I'll call you tomorrow."

"*Vai, vai.*" Serefina dunked the biscotti in her sherry. "Maybe by tomorrow you'll come to your senses!"

CHAPTER

TEN

Paavo walked slowly along Third Street in the run-down Old Bayshore part of the city. The collar of his black leather jacket was turned up against the brisk night air. Fog swirled around the streetlights, dimming them, but despite that he wore black-rimmed Ray-Bans. Most men did in this part of town.

Black Levi's, worn black boots, and a blue denim shirt completed his disguise. The sleeves of the shirt and jacket were folded back to show a heavy silver link bracelet instead of the practical black leather watchband he usually wore.

He walked with an easy, loose-limbed swagger, and had combed his hair so that the front flopped onto his forehead. What was funny about this, he thought, was how little disguised he truly was. He had grown up on these streets, dressed much like this. At times, it seemed that dressing up each day to play Mr. Homicide Inspector was the disguise and this was his reality . . . or should have been.

He stopped at an alleyway just outside a dive called El Torero. Slowly, he lifted a cigarette from his shirt pocket and, taking his sweet time, lit it.

He paid no attention to the cigarette, though. The few people on the street continued on their way without a backward glance at him, no car drove by more than once, and there wasn't the least flutter in the curtains and shades covering the windows above the street-level shops.

He took a couple more drags of the cigarette, then let himself be swallowed up by the darkness of the alley.

Leaning against a cobblestone wall and facing the street, he waited. The wait wasn't very long.

"Hey, my man," a voice said.

Paavo dropped the cigarette, crushed it out, and glanced back. A youthful black man stood behind him, nervously bouncing from one foot to the other.

"Glad you made it, Snake Belly," Paavo said.

"I always do. Smooth, slick, and deadly, that's me," he said, his voice vibrating in rhythm with his feet. "So, what you need me for, big man?"

A couple of years ago Paavo had worked hard to prove that Snake Belly, aka Jerome Walker, was innocent after some so-called friends set him up to be the fall guy for killing a rival gang member. The real killers went to jail, and Snake Belly, hardly a model citizen himself, promised to help Paavo whenever he could. It didn't do either man's reputation any good to let others know about their little deal, however.

Paavo stepped to the side so that, like Snake Belly, he could keep a sharp eye on the alley's entrance. "Something's going on in the city, and it's causing trouble—deaths. It involves gambling."

"So what else is new?" Snake Belly was clearly unimpressed.

"In particular, numbers."

"Ah, yes." His bored expression changed completely and a wry smiled appeared. "Now I'm beginning to comprehend, my good man. Yes, sir. There is some mean shit going on there. You got that right."

"Tell me about it."

"Nobody's saying nothing. Leastways, not yet. But some big money is on the street, probably Vegas money. And all of a sudden numbers is *hot*."

"Who's behind the Vegas money?" Paavo asked. "The mob?"

"Don't seem to be. The mob would be smoother, more connected, you know? Whoever this is, they're making waves. Some bad waves, too. They're some real bad dudes."

Paavo handed him two twenties. "See what you can find out. Two nights? Same place?"

"I'll be here," Snake responded.

Snake Belly left and Paavo was alone. Suddenly he was walking down Third Street again, Ray-Bans shielding his eyes, a cocky sway to his step, and an attitude that said keep clear.

The next afternoon at the mission, Angie assisted the volunteer in charge of Auction Central, Mary Ellen Hitchcock. An apple-faced, brown-haired woman, with little makeup and frumpy albeit expensive clothes, Mary Ellen was in her thirties, with two children in private school, and on her second husband—this one a lawyer, instead of the schmuck doctor, as she called him, whom she'd been married to the first time around.

Mary Ellen confessed to Angie that once upon a time she had spent her days like a lost soul, volunteering time and services at one charitable organization after another. Then one day, after picking up her prescription for Prozac (which she'd grown to rely on more and more), she walked out of the drugstore and bumped into Reverend Hodge. They began talking, and he invited her to come to the mission to help. Now she worked here exclusively, and as often as she could. She didn't need medication any longer, not even an aspirin.

There was something about the reverend, she said, that just made you want to help him. "How could you not trust a face like his?"

Mary Ellen showed Angie how to log in donations and give the donor a receipt with the highest possible donation value shown on it for tax deduction purposes.

Angie watched more than one donor's face light up when someone would bring in, for example, a Waterford bud vase that the giver valued at three hundred dollars and Mary Ellen would cry out, "You're too modest. This is worth at least four hundred. Let's make it four-fifty to be safe."

A fifty percent increase was the norm.

"I can't get over the quality of the items that have been donated," Angie said.

"This is nothing. Take a look in the back room."

Angie opened the door to the room. "Oh, my God!" She walked up to a dress hanging on a rack. "This is an original Dior. From the sixties, I'd say. A classic. It's worth more today than it cost originally." She held up the short, glittery black dress with a pouf of netting flaring out from about midthigh to knee. "Though I'm not sure anyone would wear it. Maybe a museum will want it? Or a vintage clothier?"

"You've got a good eye, Angie," Mary Ellen said, following her into the room. "Excellent, in fact. Here, you'll appreciate this. A ruby necklace once worn by Elizabeth Taylor."

"You're kidding!" Angie hung up the dress and took the necklace. She studied it. "If Liz wore it, she was wearing red glass."

"Very good!" Mary Ellen cried. "Actually, she once owned the real one, and this was just a paste job to fool thieves. Here's a photo of La Taylor with the necklace. The souvenir value should make it worth several hundred dollars, perhaps more."

"These are real," Angie said, lifting up one Rolex watch after another. Five watches lay in a cardboard box sitting on a two-shelf bookcase.

"Yes. We'll have to find a decent way to display them. But Angie, here's a photo of our *pièce de resistance*." She handed Angie a snapshot of a Picasso charcoal sketch of a woman holding a guitar.

Angie's breath caught. "Is it genuine?"

"Quite. He did many studies of this model. Not all are in museums. Reverend Hodge has it safely hidden away somewhere or I'd show it to you. This was an early study, but still, we expect this work might go for as much as a hundred thousand dollars."

"My God!"

"We have vintage wines, antique vases including a Ming, furs, jewelry. If people are feeling generous, we might bring in close to a million dollars."

Angie was speechless.

"It's going to be an outstanding auction, Angie. I can't tell you how happy I am to be a part of it. Sheila Chatsworth and I have carried most of the responsibilities. She might seem a bit pompous, but she's got a good heart and she can really get people to come through with huge donations. She'd grown a bit too friendly with the cook's sherry before meeting the reverend. Then, suddenly, she quit—cold turkey."

"Good for her."

"Isn't it? The other volunteers tend to come and go at will. We can't count on them too much, but you seem different. You're a take-charge person."

"I try to help."

"You do. I hope you too will come to feel truly blessed," Mary Ellen continued, "to work for the reverend and his benefactor."

Angie had wondered about the mysterious benefactor. "The reverend mentioned that someone had given him money to start up the mission, but he didn't say any more about the man. . . ." Her voice trailed off in hopes of encouraging Mary Ellen to fill her in.

Not much encouragement was needed. "He's incredibly sexy. And mysterious!" Mary Ellen said as she stepped back into the main room. "Even though he lives right upstairs, we rarely see him. But if you ever do see him, you'll know it. He's got a stare that's to die for."

"The reverend's benefactor is sexy?" Angie could scarcely imagine such a thing. "I expected him to be some rich old gentleman."

"Odd, isn't it?" Mary Ellen mused. "Two men opposite in every way. They met in Las Vegas and Reverend Hodge apparently saved the man's soul."

"Las Vegas? Don't you mean Minnesota?"

"Believe me, he is *not* a Minnesota-type guy." She breathed deeply. "He has the look of a man who needed saving. Oh, dear, look at the time! I've got to go over to the café and help serve the lunch crowd."

Angie's head was swimming. "You work next door as well as volunteer here?"

"I volunteer there, too. The mission gets a cut of the profits."

As Angie watched Mary Ellen—she always thought of jams and jellies—head for the café, she realized she was quite curious about the mysterious, sexy benefactor—and the fact that despite all this talk about charity and good deeds, she still hadn't seen a single needy person at the mission.

●   ●   ●

Paavo sat down at Joe Nablonski's desk. Years ago, they'd been patrol cops together at the Richmond station. Nablonski had always wanted to be a homicide inspector. The top dogs in the Bureau of Inspection, homicide inspectors were the highest level of inspector, the position the best and the brightest aspired to—and once in a while made. Nablonski did all he could in Vice to show Homicide he was ready to join them.

"I'm trying to find out about numbers running in the city," Paavo said after all the usual how-ya-doing's were dispensed with.

"Numbers?" Joe sat back in his chair, his hands folded across his large stomach. "Funny you should ask."

"Is it?"

"We never had numbers in this city worth speaking of—it was always strictly East Coast stuff—until recently. All of a sudden, we're up to our eyeballs in it. We even busted a mom-and-pop grocery for gambling. Not that we went looking for them. They put a sign in the window, advertising. Would you believe it? They thought since the state lotto was legal, a private lotto was okay, too. We look the other way sometimes, but you can't let them rub your face in it."

Paavo leaned forward. "You're saying numbers is being played, but no one cares much? Is that it?"

"What I'm saying is, sometimes we leave it alone. Like, few things give a vice squad a black eye faster than busting a poker game at a senior citizens center, you know?"

He knew. He'd seen it done and had winced along with everyone else.

"But we're not sure what's going on with numbers in the city," Joe continued. "A couple old-time bookies are missing. We heard they both started running numbers and then—pfft—they're gone. Nobody even admits to knowing them. Then, you know, Patrick Devlin was killed, and it looked like a professional hit. I think everybody's scared. But I don't know exactly why."

"What leads do you have?"

Joe stared out the grimy office window, his lips working silently, as if his next word was the last thing he wanted to admit. Finally he answered, "None."

Paavo showed no reaction, but Joe hurriedly explained anyway. "I'm not giving up. We're still looking. Something's got to break. Things are out of kilter. People are nervous. It won't stay like this for long. Something—someone—will snap. I just hope when it happens, it doesn't take too many with it."

CHAPTER

E L E V E N

On Twenty-fifth Avenue just past Clement, patrol cars with flashing lights blocked the street, and cops on foot kept away passersby.

As Paavo and Yosh approached, they could see the victim slumped over the steering wheel of his green Jeep Cherokee, blood and torn flesh where his face should have been. The driver's-side window had been shattered.

"Do we know who he is?" Paavo asked Officer Lorraine Fong after introducing himself.

"The people who live around here," Fong replied, "all say the dead man is Dennis O'Leary, owner of the pub on the corner, A Kiss of the Blarney."

"Any witnesses?" Yosh asked.

"Those folks sitting on the doorstep saw it." Fong pointed at a middle-aged couple. "They said it was a drive-by."

"Thanks," Paavo said. "We'll talk to them."

"I'll see what I can find out here." Yosh put on his

latex gloves. He tried to open the car door, but it was locked. "Great start." He pulled a jimmy out of the small satchel he carried—crime scene bag of tricks, he called it. In two seconds, he popped the door lock.

A wallet and registration showed the victim to be O'Leary. Yosh went through the car's glove compartment and the victim's pockets while Paavo took a statement from the witnesses. The husband and wife had an apartment over the pub and had been eating breakfast by the window when they saw O'Leary pull into the parking space. Seconds later, a full-size beige Chevy sedan pulled alongside. They heard a loud bang, then the Chevy sped away. They told themselves it was a backfire, but both ran downstairs to see if O'Leary was all right. He wasn't.

As Paavo finished obtaining the statement the coroner's team arrived. "Grab O'Leary's keys, Yosh," Paavo said. "We may as well go inside the pub and see what we can learn in there."

They entered a pub filled with knickknacks and wall plaques extolling the virtues of Ireland. The two walked around, checking all the little treasures in the room, their steps echoing in the large empty space. The hollow aura of death surrounded them.

"Darts, sad Irish ballads, and drinking songs," Yosh said. "I wish I'd known about this place earlier. It looks like it would have been fun to come here." He stopped in front of a menu tacked on the wall. "Corned beef and cabbage twice a week. Plenty of Guinness. What more could you ask for?"

"A live owner," Paavo said.

"You're a laugh a minute, partner," Yosh said with a shake of his head. "So, what does it look like to you?"

"Personal. The guy was hit right outside his business. What else could it be?"

"One other possibility to keep in mind these days."

"What's that?"

"Bad luck."

Paavo's attention became fixed on a stack of hand towels by the cash register. He'd noticed them earlier, as well as the ones by the sink. Towels beside a sink made sense, but why next to a cash register? He lifted up the cash register stack and beneath them found some papers with rows and rows of columns with numbers and initials.

"I don't believe it," he muttered.

Yosh walked over to see what was in Paavo's hand. "Shoot. Don't tell me Dennis O'Leary was involved in numbers running, too. Just like the liquor store owner and that guy Calderon and Bo found with your phone number."

"Right," Paavo said. "Patrick Devlin, Haram Sayir, and now O'Leary. I wonder if they knew each other."

Yosh wasn't really listening. "Numbers . . . used to be called 'policy' back East, I understand. It's like a throwback to the old days," he reminisced. "Baby-face Nelson, guys like that. Did you know he was gunned down while—"

"What the hell?" Paavo shouted.

Yosh stared at his partner in shock. Paavo never shouted. "What's wrong?"

He didn't . . . couldn't . . . speak. He simply picked up a list of names under the numbers tally sheets and pointed to the last name on the list. Paavo Smith.

"I hate to have to talk to you about this, Smith."

Paavo knew it was serious from the minute he walked into Lieutenant Hollins's office and saw that he'd taken the cigar out of his mouth. Hollins never lit it in the office—the city's no-smoking ordinances didn't allow it. But he chewed, sucked, licked, and did everything just this side of obscene with a stogie in anticipation of lighting up. Watching Hollins, Paavo finally understood the old saw "A woman's just a woman, but a good cigar is a *smoke*."

Now, though, the cigar was out of sight, and Hollins—round-faced, balding, gray hair, intense hazel eyes—sat up straight and faced Paavo. "Have a seat," he commanded.

"Yes, sir," Paavo said.

"Will you explain to me what's going on?"

"I wish I could, Chief."

"Do you know any of these gamblers who seem to have your name and phone number?"

"Not at all."

"Any idea why your name keeps turning up?"

"None."

"What did your investigations show?"

"I've been investigating from two angles—internally, to figure out what happened to Peewee Clayton's evidence, and externally, to figure out what's going on with all the dead numbers runners. Clayton was my case, and everybody knows he was involved in gambling; now some numbers runners have my name. I assume the two are connected."

"But how?"

"I don't know yet. In particular, I can't figure out why Clayton, who's a small-time lowlife if ever I saw one, has the clout to be involved in so much activity.

"That aside," Paavo continued, "looking at our internal security here at the Hall, I found some problems. The bottom line is, if you don't check up on what your people are doing at least once in a while, the best of them, even cops, will start to develop shortcuts, start to grow lax in little ways; that could easily add up to a major lapse of security."

Hollins nodded. "We used to do security reviews all

the time. Not only in the Bureau of Investigations, but throughout all the departments. Throughout the Hall, in fact. But no more. The damn budget's so tight we can't even do what we need to, let alone what we should. But it shows that we'd better move security back onto the need-to-do list."

"Someone did a good job planning the switch, and had to be plenty patient besides," Paavo said. "From all appearances, it was done by someone who knows the inner workings of the Hall. But who it was, I have no idea yet."

"And what about your external investigation?"

Paavo shook his head. "Nothing."

"I need an explanation, Smith, and I need it soon," Hollins warned. "Too many people are asking too many questions."

"I know."

"You understand what it could lead to if we don't have any answers."

Paavo seethed. "Yes, sir."

"I trust you, Smith, but not everyone knows you like I do. I'm sticking my neck out on this. So get busy."

Reverend Hodge was standing beside Mary Ellen Hitchcock when Angie entered his office. "You're sure it's authentic?" Hodge asked, studying a card encased in clear Plexiglas.

"Absolutely. These certificates prove it."

Angie stepped closer. The card showed a man in a baseball uniform . . . Babe Ruth. Even a sports illiterate like her knew that card was worth a small fortune.

"I'll take care of it," Hodge said. "Thank you, Mary Ellen."

"Are you sure? I don't want to trouble you with these valuables—the Picasso, the diamond necklace, now this."

"No trouble." He put it in his desk drawer. "It makes me feel like I'm doing my part. And you do yours."

She spun around and noticed Angie. "We've received a wonderful donation." Her eyes sparkled. "I'm simply ecstatic." She practically waltzed out of the room.

"Now, Miss Amalfi." Hodge adjusted his glasses, then smiled. "Just the person I've been waiting to see. Tell me how you're going to feed us at the auction. And what the centerpiece will be."

"Well, I haven't exactly settled on the centerpiece yet—"

His smile disappeared. "Oh?"

"—but the menu will be simply wonderful," she said quickly.

"It will?" His beetle-shaped eyebrows popped up high.

"Perfection personified," she said with a confidence she didn't completely feel.

He sat down again and gestured toward the guest chair. "Out with it."

"Okay." She also sat. "For hors d'oeuvres we'll have mushroom and squash timbales; tarte flambée made with cheese, bacon, and onion; grilled sea scallops with wild mushrooms; focaccia with a variety of toppings; smoked salmon with white caviar sauce; citrus gratin with zabaglione topping; and of course all the regulars— a variety of cheeses, cold meats, and salads for the less adventurous eaters."

"Uh, right." Reverend Hodge's brow wrinkled as she spoke.

"I haven't completely settled yet on the dessert table, but right now I'm leaning toward a nice chocolate tarragon mousse, lemon tuiles, and prune croustade. I'm not sure what else."

"Prunes?"

"These are delicious," she assured him with a smile.

He nodded skeptically. "Well, I'm sure if I knew what all that was, you'd be making my mouth water."

"Everyone will love it," Angie said. "The happier and more satisfied the people are, the more generous they'll be."

"Generally, that's right," he muttered, frowning. "I just hope they'll want to eat all that stuff they won't even know how to pronounce."

She felt her blood pressure rising.

"I mean," he continued, "some people are pretty fussy, and all this talk about prunes and zabaglione and—"

"*There you are, you low-down crook. Start sayin' your prayers for real this time!*"

The reverend looked up, then did a swan dive under his desk.

Angie spun around in her chair, and the sight caused her to hurl herself back against the wall. A scarecrowlike man with grizzled hair, missing a few front teeth and wearing stained and dirty overalls and a flannel shirt, was pointing a handgun in their direction.

"Come out of there, you two-bit polecat, or I'll blast right through your fancy-Dan desk!"

"Brother Tweeler." Hodge, on his knees, popped his head over the desktop. "You seem upset. Can we talk?"

"Ain't got nothin' to say, 'ceptin' I want my money, an' I want it now."

Hodge glanced at Angie, beads of perspiration on his brow, then back to Tweeler. "I have no idea what you're talking about, Brother. Why don't you put the gun down, and we can discuss this more calmly?"

"I hate to say a man of the cloth is lyin', Reverend, but what you're sayin' ain't worth shit. My numbers done come up, and I want my five hunnert bucks."

Angie inched toward the door. "Excuse me while I—"

"Stay put!"

She flattened herself against the wall.

"I assure you, Brother Tweeler," Hodge said, on the verge of tears, "I know nothing about any money you're owed. But if it'll make you happy to borrow five hundred dollars from this mission, I'll give it to you. There's no need for violence here."

"Who said *borrow?* I didn't hear nobody say borrow." He glanced at Angie. "Did you hear somebody say borrow, miss?"

She shook her head emphatically.

"It's my money, Hodge!" Tweeler raised the gun again and Hodge ducked.

"Yes, well . . . I'll give it to you," Hodge called from under the desk. "I mean, Miss Amalfi is here. We can't endanger the lady, right?"

Tweeler glanced at Angie. "She ain't the one in danger, Rev. Get your butt out in the open like a man!"

Hodge peeked over the desktop once more. "You want me to moon someone?"

"I want my money. Now!" Tweeler thundered.

"Reverend Hodge, *please!*" Angie cried.

"Okay, okay." Still on his knees, Hodge opened a desk drawer and lifted out his money box, then cautiously stood up.

Tweeler frowned. "If those guys who work for you would have paid up like they was s'posed to," he said, "none of this would have happened."

"You've got something wrong." Hodge's hands shook so much he could scarcely open the box. "No one works for me. We're all volunteers in the army of the Lord. Our mission is to give, not to receive."

"Stuff it, Hodge."

Hodge counted out five hundred-dollar bills. "This money was supposed to buy food for the women and children, the old men, the disabled veterans who come to the mission. The sick, the weak, the—"

"Buy food, my ass! It's all over the street that this place is filled with goddamned numbers runners. And crooked ones at that! They changed my number, and now they say I ain't a winner. But me an' Charlie Junior"—he held up his gun—"know I'm a winner."

"You heard it on the street?" Hodge asked innocently as he stood up.

"Course I did! Where the hell else would I hear such a thing?" Tweeler grabbed the money from Hodge's hands and began counting it himself.

"The street?" Hodge asked again. "But I never go on the street. It's dangerous out there. Drug dealers, hookers, guns. How could they know me or anything about me? It doesn't make sense."

"I hate to tell you, but the way you talked about them folks on the street, they sound just like the ones in this here mission to me." Tweeler looked as if he was trying to remember what came after two hundred.

"But it's not true! We aren't like that!"

"Then how'd I up and win this money?" Tweeler said, two hundred dollars in one hand, three hundred in the other, and the gun still too close to him on the table.

"I don't know. All I know is I've got some partners and others who'll be plenty upset that I gave you all that," Hodge cried, his hands against his cheeks. He looked as if he was going to give the Macaulay Culkin scream from *Home Alone*.

"My heart bleeds. Three hunnert." A hundred-dollar bill shifted hands.

"But Brother Tweeler," Hodge said, cautiously tiptoeing around the desk toward the man, "we're trying to do good here. If you take that . . . it's stealing."

Tweeler struggled until all the bills were in one hand, then he put them in the breast pocket of his flannel shirt. Sharp eyes peered at Hodge, but then he said, not so sharply, "Huh?"

"Stealing's wrong, especially from a rescue mission. A *religious* rescue mission. You'll pay for it later . . . somehow . . . sometime when you least expect it. Zap!"

Tweeler's eyes widened. "Zap?"

"That's right. You've got to do good things in the eyes of the Lord, Brother Tweeler."

"I do good things!"

"Taking this money?"

"Well . . ."

"Brother, if you do good, good things will come to you. This is a mere five hundred dollars. But if you're a truly good man, you'll get far more than this. You'll have more riches than you can count."

"I don't need more. I had trouble countin' to five hunnert."

"Don't ruin your life, Brother. Within you live dreams and hopes and a blessed assurance of your own rightness. Don't let these few shackles prevent you from finding the real you."

He gently took hold of Tweeler's arm and maneuvered him so that he faced a blank wall, and then he passed his hand along the line of the wall, as if creating a broad mural. "You could travel, Charlie. Just imagine taking a plane—or a train, if you're afraid to fly, like I am—to someplace far away. Someplace warm and friendly." His hand was like a giant paintbrush. Angie found herself staring at the blank wall as though at passing scenery. "You could buy a new suit there if you wanted one—not that there's anything wrong with your overalls, of course. You could buy a hat—a ten-gallon one, even. On your pinky finger there'd be a gold ring with a big square diamond. And when you pulled out your roll of money, that ring would flash and simply dazzle everybody! You'd go strutting down the street dressed to the nines, and the women—the women, Charlie—they'd notice you. They'd surround you, hanging on your every word. They'd do it first because of the money. But you know what, Charlie? You know what?"

Tweeler shook his head, staring at the wall, trying hard to see the paradise Hodge was describing.

"After a while," the reverend said softly, soothingly, "they'd hear nothing but your words. They'd look into your heart, and they'd be after you for yourself. For *you*. Rich ones, poor ones, all wanting you. You'd choose a rich one, of course, and spend your life in a soft bed, with all the sex and the Johnnie Walker Red Label you could ever hope for."

"You think so?" Tweeler whispered.

"Have faith, Charlie. Have faith that your will—and the power you have to change your life—are going to make a difference. You could become whoever you were always meant to be."

"Yeah," Tweeler whispered, smiling hard at the wall, looking as if the vision painted there was so real he could all but taste it. "Oh, yeah!"

Hodge plucked the five hundred dollars from Charlie's breast pocket. "God be with you, Brother." He whisked Tweeler out of his office and locked the door.

He turned around, took a wobbly step toward his desk, then fell over in a dead faint.

"Do you feel better now, Reverend Hodge?" The reverend sat on the floor, his back to the wall, feet straight out before him. Against his head he held a cloth Angie had found in the kitchen and dampened with cold water.

He moaned, then whispered mournfully, "Thank you."

Angie knelt down beside him. "Who was that horrible man?"

"He's a very troubled soul," Hodge replied. "A compulsive gambler who's lost everything. He thinks everyone is stealing from him. Now he's even blaming the mission."

"He was talking about the numbers racket," Angie said. "Paavo's been talking about numbers, too. Maybe Tweeler is right that something is going on somewhere near here."

"Maybe so, but certainly not at the mission. Anyway, last week, he was complaining about poker. The week before that, craps."

"But numbers—"

"He lies, Miss Amalfi, I'm sorry to say."

"Oh. I thought we were on to something," she murmured, disappointed that the potential lead had fizzled so quickly. "But you handled him wonderfully. I had no idea you were so clever. Your talk turned him around completely," Angie said, still a little dazzled by the way the reverend had dealt with the situation. Until he passed out, at least.

"We must take the good with the bad in this kind of work," Hodge said.

An image of the many troubled and sad cases the reverend must see in this line of work came to her. "Why do you do it?" she asked suddenly.

He seemed surprised by the question. "It's ... it's the angel on my bookshelf."

She looked at the small carved wooden angel. "It looks very old and very special."

"It is. It was given to me many years ago by a holy man as I sat by the shore at Galilee."

"My goodness, really?" She was impressed and a little awed.

"He said to keep it with me as a reminder to do good

works. So here I am." He caught her eye, then grinned. "Running a rescue mission, I can give people a serving of hope along with meat and vegetables when they come here."

"That's very kind," she said.

He nodded. "Cheap, too."

CHAPTER

TWELVE

Serefina Teresa Maria Giuseppina Amalfi entered Angie's apartment as if she owned it, which in fact she did, since she and Angie's father owned the building that housed the apartment. Angie paid them a fair market rent. Almost.

"Angelina, *una tassa di caffè, per piacere.* I've had such a terrible night. I couldn't sleep. Now my head hurts. *Dio, aiuto!*"

"I'll get some," Angie said, hurrying into the kitchen for some Italian roast. "Would you like to eat anything?" she shouted. "I've got lots of chocolate candy—dark chocolate truffles, white chocolate truffles, Grand Marnier truffles, ripple divinity, chocolate almond fudge—"

"Stop, please. No more chocolate! Do you have any more of Gina's biscotti I gave you the other day?"

Angie was getting really sick of hearing about Gina's wonderful biscotti. "I'll find some. They might be a little stale."

"*Non importante.*"

"Now, tell me what's wrong, Mamma," Angie said, carrying a tray with biscotti and coffee out to the living room.

"I finally found out what was bothering your father." She sighed. "I knew that Frankie meant trouble. Those Tagliaros, nothing but trouble. Both start with *T*. What do you expect?"

Serefina picked up the coffee cup, took a sip, sighed again, then dunked the biscotti into her cup and watched the cookie grow soggy. She quickly lifted it to her mouth, chewed, swallowed, and then heaved yet another big sigh.

"Mamma, I've never seen you like this." Angie, getting over her irritation about Gina, now was worried.

"I don't want to trouble you," Serefina said woefully.

"It's no trouble."

Serefina folded her hands. "Well . . . maybe you can help."

That was a switch. "Me? Why, I'd love to help you if I can."

"You're right. Not you."

I should have known, Angie thought.

"Paavo," her mother said.

That was even more surprising. "Paavo? You're kidding."

"It's your father who needs help." Serefina pulled her lace handkerchief out of her purse and dabbed her eyes.

"Papa?" Now Angie was even more confused. "But Papa doesn't even like Paavo."

"What can I say?" Serefina fluttered her handkerchief. "Anyway, Frankie Tagliaro owns a restaurant, the Isle of Capri, out in the Richmond district."

"I've heard of it, but I've never eaten there."

"I'm not surprised. It's not much of a place. At one

time he even used a Chinese cook. The food was good as long as you didn't care that your ravioli tasted like wontons."

"That happens."

"*Sì*. Anyway, this Frankie, he asked your father for money. Eighteen thousand dollars! He owes the money to some men, and if he doesn't pay them, he's got troubles." Serefina lowered her voice and bent close to Angie. "I could tell, the more he talked, the kind of men he was talking about."

Angie's eyes widened. "You don't mean . . . Mafia?"

"You watch too many movies. These are *crooks*."

"Oh," Angie said. Translation: these were WASP bad guys.

"He told your father he can't get any more money out of his business," Serefina continued, her hand against her breast. "The restaurant isn't making it— maybe because he serves lousy food, who knows? But if he doesn't pay . . ." She drew her forefinger across her throat.

"This is crazy. It's not Papa's problem. And I got the impression Tagliaro hadn't talked to Papa for years."

"True, but your father said Frankie sounded scared. Now he's worried." Serefina shut her eyes a moment, pressing her hand to her forehead, and Angie could see the dark shadows under her eyes, the lines of strain around her mouth. Despite all Serefina's blustering, she was truly worried. "Your father can't let an old acquaintance who came to him for help be killed," she said softly. "Even if he never liked the guy. It's a question of honor."

"Honor? What's the honor in giving money away for no reason? I'll go meet this Frankie Tagliaro myself," she said, "and order him to leave my father alone!"

"It's too late," Serefina protested. "He got on his knees, begging for the money. He even cried. Your poor father, how bad he felt! Eighteen thousand dollars! To a stranger! I cried, too, when I heard that. *Dio!* What are we going to do?" Serefina flung out her arms, and the biscotti flew from her fingers across the room.

Angie scrambled for the biscotti. "We could shoot him."

"Angelina, you've been with your friend the cop too long." Serefina drank more of her coffee. "But I know what we *could* do. Let's get Paavo to throw him in jail!"

"What?"

"Yes! If Frankie's in jail, then the crooks can't get him, and your father doesn't have to give him the money. It's a good idea, Angelina. Paavo can do it. He's smart."

"He's in Homicide. He doesn't go around throwing restaurant owners in jail."

"Maybe it's time for him to start."

"Nothing like a little evidence to brighten one's day," Yosh said cheerfully as he drove himself and Paavo out to Peewee Clayton's house. The "little evidence" was an annotation in Dennis O'Leary's numbers tally sheets that said simply "Peewee." True, there might be more than one Peewee in the city. But O'Leary's patrons had identified this Peewee as being a regular.

"Look over there, Yosh," Paavo said, pointing toward the left. "Our boy is about to take his evening constitutional."

Peewee walked jauntily down the street to the corner, then stopped and waited at the bus stop.

"Hey, all right, pal." Yosh swung the car into a driveway and out of Peewee's sight. "Let's see where he's off to."

The bus soon came, and Yosh stayed a reasonable distance behind it. Peewee got off twice, each time running into a mom-and-pop grocery store. The second time, instead of waiting for yet another bus to show up, he walked up to a black 1972 Firebird parked on the street, unlocked the door, and drove it to one pool hall, one bar, two liquor stores, and a doughnut shop.

"Nothing like following a numbers runner to find out who to turn over to Vice," Paavo said with grim satisfaction.

"You think that's what this is, do you?" Yosh asked.

"He's not shopping for his mother," Paavo said.

"He keeps this up, we might be able to follow him straight to the banker," Yosh said.

"It couldn't be that easy. There's usually a switch somewhere. We've got to watch Peewee carefully—see where it's made."

"I'm all eyes, partner," Yosh said.

Peewee's journey was structured to look as though he were buying goods at each stop. Eventually, he parked the car in a lot and, carrying a Macy's shopping bag, disappeared into a BART station.

Paavo and Yosh did the same. They huddled on the stairway, trying to stay hidden while keeping an eye on him, since there was no place to hide on the train platform.

Finally, Peewee got on a Fremont-bound train. They raced down the stairs and jumped on at the last moment, making sure he stayed on it. They moved closer to the car he was on as the train moved. It wasn't too long before it zipped underneath San Francisco Bay, headed toward Oakland.

Paavo hated riding BART. As strange as it felt traveling in any subway's hole in the ground, traveling in a tube skimming the bottom of the bay was even worse. Too many submarine movies about water pressure and leaks sprang to mind. The underwater ride was only five minutes or so, but he felt as if he should hold his breath the whole way. He'd rather face a murderer than a BART train headed for the East Bay.

But if he could keep track of Peewee, this might be the big break he needed in this case. The break that would give him some answers for Hollins.

They didn't see Peewee get off at the West Oakland or Eleventh Street stops, but just as the train began to pull out of the MacArthur station, they saw him sprint away from the tall, overweight woman who had shielded him from their view. He ran down the stairs. They tried to open the car doors, but it was too late.

They noticed, though, that Peewee no longer held his bag of goodies. The switch had to have been made on the train or at one of the stations. Getting the money from the runners to the counting house was the trickiest part of the numbers business. Other crooks, as well as the police, had an abiding interest in the cash-filled counting house location—the police to shut it down, and others to rob it. Since the easiest way to find it was simply to follow the runners, the runners had to be experts at quick shifts of money from one to another. Only the most trusted lieutenants of the banker made the final delivery.

Peewee had skunked them.

At the next stop, Yosh and Paavo got off the train, crossed to the opposite side of the platform, and spent a long, miserable return trip to San Francisco.

CHAPTER

THIRTEEN

"We've got three main questions, Angie," Paavo said as he pushed his chair back a bit from the dining table. Angie had prepared what she called one of her "simple" meals—rigatoni, veal cutlets, and a radicchio salad. "Who is Peewee working with? Why are numbers runners and gamblers turning up dead all over the city? And why in the hell does my name keep showing up in the middle of all this mess?"

The anger on his face tore at her. He was a proud man, and being the brunt of whispers and innuendos ate at him. She stood and began stacking the dinner plates. Paavo picked up some condiments to carry to the refrigerator. "No." She placed her hand on his, then lifted them from him and kissed him lightly.

"Go relax on the sofa," she said.

He did as she asked, and she put the Fifth Symphony of the Finnish composer Sibelius on the stereo, then continued cleaning up the dinner dishes.

Paavo leaned his head back against the sofa and

shut his eyes. Earlier that evening he had stood outside Angie's apartment for a long time, wondering if he should go in. He was in such a foul mood after facing Hollins and his questions, and then losing Peewee, he knew he wouldn't be good company for her. Heck, he didn't even want to be with himself tonight.

But then, when he'd seen her, held her, the world seemed a little bit better. Finally, he felt himself beginning to relax. He tried to clear his mind of work, shut his eyes, and simply enjoy his strange affinity with the music Angie had put on the stereo. Not that he was Finnish—he was pretty sure he wasn't, despite his first name. In fact, he had no idea what nationality he was, which made him more of an outcast than ever in this multicultural age when everyone else seemed to be a something-hyphen-American.

An elderly Finnish gentleman had raised him and his older sister, Jessica, when their mother abandoned them. Aulis Kokkonen had been the first to call him Paavo, and Aulis, in turn, was the only man Paavo had ever called father. There was a quality to Sibelius's music that reminded him of Aulis, and of the mystical land, the sagas and myths, that Aulis used to tell him about when he was a boy.

With a sigh, he walked over to the large picture window. Angie's apartment was on the twelfth floor of a building near the very top of Russian Hill. The northern sector of the city stretched out before him, and the view of San Francisco Bay extended from the Golden Gate Bridge to Treasure Island.

It was all of a piece, he thought, this coming to Angie, her apartment, her world. High in this aerie, this small, inviolate place, he could look down on the city far below and pretend it was no more than a thousand bright lights that held not a hint of crime or violence or poverty. Up here, he could relax and allow himself a moment, at least, of warmth and love.

"Better?" she asked, placing her hand on his arm.

He turned to her, reaching out to touch her face, the thick brown waves of her hair, to run his thumb against her bottom lip, to cup her jaw with his hand. "Why do you bother with me, Angie?" His voice was low, husky. "I'm foul-tempered, I have a season in hell for a job, I don't have the time to give you what you deserve or the money to spend on you that I'd like to. Now I'm even losing my good name around the Hall—for whatever that was worth."

She stepped closer, resting her hands against his broad chest. "You have your good name among everyone who counts, and always will. And you give me more than you'll ever know, just being here for me."

"I love you, you know." He kissed her lightly. "That's why I want everything to be perfect for you, why I want—"

She put her fingertips to his lips, stopping him. "It's all right. This will all work out. You always tell me to have patience. There are times, Inspector, when you need to take your own advice."

"Angie." He ran his hands up her arms to her shoulders, then down her back, easing her closer and closer until he could feel the contours of her body molded snugly against his own. "You're growing wise, woman. That's very sexy."

"In that case . . ." She kissed him as she started backing him toward her bedroom. "I know a place I can be a veritable *Encyclopaedia Britannica.*"

Angie lifted her head off the pillow and looked at the fluorescent readout on her clock radio. "It's only eleven, Paavo," she said. "If you stayed here tonight, we could fall asleep soon, and you might even get a good night's sleep for once."

He put his arms around her. It was becoming more and more difficult for him to leave her each night—almost half the time he didn't. They were going to have to come to some resolution of this situation soon, but with the possibility of his job on the line, he didn't think that this was the right time to talk of long-term commitments. He wanted to leave as little room as possible for regrets later.

But she was soft and warm, and it took him no time at all to realize that he could no more get out of this bed and go home than fly to the moon on his own power. He forced himself away from her for just a moment and sat up. "I'll check my messages, then we can shut down the apartment and . . . sleep. . . ."

She ran her hand over his belly. "Sounds good."

At her touch he nearly said to hell with the messages, but then she withdrew her hand, got up, put on her velour robe, and went out to the kitchen to turn off the coffeepot, shut off the lights, and lock up the apartment. She flipped on the small TV in the bedroom as she went, knowing he liked to check in on the local news each night. Half the time, it seemed almost as important to keep up with the political scene in the city as with the crime scene in order to do his job right.

As he listened to his messages, none of which couldn't wait until the next day, he watched the newscaster Emerald Yeh talk about a foiled bank robbery attempt, a traffic accident on the Golden Gate Bridge that snarled the commute, and a dog who rescued a kid who had toppled into the water fountain at Yerba Buena Center. Not a big news day, thank goodness. He was more ready than ever to . . . relax . . . once more with Angie.

He curled the pillow under his head, so that he was

propped up slightly when she came back into the bedroom. Makeup off, her hair mussed, her mouth soft from being kissed, the long robe covering her, making her seem to float by—she was more beautiful than ever. "Everything's off, and the deadbolt is on the front door," she said as she reached his side of the bed. She shut off the lamp and he took her wrist, drawing her toward him. When their lips met, he felt her hunger. It matched his own.

"I like the way you think, Inspector," she whispered.

It was all the encouragement he needed. His arms wrapped around her and he twisted so that, with a laugh, she sprawled across the bed, her back on the mattress and her legs over his. Her laughter disappeared quickly, though, as he slowly unknotted the robe, then drew the sides open, kissing her, his hands roaming over every soft, subtle, feminine inch.

"Let me turn the TV off," she said, pushing back his shoulders as she struggled to get up. "I don't want you to suddenly begin paying more attention to Emerald Yeh than to me."

"Not to worry." He didn't think there was any need whatsoever for her to turn off anything, not the way she'd managed to turn him on.

Holding her robe together, she hurried across the room to the TV. A short community service announcement began about the Random Acts of Kindness Mission and the big charity event it was going to sponsor. "Oh, look, Paavo. This is about the mission."

"Heaven is not the place for selfish people. . . ."

"That's him, Paavo. That's Reverend Hodge!"

Paavo sat up to see this wunderkind Angie had talked so much about. The reverend was facing the camera and speaking.

"Here is one of the least selfish people I know, a man who has completely changed his life for the better and now gives

freely of his time and money for our endeavor. My friend, my benefactor, and my number-one volunteer, Alexander Clausen."

Angie backed away from it, not able to believe what she was seeing. She glanced quickly at Paavo. He stared at the TV, unflinching and still. Hodge's benefactor wasn't a particularly large man, not even particularly dangerous-looking, but he made Angie's skin crawl.

He had short blond hair combed forward to frame his face, deeply tanned skin, and a large mole that looked like a big black bug on his cheek. Angie knew him as Axel Klaw.

"Perform your own random act of kindness," Clausen said, *"by giving generously to the big auction."*

The camera switched back to Hodge.

"And I'll even throw in my book and tape—a thirty-nine-ninety-nine value—for the special price of only nineteen-ninety-nine, if you call now. Our toll-free number is . . ."

Angie slammed her hand against the off switch. She bent her head and waited until the trembling left her limbs. Then she turned to Paavo.

He still hadn't moved.

"I had . . . I had no idea," she cried.

"You've never seen him there?" The blue eyes that met hers were shards of ice.

"Of course not! I heard that the reverend had a partner, but no one mentioned his name. I'm not sure I would have recognized it anyway. I thought his name was Axel Klaw."

Paavo visibly shuddered. She walked over to him and tried to hold him, but he shrugged her off. She hung back awkwardly, not sure what to do.

Memories of the last time she had seen Paavo and Klaw together rushed back at her, tying her insides into knots of fear. She and Yosh had blundered into the office of Klaw's pornography studio in Berkeley and seen Paavo and Klaw facing each other across a desk. Each had his gun drawn; each had been waiting for the other to make the first move.

He could have died right before her eyes. She shut her eyes now, trying not to remember. But she did remember. She'd seen another side of Paavo that day, the cold, hard side of a man who was willing to kill or be killed. It had stunned and frightened her. It still did.

"Paavo," she whispered, scared to death that he might go after Klaw again.

He glanced at her. "Those are the good people you're helping, Angie? The good people you've surrounded yourself with?"

Why was he angry with her? "I told you I didn't know."

His jaw tightened. "If Klaw's involved, it's no place for you to be. Stay away until I check out this so-called mission."

She sat on his side of the bed. "Don't go there, Paavo. Please. Let me talk to Reverend Hodge." She took his hand. "I'm sure he doesn't know about Klaw's background. I'm sure it's all perfectly innocent! Why, just today, a man came to see Reverend Hodge. His name was Charlie Tweeler—"

"Angie!" He pulled his hand from hers and grabbed her arm tightly. Too tightly. "Nothing involving Axel Klaw is innocent. I'm asking you to stay away from the place."

She stood up and took a step back, out of his reach. Her eyes smarted as she spoke. "I'm working with the caterers. I can't simply abandon the reverend and the other volunteers."

"Good people can be duped, Angie. Especially by a con artist like Klaw."

"No, Paavo. You're wrong about them."

He got up and started to dress.

"What are you doing?" She reached for his arm, trying to still his movement. He kept on.

"I'm going out."

"I told you I had no idea about that man!" She was close to tears.

He buttoned his shirt. "I'll ask you once more to keep away from the mission until I find out what's going on."

"You're not being reasonable!"

Cold eyes lifted to hers, and she recoiled from the implacable harshness in them. He had never looked at her this way, and her heart twisted with a sharp pang. This wasn't the lover who had held her so tenderly in his arms only minutes ago, but a hard-eyed stranger.

He didn't say anything as he strapped on his shoulder holster, slid in the gun, then put on his jacket. "I'll call you," he said as he unbolted the door.

"Don't do this!" She threw her arms around him, but he removed them and walked out the door in silence.

Somehow he found his way home that night. He didn't remember much about leaving Angie's apartment. He recalled that she'd tried to convince him that he should stay, that she had been as surprised by seeing Klaw as he was.

Paavo knew she wasn't lying, but that knowledge didn't make the black rage that filled him any easier to handle.

He had removed Angie's arms from around his neck, trying not to catch her eye as he did so. It hurt. She was soft and loving, and he ached for her, ached for the warmth only she could give. But he needed to be alone. That was something Angie didn't understand about him, and probably never would.

His need to be alone.

She didn't understand that before he'd met her, except for a few years with Aulis Kokkonen, he'd been alone ever since Jessica's death.

So he tore himself away from Angie, away from the confused, stricken look on her face. He drove down from her insulated hilltop, down into the heart of the city and out Geary Street to his cottage in the Richmond.

As he drove, thoughts of this evening disappeared, and the ugliness of twenty years ago washed over him.

When he was fourteen, he had watched his nineteen-year-old sister, Jessica, go out with a man whose name, then, was Alex Clausen. He was a splashy dresser, high-living, flashing what seemed to be a lot of money, especially to a couple of teenagers.

Jessica was working part time and taking classes at City College when Clausen turned his attention to her. Paavo protested that the man was too old and too fast for her—Clausen must have been all of twenty-six or so at the time—but Jessica wouldn't listen. She was tired of living hand to mouth, she'd said. She'd found someone who had money and who spent it on her, someone who could make her laugh and show her a good time, and she wasn't about to turn her back on him.

Paavo never learned everything Clausen was involved in, but he did know that Clausen was a dealer in hard drugs. Jessica swore to Paavo that she had never touched the stuff and never would.

Then, one night, she was found dead from an overdose of heroin.

Clausen claimed he wasn't with her the night she died, and others corroborated his story. Paavo, though, had seen her leave the apartment with him. At fourteen, he didn't know how to make people believe him, didn't know how to make them see that Alex Clausen had been involved in his sister's death. All he knew was that

Jessica wouldn't have tried heroin for the fun of it, that there was more to the story.

Twenty years. Christ, he should be over it by now. He was a homicide inspector. He saw drug deaths, murders, suicides nearly every day.

But even a homicide cop couldn't shrug off the memory of his own sister's senseless death at the hands of a man such as Klaw. In fact, knowing what he knew about drug deaths made it even worse. The convulsions, the pain, the blood from the eyes and nose . . .

When he walked into his cottage, his big tom, Hercules, greeted him with a cry, then stood and slowly stretched before leaping off the sofa and getting himself tangled up in Paavo's feet—his way of demanding his dinner. Paavo picked up the cat and petted him as he carried him into the kitchen, grabbing a can of 9-Lives Seafood Stew from a cupboard as he went.

With Herc fed, he went back into the living room and turned off the lights, but instead of continuing to the bedroom, he slumped into an easy chair.

Jessica used to drink when she went to parties with friends. Still, it was a big jump from alcohol to heroin. He didn't believe she'd have agreed to take the stuff unless she'd had so much to drink she didn't know what she was doing. That was a tried and true way to get someone hooked. Start with just a little now and then at a party, among friends. Progress to just a little because there *wasn't* any party going on, and wasn't that depressing? Enjoy just a little now and then to be ready for a party in case one happened. Need just a little now and then to get through each and every day. Demand just a little, just because . . .

Had that been what Axel Klaw had planned for Jessica? That kind of deterioration, that whirlpool into hell? Now he was back in San Francisco, within Paavo's reach, and this time he wouldn't get away.

Jessica. How many nights had he lain awake wondering what she'd be like today, and how his own life would have turned out if she'd lived?

He heard the *thwack* of the rubber cat door slamming shut. Hercules, now fed, was wandering off to check out the neighborhood. It was all right. Paavo needed to be alone tonight.

He had always been alone. He still was.

CHAPTER

FOURTEEN

"He was a drug peddler, a pornographer—for all I know, he was a pimp besides!" Angie paced back and forth in front of Reverend Hodge's desk, flinging her arms as she spoke. When she thought of the way Paavo must have felt when he saw Klaw on TV last night, she became furious all over again. "How can you let a man like that be a part of something so beautiful?"

Reverend Hodge slid his chair closer to the wall. "Miss Amalfi, you're so agitated!"

"You think *this* is agitated?" She put her face near his. "You haven't seen anything yet!"

"Calm down, please. I assure you, Mr. Clausen is not the kind of man you suggest he is."

She stuck her finger against his skinny chest. "Axel Klaw is his other name, and he's evil and ruthless. My friend hates Klaw. The two of them nearly killed each other the last time they met, and it wasn't very long ago. Not long enough for Klaw to have gone through this miraculous metamorphosis into a Lord Bountiful, that's for sure."

"Please." Hodge eased out of his chair and backed away from her, rubbing the spot she'd jabbed. "You look stressed and exhausted. Maybe you should have a bowl of chicken soup?"

She clutched her head. "I look stressed and exhausted because I am! Don't you understand? I spent all night worrying about my friend. I love him! I don't want him hurt!"

He backed up more. "Maybe you should get married to him. When married people go to bed, they fall asleep immediately."

He was treading on really thin ice now. "Maybe I *would* be getting married if Paavo weren't so troubled." Her tone was lethal. "And one of the things he's troubled about is Axel Klaw!"

"Miss Amalfi," the reverend said, "sit down, please." He grabbed a chair and wheeled it up behind her, hitting her in the back of the knees. She sat. He returned to his desk and also sat, then gave her a long, weary look. "Believe me when I say to you that Alexander Clausen is no longer this Axel Klaw creature. He's a changed man. He's been redeemed, saved. Born again."

Angie pressed her hands to her face, trying to steady herself. "How can I believe there's anything good about the Random Acts of Kindness Mission when your benefactor is a criminal? Remember Brother Tweeler? He said there was numbers running going on here. I didn't believe him. I believed you! But now I'm wondering. With Klaw here, anything's possible."

"It's Clausen, Miss Amalfi. Clausen, not Klaw. He confessed to me all about his past," the reverend said, his hands clasped. "How sordid and ugly it was. But even then, he never did anything wrong. Oh, he was no angel, and he was around men who did plenty of bad things. But not a single illegal deed was dealt by his hand. Don't you believe me?"

"I don't." She folded her arms.

"Tell me, was Mr. Clausen ever imprisoned?" Hodge asked.

"I don't know."

"He wasn't," Hodge said confidently.

"I told you he was clever!" she protested.

"Also, if he's so evil, why isn't your boyfriend here right now to arrest him?"

"Paavo said Klaw always got others to do his dirty work."

"Ah, I see. So this Mr. Klaw is not only a demon, he's a Svengali besides."

"Something like that."

"Before I ever came here, Miss Amalfi, before I ever started this adventure called the Random Acts of Kindness Mission, I knew Alexander Clausen. He publicly apologized for all his past sins. Can you imagine the bravery it takes to make a public apology? He's now completely, one hundred percent on the up-and-up, and he's even given—"

"Reverend Hodge, you're making me blush!"

Angie spun around at the familiar voice. Her whole body went cold at the sight before her.

His eyes snaked over her. She felt in need of a bath just from his gaze. "Can it be? Angelina Amalfi, if I'm not mistaken!"

"Axel Klaw," she replied.

"Clausen now. I've given up that tired, harsh name, that life. I've been reborn! Thanks to the reverend."

His words were too glib. Angie's skin prickled. But strangely, she found herself wishing his words were true, that the ugliness and evil between him and Paavo could vanish.

"Let me introduce my friends to you, Miss Amalfi," he said.

She'd been so busy taking in every aspect of Klaw, searching for any sign that he had reformed, she hadn't even noticed anyone else enter the room. Klaw turned first to the woman in the doorway. "This is Lili Charmaine. My muse."

"Get outta town!" Lili gave a deep-dimpled smile to Klaw, then turned to Angie. "Hi." She wore a skintight ivory dress. The gold zipper up the front strained to keep its teeth together, and Lili had plenty for the dress to strain against.

"How do you do, Miss Charmaine," Angie said, holding out her hand.

"Hey, that's way classic." Lili wiped her palm against her thigh, then limply shook Angie's hand. "You can call me Lili. That's not with a *y*, but with an *i* with a little heart instead of a dot over it." Her voice rose at the end, as if she were asking instead of telling.

"So that's Lili with two *i*'s?" Angie asked, more than a little dumbfounded. The woman talked like an over-the-hill Valley Girl.

"Huh?"

"This is Van Warren, my accountant," Klaw said quickly.

For a moment, Angie thought Klaw was mistaken. No one was there. Then the man stepped out from behind Lili-with-an-*i*. Angie had never before seen an accountant who looked so much like everybody's stereotype of one. He was nerdy and nebbishy, a small man with brown hair slicked straight back, horn-rimmed glasses, a dark gray suit, and a light gray tie. Yet when she looked at him more closely, she saw that instead of accountantlike rounded shoulders, his shoulders were square, and his compact body appeared hard, not flabby.

He noticed her perusal, and for an instant she thought she detected a hardening of his eyes. But then it was gone.

"Hello, Mr. Warren," she said, holding out her hand.

"How do you do?" His handshake was even more limp-wristed than Lili's. He bobbed his head, meek and even bashful. Her first perception of him had obviously been in error. Nerds might work out at a gym now and then, but even that wasn't enough to remove their basic nerdiness.

"I'm fine, thanks," Angie said, pulling her hand free.

"I'm so glad, Miss Amalfi," Klaw began, "that we can meet here under better circumstances than we did in the past. It is my fondest wish that, in time, you will come to forget the man you thought I was, and learn to accept the man I have become."

Her back stiffened. "Reverend Hodge tells me you've changed. I hope, for your sake, he's right."

Klaw smiled down at her. "Now I'm remembering what a suspicious soul you are. And brave, too, ready to take on all the Furies if it would help those you love." He glanced at Hodge. "A commendable attribute in a woman, don't you agree?"

"Everything about Miss Amalfi is commendable," Hodge said, smiling warmly at her.

"Reverend Hodge!" Sheila Chatsworth, red-faced and flustered, burst into the office. "There's someone to see you. Police!"

"Police?" Hodge jumped to his feet just as Paavo and Yosh strode into the room. Angie also stood, her heart racing at the thought of Paavo and Klaw face-to-face again.

Paavo didn't say a word, but cast his gaze from one to the other, then focused a long time on Klaw. Klaw stared back. The hatred and tension between the two was tangible. Angie could feel the others back away from them. Klaw blinked, then raised his jaw. "We meet again, Inspector."

Paavo didn't respond, but glanced toward Angie with as cold a look as he'd ever given her. He had asked her not to come here and was angry that she hadn't taken his advice. He didn't seem shocked to see her, only dismissive, and that hurt more than his anger.

He faced Hodge and held out his hand. "Reverend Hodge, Inspector Smith, Homicide. This is Inspector Yoshiwara."

Hodge, looking tinier than ever beside the two big detectives, shook their hands. "Gentlemen, what can I do for you?"

"Nothing at all," Paavo said. "We're just here to see what we can donate to a worthy cause. We were inspired by your TV appearance last night." Despite his friendly words, his tone caused chills along Angie's back. She could see that Hodge, too, was worried about the confrontation looming.

Klaw spoke. "I realize it's hard for you to believe, Smith"—his voice was a growl as low, mean, and dirty as any movie gangster's—"but I'm a changed man. Since meeting Reverend Hodge, my life has turned around. He's shown me the true way."

Paavo glanced at Hodge, taking quick measure, then turned back to Klaw with a sneer. "He's a miracle worker. Is that what you're saying?"

Klaw laughed too loudly. Hodge and Klaw's two friends joined in with nervous chuckles. "I can see why you think it'd take a miracle to redeem me. But thanks to Hodge, I'm sorry for any wrongs I may have done anyone in the past—truly sorry. I hope to find forgiveness."

Paavo's glance caught Angie's for a moment, as if to check on whether she'd been taken in by Klaw's lies. She tried to let him know that she was with him, that

Klaw didn't fool her. "You're a good actor, Klaw," he said, his eyes narrow. "But then, I always knew that."

Klaw opened his arms. "This is no act. I mean everything I'm saying." He turned to the others. "You believe me, don't you?"

Hodge, Lili, and Van Warren all nodded vigorously.

"Miss Amalfi," Klaw said, a pleading tone to his voice, "maybe you can convince him. You've worked with Reverend Hodge. You've seen the good works he does. Please, talk to Inspector Smith for me. Will you do that?"

Stricken, Angie looked from Klaw to Paavo.

"Leave her out of this, Klaw," Paavo ordered, his tone lethal.

"It's all right, Paavo," Angie said, alarmed. "Maybe this leopard has changed his spots. Reverend Hodge may have worked a miracle."

He gazed at her with tense fury.

"Please," she said softly.

He turned to Klaw. "I've never seen a miracle before."

He and Yosh strode to the door to leave, but he glanced back at Angie. "Are you coming?"

She shook her head, then bowed it, unable to bear the look in his eyes. But she had to stay; she had to keep an eye on Klaw. This was the best place to do it.

She felt, rather than saw, Paavo's whole being harden. Then he left.

For the rest of the afternoon, Paavo investigated Dennis O'Leary's murder, talking to the dead man's friends, employees, and neighbors. Clearly, somewhere there existed a mysterious numbers runner who came by each day to pick up the money collected and leave the payoff for any winners. But no one knew which of O'Leary's many customers was the runner, or runners. Runners often worked in teams to appear less obvious, since they didn't like to be fingered—they carried too much cash for it to be safe.

Investigating O'Leary's murder deep into the evening helped Paavo block out, to a slight degree, the ugly scene at the mission. Now, though, back at his desk, it flooded over him full force.

He could accept Angie's being there. She'd never listened to his advice yet, and there was no reason for her to start now. But he couldn't accept her staying there. She had to have seen what a liar Klaw was.

What a liar he always was. And how evil.

Even in Homicide, it was rare to come into contact with a person who was truly evil. But a few times in his life he had met someone who was, and one of them was Axel Klaw.

Paavo called up Klaw's rap sheet on his computer. It was disturbingly clean for a man who'd spent his life on the wrong side of the law. Despite a number of arrests, Klaw had had no convictions until four months ago, when he did a week-long stint in Las Vegas for passing bad checks. In San Francisco, the man had sold drugs, made porno films, and caused the death of at least one young woman, and the best anyone could do was nail him for stiffing a casino. What was wrong with this picture?

After finding out all he could about Klaw, he turned his attention to the Reverend T. Simon Hodge. The way this real-life Elmer Gantry had appeared and had quickly become a force for the poor in this city bothered him, as did Angie's trust in the man.

Hodge had gotten the money somewhere to rent and renovate the interior of the building housing the mission and the next-door café. Hodge said his benefactor was Klaw, but Klaw wouldn't do anything unless it brought him money. What had Klaw come up with that would cause a rescue mission to pay off big-time?

Angie was helping with an auction. Could Klaw be planning a heist? It seemed like way too much work and too complex a plan for a mere robbery. There had to be a lot more to it. And the possibility of the reverend's being a part of the plan was almost certain.

Paavo checked for T. Simon Hodge, Simon T. Hodge, even T. or H. Simon. Nothing whatsoever turned up. No Social Security number. No credit cards. No driver license. No birth certificate. It was as if, prior to coming to San Francisco, in the eyes of the law T. Simon Hodge didn't exist.

CHAPTER

FIFTEEN

"*You're stepping all over* each other!" Lieutenant Hollins's face was the color of an eggplant.

He had three teams of inspectors in front of him—Benson and Calderon, Mayfield and Sutter, Smith and Yoshiwara. "You're supposed to be good at your jobs. But this is making you look like a bunch of ignoramuses! How many times are you going to go ask the same people the same questions? Can't you six talk to each other? Can't you work together? Doesn't it enter your little pea brains that if one of you is working on a dead numbers runner, and another is working on a dead numbers runner, and a third is working on a dead numbers runner plus a guy with ties to illegal gambling that just might include numbers running, maybe you're all talking to the same people?"

"We talk all the time about these cases," Calderon said. "We know what we're doing."

"You talk, yes," Hollins said, "But now I want you to brief each other—and me. Got it?"

They got it.

"Calderon, Benson, you're first."

"Patrick Devlin was a numbers runner," Calderon began. "He made the rounds of numbers writers in the Richmond, picking up new bets and making payoffs to the winners. He lived alone in a nice apartment in the Marina. No information about where he went the night he died, or who he saw. The body was a clean kill. The work of a pro." Calderon stopped. A dead end.

Sutter and Mayfield reported next on the liquor store owner. "Haram Sayir was a numbers writer," Rebecca said. "His customers bought liquor and a lotto ticket. He kept ten percent of each bet and took a percentage of any winnings. His little side business probably brought him between seven and eight hundred dollars a month."

Sutter spoke up. "Sayir was killed in the middle of the afternoon. No one knows why. One bullet wound to the back of the head, very professional. No witnesses."

The other inspectors shook their heads sympathetically. Another dead end.

Paavo and Yosh spoke last. "Dennis O'Leary was also a numbers writer," Paavo said. "Drive-by shooting in broad daylight. No one saw the shooter."

Everyone nodded. They knew the story.

Yosh spoke next. "We've kept surveillance on Peewee Clayton. He's also done some numbers running, but we haven't seen him travel much. We've begun gathering another round of evidence to prove Peewee murdered Sarah Ann Cribbs. So far, though, nothing is as good as the original blouse and beer bottle. So there we are," Yosh said. "Nowhere, like the rest of you."

"Enough of this gloom." Hollins stood. "Let's look at this logically. First we have the numbers writers who take the bets and record them—O'Leary and Sayir.

Next are the runners—Devlin and Clayton. At the top—the level we haven't talked about at all yet—is the banker, the one who receives all the cash and makes payouts. He's the money man in the city."

"It wouldn't make sense for the banker to be involved," Yosh said. "He wouldn't kill his own people."

"What if we're looking at a new banker moving in?" Paavo suggested. "And we're seeing a turf battle?"

"Good theory," Hollins said. "All right, you guys. Enough theory. Enough dead ends. Find me some facts."

"It's a disaster! A complete disaster!" Reverend Hodge wailed. "Only six hundred tickets have been sold so far." He stood in the doorway of Auction Central. His volunteers stopped working to stare at him.

"It's still early," Mary Ellen ventured.

"Early? It might be too late—that's what you *should* be saying. Can you get the caterers to cut back, Miss Amalfi? If we have to pay for food for fifteen hundred, but only six hundred show up, we'll be turning our profits into garbage."

"But what if the rest of the tickets are sold?" Angie asked. Despite how horrible she felt after refusing to leave the mission with Paavo, she had forced herself to return again to observe Klaw and—she hated to admit it—Reverend Hodge as well. She wasn't sure whom she could trust. "I think Mary Ellen's right. You still have time. Besides, you'll be offering tickets at the door, right?"

"Nobody sells nine hundred tickets at the door. Going to a fancy charity auction isn't a spur-of-the-moment decision. It's not like taking in a movie."

Sheila Chatsworth stood up, her back stiff. "We're

going to sell out, Reverend. You can bank on it." Two
volunteers working with Sheila murmured their agree-
ment.

"Tell people it's close to being sold out," Angie suggested, "and that they need to hurry if they want to be
sure they get in. Sometimes that strategy works. Of
course, sometimes it backfires and people stay home."

"Oh, that sounds like a spiffy idea." Hodge frowned.

"Well, pardon me," Angie said. "If you can do better—"

"We meet again." Klaw stood in the doorway, sur-
veying the activity, but his words were addressed to
Angie.

"So we do," she replied. Her knees shook at the
sight of him, but she reminded herself that he was the
reason she was here. She had to keep an eye on him.

"You've got that deer-in-the-headlights look, Angelina,"
he said with a smirk. "Don't worry. I'm really a nice
guy." He looked over his shoulder. "Isn't that so? Come
and tell Angie what a gem I am."

Lili and Van Warren stepped into the room. "Yeah,
he's way bad," Lili said with a smile. Warren stayed
silent.

Klaw walked up to the table where Angie sat and
stood over her. "Did you tell her I'm a man who
believes in good works, Hodge?" he asked, his gaze
never leaving Angie's.

Hodge perked up at his name, then nervously
cleared his throat. "Of course, Mr. Clausen."

Klaw stared down at her, carefully detailing her hair,
her face, her throat. His eyes went back to her hair
again, to a lock that strayed near her eye. She held her
breath as his hand slowly began to reach toward it, to
touch her—

"Mr. Clausen," Warren said, "it's time for you to
leave."

Klaw jerked his hand back and glanced at his wrist-watch. "You're right." He turned to leave the room.

"What gives?" Lili demanded. "Do you have some new babe or what? You disappear at noon, like, every day now."

Klaw cupped her chin as he passed and planted a hard kiss on her pouting mouth. "I wouldn't dream of cheating on you, darling."

Angie used every wile she had, real or imagined, to talk Paavo into going out to dinner with her that evening. Including bribery. She picked up a glass Reverend Hodge had used at the mission and put it in her purse. It should have some clear fingerprints on it.

Angie knew Paavo was upset with her for going back to the mission, and last night, although he'd phoned, their conversation had been short and strained. But this afternoon she convinced him that she was miserable—no, beyond miserable—having him angry at her, that they had to get together to put this behind them. What she didn't tell him was that, besides all that, she had promised her mother she'd do something about Frankie Tagliaro.

Since Serefina's visit, Angie had gone to see each of her four older sisters and talked to them about Frankie Tagliaro's troubling request to their father. All of them agreed with Serefina: Angie should find out what Paavo thought they should do. Her family didn't know, though, about the strange business going on connected with his work and how distracted he'd been lately.

When Paavo came by to pick her up, she gave him the glass, but neither of them spoke much. She could see that he was still hurting, and she wasn't about to agree to stop going to the mission. They left her apartment quickly.

"The Isle of Capri?" he asked incredulously as he

drove past the restaurant she'd selected, in search of a place to park.

She understood his surprise. Even from the outside, the restaurant had an air of sleaze about it that you could cut with a knife. No wonder it was losing money. "I understand the food's excellent."

He frowned. "You can cook rings around any Italian restaurant's food, Angie. Why bother to go there? Wouldn't you rather try the new Scandinavian restaurant you were talking about the other day?"

He knew her better than she'd thought. "I'm not in the mood for fish tonight." What a lie. Just then, a car pulled out of a parking space up ahead. "Ah! What luck. Obviously, we were meant to eat here."

"Okay." Paavo took the spot, his lips pursed with resignation. "If this is what you want."

As they walked back along Geary Street toward the restaurant, Angie saw a man double-park, run in, and, a moment later, run back out again.

Crooks!

"Oh, dear," she said, trying to come up with a plausible excuse for what they had just witnessed. "I hope that doesn't mean we need reservations."

Paavo glanced at her dubiously. She could all but see his suspicions rising about the place, and they hadn't even stepped in the door yet.

The restaurant, a dark, drab room in need of a complete remodeling, was empty.

On the other hand, at the bar, every stool was taken. The area was alive with talk, laughter, and the distinctive clatter of liar's dice.

"Two?" The cocktail waitress put down the small tray she'd been carrying and picked up two menus.

Paavo nodded, still eying the bar scene.

The waitress led them to the dining room. "Is the owner here tonight?" Angie asked.

"He's in the back," she replied. She held out a chair, but Angie walked to the opposite side of the table. From there, she had a view of the bar and Paavo didn't. She sat.

"I'd love to meet him," Angie said. "I sometimes do restaurant reviews for *Haute Cuisine* magazine, and it helps to personally get to know the city's successful restaurateurs."

"Really?" The waitress squealed with delight. "Mr. Tagliaro's gonna wanna meet you right away. I'll go let him know you're here."

She hurried off.

"This restaurant is *successful*, Angie?" Paavo was clearly uncomfortable at having his back exposed while he faced a wall with a huge connect-the-dots-style painting of the Leaning Tower of Pisa. He started to turn around.

She clutched his hand in both of hers, stopping him. "We'll find out, won't we?" she said quickly. "I appreciate your coming here with me so much, Paavo. I know how stressed you've been by seeing Klaw again, by whatever this madness is that's going on at work. I don't want to cause you any more anxiety."

His gaze turned wistful. His fingers curled around her hand, and his thumb lightly rubbed her knuckles. "I'm glad you called today." Big blue eyes captured hers. "We'll make tonight just for us."

She would have been ecstatic at his loving words if she hadn't been so nervous about facing Tagliaro. "Anytime, Paav."

He gawked at her with amazement.

"Uh, excuse me. My name's Frank Tagliaro. I heard you're a restaurant critic." Her father's tormentor was medium height, darkly tanned, with black eyes and black curly hair slicked upward and piled high above his forehead, like a middle-aged Dean Martin during his

Rat Pack days. He wore a shiny black shirt, the top three buttons open and showing a thick gold link necklace against a hairy chest.

Angie shook the sleazeball's hand. "My name's Angelina Amalfi. This is my friend, Inspector Paavo Smith."

Paavo stood as he and Tagliaro shook hands. "Inspector? You with the police department?"

"Homicide."

Tagliaro smiled. "Oh, good. Good. A lot of cops stop by here pretty regular. Not that we offer them free drinks or anything—we don't want to get them in trouble, you know. Ha, ha! But they keep an eye on the place for me."

"I'm sure they do." Paavo sat back down.

Tagliaro turned his attention back to Angie. "Amalfi, did you say? You aren't related to Sal Amalfi, are you?"

Her eyes narrowed. "He's my father. Do you know him?"

"Do I know him? Like a brother. So you're his daughter. *Come bella!* He's got to be real proud of you."

"He's proud of all five of us."

"Five? Oh, yeah, that's right. So, what can I tell you about the restaurant?"

She folded her arms. "Has it been here long?"

"Three years last February."

"Interesting. Most restaurants don't last half that amount of time. You'll have to let me in on your secret." She smiled sweetly.

"Secret?" he asked.

She continued her inquiry. "Who's your cook?"

"My brother-in-law, Pietro Castagnola. Ah, I can see by your face you never heard of him. He's still young, but a good cook. He cooks like my mamma used to, God rest her soul. You want to meet him?"

"No. Meeting you is quite sufficient. I'll let his food provide his introduction."

"The food..." He pulled the menus from their hands. "I'll do the ordering for you. For *la figlia di mio paisano Salvatore*, nothing but the best. *Bene?*"

"*Molto bene*," she replied.

"Susie, come with me," Frankie said to the waitress. "I got to pick out a bottle of wine for these people from my own private stock. A good one." Tagliaro winked at Angie, then hurried off toward the kitchen, the waitress running behind.

Paavo eyed her. "What's this about, Angie? Did you know he was friends with your father?"

She drummed her fingers on the table. "I wouldn't exactly call them friends."

"No. That was obvious. What's wrong?"

"Nothing." Frowning, she peered at the kitchen door Tagliaro had disappeared through. "I just hope we can enjoy the meal."

Before long, the waitress brought out a bottle of fifteen-year-old Robert Mondavi cabernet sauvignon—not outstanding, but acceptable—along with a rather routine antipasto platter. They next moved on to crab cioppino, manicotti, and roast lamb with a side of sautéed zucchini. Although Angie had eaten considerably better prepared food, it wasn't as bad as she'd feared it might be. Often, just a little more salt and pepper helped tremendously.

The meal was strained, though, with Paavo being quiet while Angie chattered about nothing in particular. They were having dessert, cannoli and espresso, when the bar turned still.

Paavo turned to see his friend from Vice, Joe Nablonski, Joe's partner, and two Richmond station cops walk into the bar.

"I ain't done nothing wrong," Tagliaro proclaimed.

"I run a clean place. No problems, officers. Won't you have a drink? On the house."

"Here's our warrant to search the premises. We've got a complaint about gambling going on here," Nablonski said.

"Look," Tagliaro said, turning him away from the bar and toward the restaurant. "A homicide inspector's been here the whole time. He's having a nice meal with his girlfriend. Come with me. You know Inspector Smith?"

Nablonski's eye caught Paavo's as Tagliaro pushed him into the dining room.

"What's going on?" Paavo asked, standing.

"We got a tip about this place," Nablonski replied. "Search warrant, the works. We're closing it down while we check it all out."

Paavo looked surprised. "Fast work. What's the problem?"

Nablonski opened his mouth, then hesitated just long enough to show his discomfort. "Gambling. Specifically numbers. Seems this is a numbers drop."

Paavo glanced piercingly at Angie, at the bar.

Nablonski self-consciously tugged at his ear. "Listen, Internal Affairs is on their way over, too. I don't know why all this is coming down in quite this way, but why don't you and the lady get out of here?"

"Internal Affairs doesn't show up at raids," Paavo said.

The two cops stared at each other a long moment. "I agree." Nablonski frowned. "Something smells real bad. I'll cover. Get going."

Paavo looked from Nablonski to Tagliaro to the two young patrol officers who came into the bar with Nablonski. Something about them was familiar. He walked over to them. "Do I know you two?" he asked.

"Officer Kellogg, sir," one man answered, standing straight and stiff, chin up.

"Officer Rosenberg, sir," the other said, standing even more rigidly than his partner.

"Kellogg ... Rosenberg. You two were the officers who found Sarah Ann Cribbs's body, weren't you?"

"Yes, sir. We were quite surprised when you wouldn't identify the evidence and Peewee Clayton got off, sir," Rosenberg said.

"What's that?" Paavo chilled at the implication of Rosenberg's words.

"We were also there, sir," Kellogg said, "when Patrick Devlin's body was found. We saw the two homicide inspectors take something from his mouth. We learned what that something was, sir."

Paavo scrutinized both men carefully. He'd never forget either one again. "You're both pretty new to the force, aren't you?"

"Yes, sir," they both responded. Rosenberg added, "We graduated four months ago."

"It's never a good idea to jump to conclusions in police work. If something appears too obvious, it's smart to get suspicious fast. Remember that." He left them standing stiffly, with shoulders squared, their mouths set in grim determination as they pondered his words. He shook Nablonski's hand, then took hold of Angie's arm and left.

"I don't understand what happened," Angie said, practically running as Paavo took long-legged, angry strides down the street to his car. "That young policeman sounded like he was accusing you of something."

Paavo unlocked the passenger-side door for her and opened it, then hurried to the driver's side and climbed in. "He was," he said grimly.

"But ..." Puzzled, she glanced back at the restaurant as Paavo pulled into traffic. This didn't make sense. She frowned, studying him. "Internal Affairs, they said.

Paavo, Internal Affairs wasn't going there to check up on you, were they?"

"That's what it sounded like."

"But why?"

"Because they've connected me with the numbers racket, that's why." He gripped the steering wheel so tightly his knuckles turned white. "And the restaurant is apparently a numbers drop."

She felt light-headed. "Numbers . . . ?"

"Don't worry about it."

"But it was my idea to go to the Isle of Capri!"

"Maybe we could convince IA of that eventually."

"Will your being there"—her throat nearly closed as the implication of what she'd done hit her—"get you into trouble?"

He didn't reply for a moment, his expression bitter. "It seems everything has that effect these days."

She folded her hands and forced her eyes straight ahead, trying to stay calm despite the pounding of her heart. "I'll explain all about the restaurant to them."

"They won't care," he said.

"What do you mean?" She clenched her fists. "I'm not going to let you be in trouble because I wanted to go someplace!"

"It's not important." As he spoke he gave a defeated shake of his head. She'd never seen him like this before. Tears sprang to her eyes.

"I'm sorry," she said. "I'm sorry for all of it—for Klaw and the mission, and this and . . . and I was just trying to help my father!"

"Don't cry, Angie." He sounded terribly weary, then reached over and touched her hand. "It'll work out. But what did you mean, help your father?"

She pulled a wad of Kleenex from her purse and wiped her eyes. "My mother told me Tagliaro went to see my father. He wanted to borrow money, said he was in trouble. I wanted to see him, to find out what kind of man would bother my father, whom he scarcely knows. I didn't want to hurt you!"

Paavo puzzled over this new information. "Do you know if Tagliaro mentioned gamblers or numbers running?"

"I'm sure my mother would have told me if he did. I just figured he'd borrowed money and was being strong-armed to pay it back, that's all." She shook her head. "Numbers. God, after all the other trouble you've had, I make it even worse for you. And I even forgot to tell you about Brother Tweeler! I mean, I didn't really forget, but I believed Reverend Hodge that it meant nothing, and then we hardly talked after seeing Klaw until tonight, and I forgot because I was so glad to see you, and— What are you doing?"

He pulled over into a parking space, shut off the engine, and faced her. Taking the balled-up Kleenex, he wiped tears and smeared mascara from her face. "Now, start over," he said gently. "Who in the world is Brother Tweeler?"

"He came running into Reverend Hodge's office with a gun, demanding money. He said he had won at numbers, but no one would pay him. He said there were numbers players at the mission. Hodge didn't know anything about it. I believe him, Paavo. I really do!" Her eyes welled up again.

She felt the tension in him build as he listened to her story. He seemed to stop breathing for a moment. Then he gazed down at her and the hard, rigid lines around his mouth softened, the firm set of his jaw eased. "It's all right, Angie. Don't cry. None of this is worth a single tear, believe me."

His words only made her feel worse, and she cried harder. "I should have thought! I'm so stupid sometimes!"

"You're not stupid at all, and if anything, you think and worry about things too much," he whispered, guiding her head to his shoulder as he pushed her hair back from her face and lightly kissed her forehead. "You didn't know, that's all. But someone did."

The sudden hard edge of his tone troubled her. "What do you mean?"

"It all fell together too quickly, too easily. The tip to raid the place, the search warrant. Those Richmond station cops."

She knew what he meant. Even here, even when she was taking care of a family matter, Paavo was targeted. She grasped his shoulder. "It's as if someone is watching you, Paavo. Someone with a direct line to the police department." Agitated and worried by this latest twist, she sat up and faced him directly. "Who could be doing something like that?"

"I've got an idea," Paavo said. "But it doesn't make any sense."

CHAPTER

SIXTEEN

"Angels are in." Connie propped her elbows on the glass counter in her shop, Everyone's Fancy. "I don't get it myself. I thought it was a passing fancy—books, movies, even TV shows. Now, all these figurines."

Angie was looking at a display cabinet full of them—from cherubic, childlike cupids to little girls with halos; delicate winged seraphim; winged males of the Gabriel variety; and a fearful Lucifer being cast from heaven. Checking the prices, she realized that the very old, intricate statue of an angel that sat on Reverend Hodge's bookcase must be worth a small fortune, even though it was only about four inches high.

She picked up the fierce, scowling Lucifer. "Hmm, reminds me of a cop I went to dinner with recently," she murmured. Then, louder, "Who'd want one of these sitting on their mantel?"

"I figure it's the moral equivalent of putting a picture of Roseanne on your refrigerator when dieting. Be good, or else!"

Angie put it down. "Creepy."

"I think it's one of those end-of-the-millennium things," Connie suggested.

"You're probably right."

"So, what brings you all the way out here to West Portal Avenue?" Connie asked.

"Two things. First, I want to find a birthday present for my sister Maria. Considering how religiously inclined she is, one of these angels might make a nice gift. Not Lucifer, though."

"She's the one married to the jazz musician, right?"

"Right. I guess that's enough to make a saint out of anyone," she mused, selecting a beautifully made porcelain angel from France and giving it to Connie to gift-wrap. "And the second reason I'm here is to talk to you about Paavo."

"Ah! Now we're getting somewhere," Connie said, tearing a length of colorful paper from the roll.

"We've got to do something to help him. I'm so worried about him I don't know what to do. He's getting into more and more trouble at work, and now he's distracted by Axel Klaw's being back in the city. He believes Klaw is up to something, but he doesn't know what. I suspect he's right. We've got to find proof, Connie. You and me."

Connie's hands stilled over the wrapping paper and she stared at Angie with dawning realization. "Isn't Klaw the guy who used to run a porno studio and surround himself with criminals?"

"That's him." Angie shuddered. "He claims he's been converted."

"Forget it, Angie. I don't do criminals." She emphatically ripped tape from the holder.

"You've got to help me. Paavo needs us."

Connie shook her head. "Speak for yourself, *kemosabe*."

"Good ol' Tonto, stalwart to the end!" Angie said sarcastically. "It's perfectly safe, and it won't take long at all. Please, Connie."

Connie finished taping the paper, then cut a length of wide satin ribbon. "Look, I'm sorry about Paavo and all he's going through, but he's a cop. He can handle it." She knotted the ribbon into a stylized half bow and handed the gift to Angie.

"This time, Connie, he needs my help. I can feel it. And I need you," Angie pleaded, clutching the package. "I really do. Just this one time. I promise I'll never ask you to do anything like this again. Won't you help me?"

Connie chewed her bottom lip guiltily. "Would I have to face Klaw?"

"Not at all." Angie's voice fairly quivered with encouragement. "It's absolutely safe."

"What would I have to do?"

"Just come with me for a little while."

"That's all?" Connie's eyebrows arched suspiciously.

"That's all."

Connie relaxed. "Well, in that case . . . okay. That's easy."

"Just one more little thing," Angie said. "We'll need to use your car."

Inspector Toshiro Yoshiwara hesitated a moment before the door of the conference room. Assistant District Attorney Hanover Judd had called and asked to meet him there . . . alone. Yosh didn't like the tone of the request one bit. He entered the room.

"We've got a problem, Yosh," Judd said. Early thirties, enthusiastic, fair, and not afraid to take on a tough case, he was one of the assistant DAs the homicide inspectors most liked to work with.

Yosh didn't even try to make his usual boisterous

cracks, but grimly sat down, ready to hear Judd out. "What is it?"

"Last night, there was a raid at the Isle of Capri restaurant out on Geary Street." Judd cleared his throat lightly. "Paavo was there. A couple of young cops who were on the scene are apparently going around telling people that a vice cop gave him the go-ahead to leave. Rumors about it have even gotten to the DA. It looks bad, Yosh."

The news caught Yosh by surprise. "I don't know anything about it, Hanover. I just got in. But I know Paavo had a good reason for being there, and a good reason for leaving."

"I agree. But that won't stop this from getting to IA. I wanted you to know, Yosh. There might be something you can do to help."

"The whole thing stinks!" Yosh said.

"I know it. But if Internal Affairs hears what those two rookies are saying, it's going to get ugly. He'll be suspended, if not worse."

Yosh slowly shook his head, realizing that Judd was putting his own reputation on the line simply telling Yosh about it, knowing Yosh would pass along a warning to Paavo. "I'll do what I can."

Judd stood. The meeting was over. "I just hope it's not too late."

Angie and Connie sat in Connie's Toyota Tercel in a parking area a block away from the Random Acts of Kindness Mission. Angie held a pair of binoculars fixed on the mission's entrance. "Lili said Klaw goes out every day around noon. Let's hope she's able to tell time."

"That smart, huh?"

"She hangs around with Axel Klaw, doesn't she?"

"Good point."

"There he is!" Angie shouted. "And he's alone." She watched as Klaw walked to a black Lincoln Town Car and got in.

"So that's him," Connie mused. "He doesn't look evil. Actually, with the tan, bleached hair, and jewelry, he's very southern California-looking."

"Start up the engine. We've got to be ready," Angie said.

"Ready?" Connie asked. "Ready for what?"

"To follow him. We've got to find out where he's going."

"Follow him? Are you crazy? What if he sees us?"

"He'll see a beautiful blonde driving a car, and with her, a kid in a baseball cap." As she spoke she put on a blue cap.

"AARP?" Connie asked.

"Mrs. Calamatti, on the third floor, was the only person I could find this morning who owned a baseball cap I could borrow. Klaw won't be able to read it, anyway." She tucked her hair up under the rim, then put on dark glasses and slid down in the seat, so that just her nose and eyes were peering over the dashboard.

Klaw started up the engine and pulled out of the space. "Let's go!" Angie cried.

Nervously, Connie stomped on the gas, shooting out of the parking space and driving fast to the corner.

"Slow down!" Angie said as Connie made a wide left turn. "You don't want to rear-end him."

"I don't want to do anything with him!" Connie reminded her. "Shoot, why is that man going so fast? Does he think someone's following him?"

"Where's a traffic cop when you need one?" Angie mumbled.

"With our luck, we'd be the ones who'd get stopped," Connie said.

Klaw stayed considerably ahead of them as he zigzagged through the downtown area. Then he turned onto California Street, headed west. The traffic, including a cable car, helped hide the fact that they were following him. That, and the fact that Connie's car was a small gray Toyota. Angie figured Klaw was the type who'd never deign to notice a subcompact.

He rode California all the way across town to the Richmond district. On Sixth Avenue, he made a right turn.

"Hurry up!" Angie yelled, clutching the dashboard.

"I've got to move over into the right lane first," Connie cried.

"Move now. Quick!"

Connie swung her car into the lane, to the sound of screeching tires and a loud horn blast.

"Okay, so I cut it a little close," Angie said. "But you can turn onto Sixth now."

Connie did, just as Klaw's car disappeared with a left turn onto Clement Street. She floored it down the block, made a sharp left, and nearly took Klaw's door off as he opened it to get out of his car. Angie ducked so Klaw wouldn't see her if he looked up to yell at the driver who nearly ran over his toes.

Shaking from her wild ride, Connie pulled into a bus stop. She and Angie watched Klaw from the rearview and side mirrors. He walked into a Russian restaurant called Vladivostok.

"I don't believe it," Connie cried, draped limply over the steering wheel. "He drove like a maniac across town to get a piroshki?"

"He's got to be meeting someone there," Angie said. "Go see who it is."

"Me?" Connie's eyes were like doughnuts.

"I can't go—he'll recognize me. But you can." She pulled a twenty and a ten out of her purse. "I'd suggest the chicken Kiev, maybe some borscht—ask for sour cream on top. You'll love it."

Connie looked at the money and the restaurant, one of the better ones in the city. "I haven't had lunch yet," she murmured.

"Russian food is quite good. Be sure to have some freshly baked black bread with lots of butter along with the soup. Strong coffee afterward, a rich dessert . . ."

"Why fight it?" Connie used the rearview mirror again, this time to check her hair and lipstick. "Wish me luck." With that, she left.

Angie moved the car to a parking space as soon as one opened up, and then sat, slumped down in the seat, the baseball cap low on her brow, for over an hour doing nothing but feeding the parking meter and watching people walk up and down the street. Clement Street was a cornucopia of smells from Chinese and Russian restaurants, plus sprinklings of Thai cuisine, Vietnamese food, and an occasional Mexican eatery thrown in for good measure. Antique shops, enormous used-book stores, and secondhand furniture stores made up the bulk of the shops along the street—along with grocery stores and other businesses found in every neighborhood where people lived as well as played.

Given the temptation around her, it was hard not to get out of the car and run into a store. Or at least a deli. But she reminded herself that she was keeping watch here for Paavo's sake.

An eternity later, Connie came out of the restaurant and headed for the car.

"You were right about the chicken Kiev," she said. "The borscht was a little salty, but once I stirred the sour cream—"

"Forget the sour cream!" Angie knew exactly what Connie was doing. "What's Klaw up to?"

"He's with a woman," Connie told her. "Young,

plain. Looks like someone just starting out in the job market."

"Were you able to find out who is she?"

"I heard him call her Gretchen when she walked in, but that was it."

"Describe her."

"She's about five-foot-seven or -eight, light brown hair, straight, pulled back in a barrette. Her face is kind of fleshy. Big cheeks, jowls, lips. Little brown eyes. Not exactly Miss America material. Dull clothes—white blouse, blue skirt. Her build is kind of . . . cylindrical. Breasts, waist, and hips all kind of blend together."

Angie sat slack-jawed. Connie was a budding Sam Spade.

"Actually," Connie continued, "you can see for yourself. There she is."

Connie's description was on the mark. Klaw escorted the woman to his car. She might have been plain, but her expression said the sun rose and set on Axel Klaw. A dog looking at its beloved master had no more adoration in its eyes.

Angie sat behind the wheel this time and followed Klaw to an apartment building in the Ingleside district, a relatively low-cost area. Klaw escorted the woman inside.

"Damn!" Angie squinted at the door. "Now what?"

"Looks like we get to sit here and wait while he has a little afternoon delight." Connie slid down in the seat, her arms folded. "Just what I need. To find out a weirdo like Axel Klaw can get it, but not me."

"Maybe he's just dropping her off or something." They sat and waited . . . and waited . . . watching the minutes on the dashboard clock go by. There weren't even shops or interesting pedestrians in this part of town.

"What's with the guy?" Angie said after a long while.

"He's living with one woman and has this other cookie on the side. Somehow the man's magnetism is completely lost on me."

"Yes, but you've got Paavo. Actually, I can see a certain attractiveness about Klaw—if you like the Christopher Walken crazed-sex-fiend look. I can see that."

Angie gave her a sidelong glance. "How long *has* it been for you?"

"Look! There he is!" Connie cried.

"No Gretchen," Angie said. "I guess she lives there."

"Or he killed her," Connie whispered.

"I wouldn't put it past him."

When Klaw pulled out of his parking space Angie waited a moment, then followed.

"Shouldn't we go check?" Connie asked.

"And if she's alive, what do we say? We're taking a survey on sex after stroganoff?"

Angie tried to follow Klaw but quickly lost him in the crush of Nineteenth Avenue traffic. Dejected, she went back to the mission, only to find his car parked in front of the building.

Finally Paavo got back the results of the tests on the glass with Hodge's fingerprints, the one Angie had given him. He tore the envelope open, eager to find out just who the Reverend T. Simon Hodge really was.

He scanned the short write-up quickly, then read it again more slowly, but the bottom line was summed up in only two words: No match.

"I'd say Mr. Klaw—actually now it's Clausen—fancies himself a ladies' man, yes," replied Reverend Hodge in answer to Angie's question. She sat in the mission's dining room, sipping coffee and turning pages of a cookbook filled with fancy hors d'oeuvres, but her mind was miles away. "Are you interested in him, Miss Amalfi?"

That brought her back. "God, no! I was just curious about him and Lili, mostly."

"She lives with him in his apartment over the mission. I won't say it's a love match, but they do seem to have a certain compatibility," Hodge ventured.

"I guess they do," she said. "I didn't realize there were apartments upstairs."

"Four. I have a small one, as does Mr. Warren. Klaw and Lili share the largest, and the fourth is empty. Are you looking for a place to live?"

"No, thanks." She turned back to the cookbook, but couldn't suppress a small sigh.

He had been passing through the dining room taking a roundabout route to his office, but now he stopped and sat beside her. "What's wrong, Miss Amalfi? You look like you lost your best friend."

She shut the book. "I have—the man I love. I'm so worried. Last night I took him somewhere with me, and the place was raided. Now he's in even worse trouble, and none of it's his fault. It's mine."

"Why would you choose a place like that?"

"I was trying to be helpful. Instead I caused more harm."

"You meant well."

"I don't see that it matters," she lamented.

"The world is a funny place, Miss Angie," Reverend Hodge said. "Those who do bad things often seem to live high on the hog. But you just wait awhile. Every time, eventually, a big butcher comes along and that hog ends up as bologna sandwiches."

CHAPTER

SEVENTEEN

Paavo stood in the doorway of an alley off Third Street. This was his third meeting with Snake Belly. Last time, the Snake hadn't learned anything new.

"Hey, my man," Snake Belly whispered from behind him. "You better watch out with all that smokin' to signal me. You're gonna get hooked. Those things can kill you. Me, I got me some good weed. You ever want to try the real thing, you let me know."

"Keep it up, Snake," Paavo said in warning. "I'm still a cop."

"Hey, you know I'm just jokin'. And anyway, you wouldn't bring harm to the man who's got some info for you, now would you?"

"Depends on what it's worth."

"That's cold, man. But I ain't worried, 'cause what I got is worth its weight in gold."

"I'm still waiting," Paavo said. "Haven't heard anything but a lot of hot air so far."

"Well, listen to this. I met me a bookie. Real

talkative guy, but it cost me a hundred bucks. I knew you'd be good for it, though."

"Better be worth every penny." Paavo knew Snake Belly would be keeping most of the money for himself—he wouldn't give his own mother a hundred dollars for information.

"It's worth it, man." Snake Belly pulled out a cigarette and took his time lighting up, clearly enjoying Paavo's impatience. Finally, he spoke. "The bookie says it's known all over town that a new banker's moved in. The guy's got plans to set up numbers in a big way. He's moving in on the old-timers. They go along with him, or they're dead."

Paavo listened in silence as Snake Belly confirmed his suspicions about the sudden rash of murders. "Who is this new banker?"

"I don't think the bookie knows. That, or he's too scared to say. This guy's got some mean guns with him. No mercy."

"Who's he killed?"

"I don't know them. Some Irish dudes, for the most part. Devlin, O'Leary. Names like that. Mean anything to you?"

"Yeah, they mean something to me."

"They wouldn't go along. Now they're dead. And everyone's really scared 'cause this new banker's got an in. You know what his in is?"

"What?"

"He's in cahoots with a cop. A good cop gone bad."

Hearing Snake Belly say the words made him sick with disgust, even though he couldn't say he was surprised. This whole situation had too many earmarks of an inside job. "Tell me about it."

"The cop covers for him, gives him the info he needs. Sets up guys who won't go along, takes good care of guys who will. Even helps them beat murder raps. Do you know who the cop is?"

Paavo felt the hairs on the back of his neck begin to prickle. "What is this, twenty questions?"

"Just asking, man."

His patience was gone. "Out with it."

"You."

This was just the Snake being funny, he told himself, but one look at Snake's eyes and he knew it wasn't a joke. "What the hell are you talking about?"

Snake raised his hands, taking a step back. "Look, man, I'm just repeating what I was told."

Paavo moved toward him. "Where did the bookie hear that story?"

"He wouldn't tell me. He seemed kind of scared to be telling me this much. Things are rough out there, especially for an old-time bookie like this guy."

"So why doesn't he join up with the new banker, too?"

Snake dropped his cigarette and stepped on it. "Probably will."

"Who's his connection?"

"He wouldn't tell me that either."

Paavo didn't want to believe any of this, but he couldn't deny the air of truth to Snake's words. "I want to meet this bookie."

"I don't know if it's possible. I ain't jiving you neither. He was scared, man."

Snake Belly sounded sincere. That gave Paavo pause. "Okay. Talk to him." Angie's story about Brother Tweeler and numbers had grated on him ever since she'd told him about it. This news made a dull, niggling notion grow into a full-fledged hunch. "Find out if the name Axel Klaw means anything to him. Or the Random Acts of Kindness Mission."

"Mission? You jiving me or what?"

"Pay what you need to get him to talk—and to meet me. I'm good for it if he's willing to name names."

"That'll be big-time money."

"I said I'm good for it."

"In that case . . . meet me here in two nights. If it's a go, I'll take you to him."

"Done," Paavo said.

With that, Snake Belly vanished into the back alley.

Angie was rarely at a loss for words, but that's exactly what she was when she answered her door and saw Paavo. He'd rushed right over from his meeting with Snake Belly. The more he thought about the connection between numbers running, Klaw's sudden return, and the troubles he was having, the more certain he became that somehow all three were connected. He had to warn her off and make her listen.

She stared at his black leather jacket, black jeans, boots, and dark glasses a moment, then stuck her head out the doorway and looked down the hall.

"What are you doing?" he asked, removing the glasses.

"Looking for your Harley."

"Very funny."

She stepped aside and let him enter the apartment. Despite the cautious, serious way she studied him, she put her arms around him and forced a smile. "Is it true what they say about bikers?"

He tilted her chin upward and kissed her. "What do they say?" he murmured.

She gave him a saucy smile. "I don't know. But we can come up with something."

Despite himself, he grinned, but then the smile fell away and he followed her to the sofa.

"So what's with the new image, Inspector?" Angie asked, still trying to force brightness on him. "You're not an undercover Hell's Angel, I hope."

He took off his jacket before sitting down. "I had to meet someone and not let the whole neighborhood know I'm a cop."

"It sounds dangerous," she said with a small frown.

"It's a lot less dangerous than what you're doing, Angie. Klaw's behind some heavy stuff. You shouldn't be anywhere near him."

Abruptly, she stood up and headed for the kitchen. "I'll put on some coffee. Are you hungry, Inspector?"

He followed her. Her kitchen looked like a candy factory, with bars and chunks of a variety of chocolates, nuts, glazed fruit, sugar, and recipes spread over the counters.

"You've got to listen. Klaw might have someone on the police force involved. I've been hearing too many things; there are too many coincidences going on."

"Maybe it's not Klaw at all," she suggested, scooping coffee into a filter. "For example, I followed him today—"

He grabbed her wrist. "You *what*?"

She removed his hand. "It's okay. Connie was with me."

"Oh, that makes it a whole helluva lot better." He threw up his arms and began to pace. The last thing he needed was to worry about Angie.

"Anyway"—she added water to the Krups, then flicked the on switch—"it turns out that he's got another woman on the side. Her name's Gretchen. He met her at a Russian restaurant on Clement, then took her to an apartment in the Ingleside. She's young and plain but obviously adores him."

He could scarcely believe what she was telling him. "You found out all that?"

She smiled smugly as she unwrapped a wedge of Brie and put it on a plate.

"And a noontime fling was all there was to it?" He followed right behind her as she reached into a cupboard for a box of English crackers.

"So it seems."

"Nothing's the way it seems with Klaw. Nothing ever is." He stopped talking, thinking about all the things going on around him that weren't what they seemed.

"It's possible, Paavo, that some other crook picked up on this numbers business as a way to get at you," Angie suggested, bringing the cheese and crackers into the living room. "It wouldn't be the first time. It might not have anything to do with Axel Klaw at all. Aren't there any other possibilities? More . . . more realistic ones, perhaps?"

"Realistic?" He took hold of her arms, stopping her flitting about. He needed to talk about this. "Klaw's damned realistic if you ask me."

"Paavo." Her fingers tightened on his shirt. "There's no reason to jump to the conclusion that it's Klaw. I mean, you're obsessed with the man, and that could be clouding your perception."

"*Obsessed?*" He drew back from her and his voice lowered, soft yet dangerous. "So that's what you think."

"I don't trust Klaw either!" she cried, stepping up to him once more. "But before you decide it's him, I want you to be absolutely sure there's no one else, no one at all, that you're suspicious of."

He rubbed his forehead, trying to contain his irritation at Angie's questioning Klaw's guilt, suggesting that he might be wrong about Klaw, might be obsessed with the man, and that he should concentrate instead on the other players involved. "A couple of young cops from the Richmond station seem to turn up almost every time something happens involving me and numbers running," he said. "Considering how many patrolmen there are at that station, the odds against that happening are phenomenal. It makes me want to know what's going on there as well."

"Maybe they're the crooked cops," she suggested. "You said this looked like an inside job. Aren't they the ones who caused Internal Affairs to go to the Isle of Capri restaurant?"

"I don't know that for sure, though the whole thing reeked of a setup. But how would they know we would go there?"

"They must be watching you. Or having someone else watch."

"Yet *another* crooked cop, Angie? There's got to be another way." He forced himself to look at the situation objectively. He didn't want to be narrow-minded and obsessed—God, how it grated that she'd say that to him. He took a deep breath. "Did you say anything about your father or Tagliaro to anyone but me?"

"Only my sisters." She looked relieved at this new approach. "They all agreed with my mother—that we should talk to you about this."

"Okay. So your father was approached by Tagliaro, then your mother went to you because of me."

"Then *we* go together to see Tagliaro," Angie added, puzzled.

Paavo began to pace, then stopped and faced her. "An idea struck me, but it's too crazy." He pondered it a moment longer. "You said this Tagliaro hadn't had any contact with your father in years, right?"

"That's right." Angie clasped her hands, her eyes never leaving his. "My mother said Papa didn't know Frankie very well, and all of a sudden, he showed up."

"Which means something—or someone—caused him to decide to go to your father." He paced again, his hand stroking the back of his neck. "If I'm the target here, which seems to be the case, it means somebody might have figured out that they could get to me through you . . . and they could get to you through your family. It's someone who knows you, knows your character. Someone who put Tagliaro up to going to your father in hopes you'd find out about it and take matters into your own hands."

"What?" Angie was shocked. "How could anyone assume I'd do a thing like that?"

Paavo decided it was best not to explain that one to her.

"It was a setup." He dropped his hand and faced her directly. "An elaborate setup. It's got to have been Klaw!"

"Don't make assumptions, Paavo, please," she urged. "God. I give up." She banged the door going into the kitchen to get the coffee.

He stormed after her. "What's wrong? I'm using pure logic."

"You're too involved." She seemed to scrutinize him, to fairly pick apart his mounting tension, his need for revenge. "Let another cop take over. Let someone else follow Klaw and see, clearly, what he is or isn't doing."

There was no way she could understand. He withdrew—physically and emotionally. "Klaw is my business, Angie. Nobody else's."

She gripped his hands. "I'll be damned if I let you get yourself killed over that man. Even if he isn't the problem, you'll *make* him it."

He looked down at her small, pale hands holding his large, hard ones. Where other people cowered at his anger, she stood up to him. *She* wouldn't let him get himself killed over Klaw. He'd have laughed if it hadn't been so touching. He didn't know what the hell to do—about her, or Klaw, or even himself. "You worry about me, and you're the one who goes and follows him," he said quietly. "He is a killer, Angie. He killed my sister. How do you think it makes me feel to know you're anywhere near him?"

She threw her arms around his waist, her soft cheek

pressed against his chest. "I'm sorry. I don't mean to worry you."

He ran his hand over her hair. "You know why you worry me, don't you?"

She gazed up at him. "Yes," she said softly.

He cupped her face. His hands seemed to quiver slightly at the emotions running through him. "If I lost you, I don't know what I'd do."

He saw the fullness of her heart in her eyes. "You won't," she whispered, then drew his lips to hers and melted in his arms.

That night he let her find out everything she wanted to know about men who wear black leather.

CHAPTER

EIGHTEEN

Angie was bending over the desk in the donation room, trying to count up how many tickets they'd sold so far. The sales were going well, despite Reverend Hodge's anxiety. Besides, they still had a week before the big event—lots of time to sell more tickets.

His irritation at the cost of the caterer and the small army needed to cook and serve the hors d'oeuvres and pastries struck her as nothing more than him being cheap. Every time she talked to the caterer, he came up with more exciting food to serve, so of course the cost kept mounting. It was now around $110,000, but who could say no to gâteau Saint-Honoré, even though the fifteen hundred cream puffs—one on top of each piece of cake—added considerably to the cost? It wasn't as if they could give someone half a cream puff. But with Picassos and diamonds to sell, she couldn't allow the food or wine to look skimpy. Considering the cost of wedding banquets, she thought she was doing pretty darn well.

She'd simply have to find cost savings elsewhere. Maybe paper napkins instead of linen would help?

Suddenly, the world went black as hands clasped playfully over her eyes.

She gave a little yelp, pulled free, and spun around with a smile, thinking it was one of the other volunteers clowning around. To her horror, before her stood Axel Klaw.

He put his hands on his hips, his feet apart, and laughed uproariously.

She wanted to tell him he wasn't that funny, but somehow, she couldn't get the words past her throat. The thought of Klaw's touching her made her skin crawl. Finally, not knowing what to do, what to say, or how to act, she grabbed her purse and ran from the room.

Klaw laughed louder.

"You got problems, buddy." Yosh shook his head. He sat beside Paavo's desk as the two filled each other in on what had happened at the Isle of Capri and on Hanover Judd's tale of rumors—most likely from those two rookies.

"We're investigating the dead numbers runners well enough between all of us. It's Klaw, Lili Charmaine, Van Warren, and now a new player—a girlfriend of Klaw's named Gretchen—that I want to find out about."

"I'm with you, partner," Yosh said.

Paavo studied him. Looking into the doings of a man such as Klaw and his friends could get dangerous. Not to mention that if Yosh tried to help him on department time and anyone wanted to get nasty about it, Yosh could end up in hot water, too. "Are you sure?" he asked.

"It's no more than you'd do for me," Yosh said, his gaze direct and open.

Paavo just nodded.

●   ●   ●

Angie's heart eventually stopped racing as she sat in the Senseless Beauty Café and talked with Rainbow Grchek. The café, Angie was pleased to learn, was proving quite successful. Office workers from the financial district and Market Street jogged or walked along the Embarcadero at lunchtime, and often stopped in for something vegetarian or low-fat. Or, if they'd had a bad day at work—which for some people was every day at work—they'd order a scrumptious pastry to lift their spirits.

"Oh, hi! What do you hear?" Angie knew that voice—the sound of fingernails scraping along a blackboard would have been more welcome. She looked up quickly, fearfully, wondering if Klaw was with his girlfriend. Luckily, Lili was alone.

"Hello, Lili," Rainbow called. "Pull up a chair."

Lili sauntered over to their table. She wore a short turquoise jacket, a white ruffled blouse, and a teeny skirt that looked as though it had been made out of a band of turquoise spandex. "No time for a calorie fest for me. I'm hitting the stores. Axel will go ballistic if I don't do what I'm supposed to, when I'm supposed to."

"You mean Axel actually wants you to go shopping?" Angie asked. "That's a switch." Unless it was to buy better-looking clothes, she almost said, but thought better of it.

"Yeah. He gives me snaps for courageous fashion efforts. Most people say, like, hello-o-o, you've already got more clothes than you can wear in, like, twenty years, but not my guy. That's why I'd do whatever he says, just to show him he's right."

"That's good, Lili."

"Yeah. Sometimes I get way bored, though, but what the hey."

"I can't imagine that he'd ask you to do boring things."

"He does. He's into athletics in a monster way."

Angie had doubts about pursuing this conversation any further. She could well imagine some of the athletics Klaw liked to pursue with Lili. "I didn't know," she said finally, curiosity outweighing good taste—as usual.

"He hangs with a bunch of joggers," Lili said.

"Joggers?" That was the last thing Angie expected to hear. "Jogging can be boring, I guess."

"He wants to open a string of health clubs." Lili clearly relished the fact that someone was listening to her. "I thought, like, okay, whatever you want to call them is okay with me."

"So they're not health clubs?" Angie was growing more confused by the minute.

Lili's gaze grew almost shrewd. "If Axel says they're salami sandwiches, that's what they are."

"Of course." Angie wasn't about to alarm Lili.

"Now you're talking. Of course, if those investors I met in Las Vegas tried to jog, we'd have to call for oxygen fast."

"I didn't know you were both in Vegas."

"Oh, yeah. I was onstage, even. Actually, Lili Charmaine isn't my real name. It's my show name. But then, I got to be so last-season, I was fired. What could I do? I gave a few shows one-on-one, if you know what I mean."

Angie got it. "I'm sorry," she said.

"It's okay. Showgirls are twenty, twenty-one. I'm thirty-two. Not that anyone could tell."

Angie could.

"That's why," Lili continued, "I'm way grateful to join the reverend. I can talk to the girls who'll come here when the place gets going. I'll steer them right. Make a difference. Does that make me sound like a retard?"

"Not at all," Angie said, looking at Lili in a whole new light.

"Axel thinks I'm mental, but I tell him that's way harsh. Then he says, what do I know?"

"I think you'd be an asset to the mission," Angie told her.

"Thanks, Ang. I'd like to show Axel and his investors what I can do."

Talk of the investors brought Angie back to wondering what Klaw was up to. "If Klaw had investors in Las Vegas," Angie asked, "why didn't he just stay there? I would have thought he wouldn't want to leave."

"You are so totally in the dark. Nobody cares about health clubs in the desert. It's way hot. If you don't, like, spend all your time sitting around and drinking, you'd wither up and die. That's why it's got a major jogger drought."

Back to jogging. Angie's head was spinning. "But you don't need a health club to jog."

"Hey, that's truly sublime." Lili stared off into space awhile. "I never thought of that."

Give me strength, Angie thought. "Does Axel jog?"

"Get outta town! No way! Actually, he sends me to meet the joggers. They're all, like, giving me stuff for him all the time."

"What kind of stuff?" Angie probed.

"Don't ask me. He'd go ballistic if I touched it. Anyway, I've got to haul ass. I'm stopping at a palm reader's."

"A palm reader's?" Angie would have assumed Lili was joking, but something told her Lili didn't joke. Did Axel have something to do with palm readers, too?

"I found a cute little shop. I was freaking. You know what she said?"

"I can't imagine," Angie murmured, realizing this had nothing to do with Axel, but was pure Lili.

"It's so fab. I'm going to meet a handsome man and get rich."

"Really? How exciting for you."

"I can't tell Axel, though—I mean, Alex. I mean, he's cute, but even *he* don't think he's handsome. Anyway, sometimes I just don't think this relationship is a major forever-after."

"I've had days like that," Angie admitted.

"Well, so long, Ang." Lili stood up to leave.

"Don't tell Axel we talked, okay?" Angie asked. "He might not like to hear you were delayed going shopping."

Lili smiled. "That's cool. Bye." With that, she left.

Lili might not care what her visits to Axel's friends were all about, but Angie was eager to find out. Health clubs? Joggers? She didn't think so.

CHAPTER

NINETEEN

Paavo made a quick about-face as he approached room 450 of the Hall of Justice the next morning. A reporter from the *San Francisco Examiner*, the city's afternoon paper, was pacing the hallway. The woman's beat was city government, and she was having a field day investigating rumors of a top homicide inspector's alleged involvement in deaths resulting from numbers racketeering.

Instead of battling his way to his desk, Paavo went down to the Police Administration offices. He still smarted every time he remembered Angie's calling him obsessed with Klaw. It wasn't obsession. But maybe he had jumped to the correct conclusion overly soon.

In the files area he looked up the records of Richmond station officers Mike Kellogg and Eric Rosenberg. Both records were so clean they sparkled. Not the slightest hint of notoriety lingered over either one of them, and they'd been among the highest scorers at the police academy.

So why were they under his feet with every step he took? Why were they watching him so closely?

He was pondering those questions when Rebecca Mayfield burst into the files room. "Paavo, I was hoping I'd find you here."

"What's wrong?"

"Sutter and I are the on-call team this week. Last night we got a summons to go to a restaurant—the Isle of Capri. The owner, Frankie Tagliaro, had been murdered. One bullet, back of the head. I thought you'd want to know."

"Ah, Angie, I'm so glad you're here," Reverend Hodge said, bursting into Auction Central. Angie sat at a desk going over the donations list. "We've got to cut back on the food bill. It's too much. Whoever heard of pâté de canard en croûte at an auction? Whoever heard of pâté de canard en croûte at anything? I don't even know what it is. All I know is, it's too damned expensive for us."

She leaned back in her chair. "It's boned, stuffed duck in a pastry crust—beautiful, elegant, and worth every penny. No one will eat much, but they'll be impressed nonetheless. You must remember, Reverend Hodge, penny-pinching is not a noble trait."

"Who's penny-pinching? I just don't want to end up in the poorhouse."

"You've got all those fine donations." Angie had been over this with him time and again. "You don't have to worry."

"But every time I turn around, the bill for the caterer goes higher."

"You told me you wanted to impress the patrons with fine food, didn't you?" she cried.

"Impressing them is one thing. Stuffing them to the gills with all this expensive food is another!"

She rubbed her forehead. "It'll be worth it. Trust me."

He pulled at his hair. "Right now, it's all I can do to get people to spend two hundred lousy dollars for a ticket! I spend all my time publicizing the damn—oops!—I mean, darn thing. Maybe this was all just a bad idea! Maybe I should forget the whole thing!"

"You're right," she said, her voice clipped.

He dropped his hands. "What?"

"I said you're right." She stood. "I quit. I'll call the caterer and tell him to forget it. You can refund all the ticket money. Mary Ellen tells me you're keeping it in some special account, so giving it back should be easy."

"Now wait, Angie." He darted to her side and got down on one knee. "Don't be hasty. I mean, you shouldn't jump off the train before it reaches the station. Give it a chance."

She slowly lifted one eyebrow. "Are you sure?"

He sighed, and his look told her he realized what she'd done. He stood and dusted off his knee. "I'm sure. So tell me, how's the centerpiece coming?"

She sat down again. "Well . . . I haven't quite settled on one thing."

"That's understandable. What are you thinking about?"

She wasn't sure how to break this to him. "Well . . . I haven't quite thought of anything yet, either."

"I see." The Adam's apple on his skinny neck bobbed up and down a couple of times. "I'm sure you'll come up with something soon. Something meaningful."

She blanched. "You wanted attractive . . . now you want meaningful, too? We've got only six days left. That might not be enough time to be too meaningful."

"Don't worry. God will guide you."

"You've got that right." She folded her arms and slouched down in the chair, knowing more hours would be spent racking her brain. "Whatever the centerpiece is, God only knows."

HOMICIDE INSPECTOR QUIZZED ON GAMBLING TIES

by Doris Grant
Examiner Staff Writer

Homicide inspector Paavo Smith came under increased scrutiny today as the investigation into his alleged gambling activities broadened. Charges of payoffs and kickbacks have been made based on finding Smith's name on the tally sheets of two murdered numbers racketeers, Patrick Devlin and Dennis O'Leary. Also, last night's murder of Frankie Tagliaro, a restaurant owner with ties to the numbers racket, became connected to the case when word got out that Smith was found at Tagliaro's restaurant during a raid a few days ago by the vice squad. Vice inspectors allegedly allowed Smith to leave the scene.

In an action bound to stir controversy even more, Smith remains the lead investigator of Dennis O'Leary's murder. The investigation is said to be stalled. Chief of Police Lawrence Creighton says the matter is being looked into. Smith had no comment.

Paavo was dialing Angie's number when he was summoned to Lieutenant Hollins's office. He had wanted to tell Angie about Tagliaro's murder so that she could explain it to her father in a way that would leave him feeling no responsibility for the man's death.

He got her answering machine and hung up. She was

probably at the mission. He'd call there as soon as he finished with Hollins.

When he walked into Hollins's office, he was surprised to find Assistant District Attorney Judd there waiting for him.

"Have a seat, Smith," Hollins said.

"Well," he said, taking the chair indicated, "I guess the two of you are here to give me the same rousing endorsement as the chief of police did in this afternoon's paper. I can't tell you how touched I was by his support."

Hollins gave Paavo a look that was filled with compassion. "We've worked together a lot of years, Paavo," Hollins said. "I know you, I know all my men, almost as well as I do my wife. And probably a hell of a lot better than I know either one of my kids. I trust all of you. I'd trust you with my life, and I want you to know that."

Paavo leaned back in the chair. Why was it that talk about trust made one instinctively wary? "I feel a whole lot better now."

Hollins ignored the sarcasm. "With that statement in the paper about your being at Tagliaro's restaurant when it was raided, everything's hit the fan. The DA's ordered an investigation. Already he's got a call from someone, a woman—she didn't identify herself—but she said he should look at the deposits made to your savings account at the Bank of America. Judd's been told to do it."

Paavo could scarcely look at Judd, whom he'd once considered a friend. Yosh had filled him in on their talk, on the way Judd had asked Yosh to do what he could to prove Paavo's innocence. Paavo might have felt differently if Judd had talked to him first instead of talking to his partner, and now his boss. He turned to Judd and said only, "Did you?"

Judd squirmed uncomfortably under the intense

scrutiny. "No. We'll let you do that. Have the statement faxed to me from the bank."

"So there's no danger of my tampering with the results, is that it?" He didn't raise his voice, didn't speak with any emotion, and that seemed to make his words, his unspoken accusation, even more chilling.

"So there'll be no question in anyone else's mind," Hollins said emphatically. "I know there's nothing to any of this nonsense. The thing is, I want to find out what's going on and who's hassling you."

"You're not the only one," Paavo said. He stood, his gaze piercing first one and then the other. "Any more accusations I should know about?"

Hollins pulled out a cigar and chewed it for a while. "We understand you were good friends with Frankie Tagliaro."

"Friends? Good Christ, who's feeding you these lies? I never saw the guy before Angie and I went to dinner there the other night."

"Why'd you pick that place?"

"Why?" Should he go into the whole story about numbers and Angie's father with these two? Would that make him sound less guilty, or more so? "We eat out at a lot of different spots." Even to his ears, the excuse sounded lame. "It was on the way to my place."

Hollins and Judd's eyes met. "Get that bank statement so we can straighten all this out," Hollins said. "In the meantime, I'm giving Yosh your cases. You're not suspended. You can come to work, ride with Yosh if you want, but don't handle anything on your own. Is that clear?"

His frustration beyond the breaking point, Paavo left without another word.

●   ●   ●

Angie needed to give serious thought to the centerpiece the reverend wanted, and decided that an iced mocha decaf latte made with nonfat milk—generally known as a Why Bother—would be the way to do it. She was walking from the mission to the Senseless Beauty Café when her eye caught a page-one story in the *Examiner:* "Restaurant Owner Murdered."

Her blood froze. Not long ago there had been a rash of murders that left the restaurateurs of the city reeling, many of whom were her friends. Dropping a quarter into the machine, she pulled out a newspaper.

Frankie Tagliaro was the dead man. Poor Frankie. He had gotten involved in something way over his head and had paid the ultimate price for it.

She wondered why Paavo hadn't called and told her about this. He must have known. A call from him so that she could tell her parents before news of the murder came out in the paper would have been helpful. The thought of her father's reaction to the news worried her.

She turned back to the mission to call home, but then realized that if there was any connection between Tagliaro and Klaw, she didn't want Klaw and his cronies to overhear her conversation. She went to her car and used her cellular phone.

Serefina answered.

"Mamma, did you hear about Frankie Tagliaro?" she asked.

"*Sì.* It was on the radio. Your father is upset."

"Tell him the murder had nothing to do with the money Frankie wanted to borrow from him."

"You're sure?"

"I'm sure. Paavo knows all about it."

"*Dio, grazie,* I was so worried. So, why was he killed?"

Good question. "The police aren't saying, Mamma."

"Then how do you know it wasn't because of the money he owed?"

Oops. "He was killed ... because ... he got Don Corleone angry with him."

"Corleone? I don't know any Corleones in San Francisco," Serefina said.

"Be grateful, Mamma," Angie whispered confidentially.

"Don't worry, Angelina. Marlon Brando and Al Pacino wouldn't hurt a fly."

"Oh, dear."

"Next time, tell the truth." Serefina abruptly hung up.

The Bank of America branch near Paavo's house in the Richmond district was one of those small neighborhood banks where, years ago, the tellers knew all their customers and probably knew more about them and how they lived than any of those customers cared to consider. Now, though, Paavo didn't recognize a soul in the bank. His salary went into his checking account by direct deposit, and between checks, credit cards, and ATMs, he managed to spend it without any banker's face-to-face intervention.

He asked for a printout of his deposits into savings for the past three months. He expected the list to be a simple one, since he hadn't made any deposits in that time. Everything he earned went into checking, and between money for property taxes and money to fix a busted water pump and put a new clutch in his car, he hadn't had enough left over to bother moving into savings.

The bank teller keyed in his account number and waited a moment, then hit a button. The printer began to clatter and in a short while produced a five-by-eight sheet of paper. He took it from her and stared, unbelieving. One transaction was listed. It was dated the day after he and Angie went to Frankie Tagliaro's for dinner. The amount was five thousand dollars.

"How was this deposit made?" he asked.

"How?" she repeated absently.

He was out of patience. "ATM? Wired from another bank? *How?*"

She looked at the codes, then excused herself and went to speak to her manager. When she returned she said, "As best we can determine, you made it."

Would this madness never end? It made him wonder if someone was running around impersonating him. "Why do you think that?" he asked, trying his best to sound patient and reasonable.

"The codes. They tell us that you came to the bank and personally deposited this into your account."

"Do you know for sure I was the depositor?"

"Well . . . we don't require a signature or ID to put money *into* an account, especially when the transaction is cash. It's your account, someone made a cash deposit, so naturally we assumed . . ."

"And if it wasn't me, can you tell who did make the deposit?"

"I'm sorry, sir. The bank doesn't require—"

"I know. Forget it. I need this statement faxed." He handed her Hanover Judd's fax number.

"There'll be a charge for this service, sir," the teller said.

It took every ounce of his control for him to thank her for her help and tell her to deduct the charge from his account.

Angie sat in the mission's dining hall. Although the reverend had big plans for it in the future, right now only the volunteers used it. She was busily going through catalogues and books on wedding receptions in hopes of coming up with some innovative ideas on centerpieces. Oh, yes—meaningful ideas as well.

"Excuse me, please, miss."

She looked up. Her mouth dropped open, and she knew she was sitting there looking exceedingly dumb.

"I want to donate this. I heard about the auction and thought this might bring in some money. I don't imagine I'll ever need to use it again." He smiled at her—big round cheeks, dimples, blue eyes.

She still stared, speechless.

"Oh, I know what you're thinking. This isn't mine. It was a prop. The wig I used in *Mrs. Doubtfire*. Do you want it?"

She nodded, still unable to shut her mouth or talk.

"Okay. Enjoy!"

Robin Williams turned and walked out of the mission. She looked down at the wig, then at her donation pad. She picked it up and ran after him, wondering how she could possibly explain and apologize for being dumbstruck. Or rather, starstruck.

She screeched to a halt when she saw Axel Klaw shaking the actor's hand. Klaw looked from her to her donation pad. "Ah, here's Miss Amalfi now with the paperwork you'll need for the IRS. We can't forget the government, you know." He took the pad and scribbled on it. "Let's see—five thousand? Who knows what it'll bring? If it goes for more, we'll send you a new receipt."

"Thanks," Williams said, then looked at Angie and waved before he turned and walked away.

"Miss Amalfi," Klaw said with a chuckle as he took her arm and escorted her back into the mission, "you really should close your mouth. There are flies around."

"I . . . I'm just . . ." She shut her mouth, then pulled her arm free. She lifted her chin. "Thank you for giving him the donation slip. I was just so surprised."

"I understand." Klaw patted and stroked her arm.

"You're doing a fine job, Miss Amalfi. And I'm glad we've run into each other this way. I want to tell you how sorry I am that our earlier meetings went so badly. I hope that in the time you've been here you've come to understand me better, and to see that I'm doing all I can to make a positive change."

"Excuse me, Mr. Clausen." Angie backed away. She didn't want to hear this, and she certainly didn't want him to touch her again.

"Please." He grabbed hold of her hand and lifted it to his chest, cupping it with both of his. "Listen to me, try to understand. When I was young, I did wrong. I fell in with the wrong people. I'm sorry for that. I'm sorry for any involvement I may have had that caused your boyfriend pain."

She looked up at him, searching his eyes, but they were flat, emotionless. She could get no reading from them, no sense of humanity, despite his impassioned words.

"Please tell him how sorry I am," Klaw continued. "Tell him I hope that someday he'll stop this persecution of me."

"Persecution?" She pulled her hand free.

"You know it's true, Miss Amalfi." He gazed at her again, and she found that despite the way her stomach recoiled at his touch, she was unable to break the hold of his eyes. "I have no hard feelings, Angie." He stepped closer. She backed up. "May I call you Angie?" He took another step toward her. She tried to stand her ground. "I forgive him, as I hope someday he'll forgive me."

"It wasn't that long ago that I saw you running a porn studio," she said, her chin high. "Was that part of your rehabilitation?"

"That was before! I'm a changed man." He clutched her arms. "Overnight, almost, Reverend Hodge made me see the light. Made me"—he leaned closer, and she felt his breath touch her face—"compassionate."

She pushed herself free, stumbling backward. "You can tell Paavo yourself about your new ways, if you have the nerve! Besides, Paavo is *never* wrong about people. What you call a persecution, Mr. Clausen, I call a desire for justice."

"Mr. Clausen is the soul of generosity and fairness, Miss Amalfi." She gasped and spun around. Van Warren, the small, beady-eyed accountant, was sitting on the sofa in the entry hall. She hadn't seen or heard him come in. "It must hurt Mr. Clausen to hear you speak so harshly of him," Warren rebuked.

She looked from one to the other, struck with the realization that Warren was as bad as his boss, just in a more weasely, less overt manner.

"I wish it *did* hurt him," she said. "But I know better than that."

Head high, she marched back into the dining hall. As she did she noticed the Reverend Hodge standing in front of the kitchen door, his gaze darting from her to Klaw, a troubled expression on his face.

CHAPTER

T W E N T Y

Angie finally found a moment to order her iced decaf mocha latte with nonfat milk at the Senseless Beauty Café and was sipping it through a straw when who should walk through the door but Paavo. He was frowning, his brow tight and pinched with worry.

"I'm glad I found you," he said as he approached.

Her first thought was that she couldn't believe he'd actually come looking for her. Her second was to hope Klaw was far away from the mission. And third was that this visit must be due to Frankie Tagliaro's death.

He sat down at her table. Rainbow was over to him like a shot. "Hi there. What can I do for you?"

"I . . ." He glanced at Angie's tall, icy drink. "I'll have one of those."

"I don't think you'll care for it," Angie confessed.

"I'll give it a try," Paavo said.

"Terrific." Rainbow gave him one of her biggest smiles. "One Why Bother coming right up."

Paavo gave Angie a quizzical look, which she was

glad to see. It was better than the hardness he'd seemed to don like a shield since seeing Klaw on television, the intensity surrounding him, the cold, angry glint in his eyes when he didn't think she was looking. "I read about Frankie Tagliaro in the newspapers, Paavo," she said.

"I was hoping you hadn't heard yet. I guess your father has as well?"

She nodded.

"How is he taking the news?"

"He was upset, but I told my mother you had it on good authority that the loan Frankie wanted had nothing to do with his murder."

"Good."

There were times Paavo went along with her tall tales with amazing ease.

"I tried to call a couple of times and then decided to come and see you," he said. "Hollins has been on my back again. Now the DA's involved, wanting to pull my badge. Sounds like he's got a good chance at getting it, too. He's even asked IA to do a formal investigation."

"No," she cried, her heart breaking for him.

"This whole business has been so crazy, and now it's touched your family. I'm sorry, I just—"

"You don't have to apologize for anything." She gave his hand a squeeze, then they broke contact as Rainbow brought him his coffee.

He took a sip and wrinkled his mouth. "What is it? I thought it was an iced latte."

"Low-fat and decaf," she explained.

"No kidding." His expression reeked of disgust.

"What do you hear, Angie!" Lili pushed open the door and walked in, swinging a Macy's bag. Her gaze riveted on Paavo and she sauntered over to the table. "Hey there. I'm Angie's friend."

Since when? Angie wondered. Lili was oblivious to

anything but Paavo. "Paavo Smith, meet Lili Charmaine. She's a guest of Alex Clausen's over at the mission."

Paavo caught Angie's eye. "Oh. How do you do, Miss Charmaine," he said, standing and taking her hand.

"That's way sublime. Let's swish in a place for me." Paavo helped her grab a chair from the table beside theirs and swing it around. She shoved it right next to Paavo, then sat, up close and personal. He didn't move his chair a centimeter as he, too, sat down. Angie was not amused.

"I'm Lili—with an *i*, not a *y*. I put a heart over the *i* instead of a plain ol' dot." She smiled. Angie hadn't seen such deep dimples since her apple doll's head dried up.

"How clever," Paavo said.

To barf!

"Angie, I'm in the freaking outer limits. Remember that palm reader?" She looked at Paavo, then back at Angie with a glowing smile. "I'm a believer!"

"Forget it," Angie said. "You're too late."

"All's fair, Angie. And he's such a Baldwin." Her dimples all but tapped out Morse code at Paavo. And the message was X-rated.

"What palm reader?" he asked.

Lili touched her finger to her chin. "I think it's called, uh . . . destiny."

Angie was about to show her destiny at the end of a knuckle sandwich.

"Say." Lili now moved her finger to Paavo's sleeve. "We're all going to a speakeasy day after tomorrow. It's really a supper club—dinner, dancing, games—but everybody dresses up like the Roaring Twenties. It's fun. They say those were wild days. As if!" She winked at Paavo. "It'd be major cool if you'd come, too. You and Ang."

"A speakeasy? That sounds delightful," Paavo said.

Delightful?

He glared at Angie. She guessed her snicker wasn't exactly silent.

"Will you be going with your friend Mr. Clausen?" he asked.

"Sure, but he gets so busy with the games, he forgets I'm there. We'll have time for a dance . . . or two . . ."

Angie glanced at the ceiling to see if the paint had started to scorch yet from all the smoldering Lili was doing. She was at the end of her patience, ready to go for the woman's throat, when she felt Paavo's hand on her thigh. She glanced his way. He began to rub her knee. "It sounds like a perfect evening," he purred in reply to Lili's suggestion.

"Terrific!" She picked up her purse and began rummaging through it. "Here's the four-one-one. You need this card to get in. I'll tell Axel—I mean, Alex—I lost mine. It's cool. I lose stuff all the time. He gets, like, all pissed off, but it doesn't mean a thing."

"You're very kind," Paavo said.

"This is so doable." She squirmed in her chair. "I'm ready."

"Good. And don't mention it to anyone," Paavo added. "So that we can surprise them."

She leaned toward him, showing lots of cleavage, and put her forefinger against lips thrust out as if in a kiss. "I'm all silence." She put down her finger. "And I'm way good at doing *exactly* what I'm told to do."

"Are you?"

She smiled, lost in his blue eyes. Angie knew the feeling. If he didn't stop playing with her knee, her glasses were going to steam up, and she wasn't even wearing any. She kicked off her shoes. He was making her feet hot. And that wasn't all he was making hot, either.

"Well, this is so cool, Mr. Smith," Lili said, making a

seductive act out of picking up her Macy's shopping bag. "I'd better haul ass. Axel is waiting." She started to walk away, then looked back and waved. "Bye-yai-yai."

Bye-yai-yai? Knee rubbing or no, that was too much. "Give me a break!" Angie cried.

Paavo let go of her and, for what seemed like the first time in days, he grinned.

The next morning, Angie waited until Axel Klaw, his accountant, and Lili left the mission, then she picked up her donation pad, held it as if she were working on some business transaction, and ducked into Klaw's office. It was fairly small, located between the accountant's office and Hodge's. Klaw went into it several times a day, but he was rarely there very long. He seemed to spend most of his time upstairs in the apartments with Lili and Warren.

Last night over dinner she'd told Paavo about her earlier conversation with Lili Charmaine, how Lili had talked about meeting Klaw and his "investors" in Las Vegas, about the so-called health clubs and joggers. She also told him about the four upstairs apartments. She and Paavo were pretty sure of what Lili and Klaw were *really* up to.

Now she just had to find some proof. Paavo said he'd take care of everything. But the police seemed to work so *slowly*, and she was here, right next door to Axel Klaw's office. How could she ignore the opportunity for just one quick peek?

She put down her pad and began a mad scramble through his desk. There had to be something that would help her understand what he was up to. On the desktop were some brochures and other advertisements for the auction, plus a photo and map of the Palace of the Legion of Honor, showing all the rooms, even the basement.

She checked the drawers. Nothing was in them other than several old newspapers, about a week's worth. This didn't make much sense. No wonder the office wasn't locked.

She looked at the maps again. She had never been too sure where Klaw's responsibilities for the auction lay—if anywhere. He might have simply been the money man, leaving everything else up to the reverend. Somehow, though, that didn't seem to be Klaw's style.

Could the maps mean he was in charge of the crew who would move the goods to be auctioned in and out of the rooms? The items to be sold represented hundreds of thousands of dollars' worth of donations. Could Klaw be planning to steal them?

But if so, wasn't there an easier way than to set up such an elaborate scheme? That kind of thievery just didn't seem to be Klaw's style. What was, though? What was Klaw planning?

"What a surprise to find you here, Miss Amalfi."

She jumped away from the desk and looked up.

"Reverend Hodge! You scared me." The reverend hadn't been around earlier. She'd searched for him before deciding to take matters into her own hands this way. "I was just looking for some donation slips that I'm missing. I thought Mr. Clausen might have them."

"I doubt it," he said. "Mr. Clausen isn't one to handle details. Come along, Miss Amalfi, before Mr. Clausen returns. I don't think he'd like your being here."

"I saw him leave, though . . . I mean . . . that's why I didn't ask his permission to look for the slips," she said as Hodge pulled her into the hallway.

"You must be careful about what you count on in life," Hodge said, shutting the door behind her.

"Wait, my donation pad."

"Hurry, Miss Amalfi. I think I hear Mr. Clausen's voice."

She felt as if her blood had turned to ice. Opening the door, she ran into the room, grabbed the pad, and ran back out, pulling the door behind her quietly.

Klaw and Warren, scowling fiercely, appeared at the end of the hallway. Reverend Hodge took Angie's arm and half dragged her toward them. "Hello," he said cheerfully. "We were just going into Auction Central to look over the wonderful food Miss Amalfi is having catered for us. Would you like to join us?"

Klaw gave her a once-over, then frowned. "No." He and Warren brushed past them, opened the door to Klaw's office, and went inside.

"Oh, my," Angie said, realizing what a close call she'd had.

"Exactly," Hodge agreed, looking over his shoulder at Klaw's office door, his expression as worried and puzzled as Angie's own.

"That's the place," Snake Belly said. He was seated in Paavo's car, an old Austin-Healey roadster. "Room three-D, like those funky old movies."

The Snake was pointing at a run-down four-story tenement, gray with soot and grime from years of neglect. Sheets instead of curtains covered a few upper windows; others were cracked and patched with tape and cardboard, and still others didn't have anything over them. The ground floor looked as though it had once been a storefront, with its deep-set entryway and large plate-glass window. The windows were whitewashed and empty.

"Let me out at the corner," Snake Belly said. "I'll wait for you there." Paavo drove to the corner. As Snake got out he patted the hood of the car. "Don't forget to feed the mice tonight, big man. They were struggling to make it up these hills."

Everybody's a jokester, Paavo thought as he found himself a red zone to park in. There were some areas meter maids didn't bother to patrol. This was one of them.

He went back to the tenement. The smell of urine and worse in the lobby was enough to make him gag. The wallpaper was stained and coming loose, and there was no carpet on the floor or the stairs. He could see the dry rot on the wood and could practically hear the chomping of termites in the walls.

The first floor was empty. Room 3D was at the top of two flights of stairs. He knocked softly on the door and waited.

He knocked a little louder.

Another door in the hallway opened. Paavo froze, turned his back to the open door, and listened for the sound of approaching feet. Instead, the door slammed shut again.

He tried the doorknob. It turned, and the latch clicked. Sliding his revolver from his shoulder holster, he eased the door open.

The room was small, stained, and filthy. Amidst the rubbish, lying crosswise on the bed, was the body of a man. Blood dripped onto the floor from the bullet hole in his forehead.

The bookie, Paavo thought. He pocketed his gun and walked into the room. Past experience told him he wouldn't find a pulse on the man. He didn't.

The body was still warm, the limbs loose. Whoever did this could still be nearby. He walked to the window, the old-fashioned double-hung variety. It was unlatched. Using the sleeves of his jacket, so that he wouldn't destroy any fingerprints that might be on it, he lifted it and stuck his head out. A fire escape led both to the roof and the street.

"Making your escape, Smith?"

He turned. LeRoy Davis and Mitch Connors from Internal Affairs stood in front of the doorway, guns drawn and pointed straight at him. They were older men, both barrel-chested and with big bellies, the type who'd gotten a little too old and a little too fat to be on the street or in investigation anymore, so now they just spied on other cops. The pace was a lot slower that way. They were like two peas in a pod except that one was black and the other white. "Jesus Christ," Paavo said, pulling himself back into the room, then straightening and holding his arms out at his side so that they could see he wasn't reaching for his gun. "What is this?"

"You should be answering questions, Smith, not asking them." Davis, his chest puffed out, put his gun back in his holster. "I'm going to trust you. Although to tell the truth, I don't know why I should."

"Trust me? That's big of you." Paavo was fuming. "I came in here to talk to the guy and found him like this. The killer probably went down the fire escape."

Davis slid his gaze from the window back to the dead man. "What's his name?"

"I don't know. Let me get the person who brought me here. He's waiting for me at the corner. He'll tell you who the dead man is, and explain that I wasn't even here long enough to have killed him."

Connors stepped closer to the doorway, blocking it, then folded his arms across his big chest. "Sure he will. We got a call, too. A call from the dead man to get over here fast because a dirty cop was on his way to see him. A dirty cop who was going to put the squeeze on him. But it looks like you made it before us."

Paavo was beyond disgusted. He could scarcely contain his fury. "You know there's no truth to that story."

"Hey, look here," Davis said, lifting a paper out of

the top bureau drawer. "Maybe this is all the proof we need."

"Watch what you're touching, Davis," Paavo warned. "This is a murder scene."

"Hey, LeRoy, listen to him," Connors said. "He sounds like he thinks he's still a homicide dick. Ain't that a hoot?"

Davis snickered. "Not for long. Not after what I found." He read from the paper he held. "'PS, three seven one five five four six.' Is that *PS* as in Paavo Smith, do you think?"

Paavo felt the blood drain from his face. "That's my phone number. What of it?"

"I thought you just said you don't even know this guy's name," Connors chided.

"I don't. Everyone knows my phone number is out there with these numbers runners—"

"You know all about numbers runners, don't you, Smith?" Davis asked.

Paavo was sick of these two and their accusations. "Look, we're wasting time. Let's go downstairs and find Snake Belly. He'll explain to you that I have nothing to do with this."

"Snake Belly? Nice guys you hang around with, Smith."

"Present company excepted," he said.

Connors frowned, then held out his hand. "Give me your gun."

Paavo took it from his holster and turned it over to him. "You can see it hasn't been fired. I want it back."

Connors pocketed it. "I don't think so. We're going to run a few tests first."

"Let's go find your friend," Davis said, stepping aside.

Paavo pushed his way past the two men and hurried down the stairs. They followed him out the door to the corner.

"He's not here," Paavo said, pacing in a small circle, feeling caged by the two hovering close by. "Even if he was here, seeing you two goons wouldn't make him want to show himself. I'll have to find him. I'll get him to come in and explain what's going on."

Davis and Connors glanced at each other.

"What? Am I under arrest or something? Is that what this is about?"

"Not yet," Connors said. "First we're going to go have a nice, long chat down at the Hall."

CHAPTER

TWENTY-ONE

Connie stood beside Angie, her forefinger lightly tapping her cheek as she studied the contraption in the middle of the kitchen. Finally she dropped her hand and made her pronouncement. "You've got to be kidding," she said.

A shave-and-a-haircut knock sounded at the door, followed by a "Yoo-hoo, Angie!"

"Oh, no," Angie groaned. "Not today. If we're quiet, he might go away."

"Is that your neighbor?" Connie asked. "He seemed harmless enough. Kind of cute, as a matter of fact. Why not let him in?"

"I'm warning you, that's like the Trojans deciding to let in the horse," Angie said.

"He can't be that bad." Connie grinned.

Angie rolled her eyes as she went to the living room and opened the door.

"Hey there!" Stan bounded into the living room, not waiting for an invitation. "What's going on?"

"Nothing, Stan," Angie said, still holding the door open. "What did you want?"

"I thought I heard voices in the hall earlier, like someone came to visit. Someone *female*," Stan said as he headed for the kitchen. "Wow! What's that?"

Angie shut the door and followed.

"Hi! Your name is Connie, right? Remember me? Stan the man!"

"Of course I remember you." Connie smiled coyly, to Angie's horror.

"I don't think I've ever seen anything like this before," Stan said, circling the machine. "Except in mad-scientist movies."

"Want to guess what it is?" Connie asked.

"Is there a prize?"

"No."

"I give up, then," he said.

"It's a candy maker." Connie smiled. "Angie bought it."

"Hey, neat," Stan said, touching the knobs and flaps that blanketed the machine. He glanced at Angie. "Does it work?"

"I hope so," she replied. "I saw it on TV—a home shopping program. They showed someone pour in the ingredients and push a button. Next thing, they showed a box of perfectly formed chocolates. It must work. There must be some truth in advertising, right?"

"I don't know if I've heard of any lately," Connie said.

"Anyway, it's got to be lots easier than making them by hand," Angie added.

"You did great, Angie!" Stan bent over to look underneath the thing at all the moving parts. "I could go for some chocolates myself, especially at this price."

"Here's a cute mold," Connie said, digging through a box of implements. "It looks like a chestnut." She held up two small shaped metal cups that when fitted to-gether formed a chestnut.

"I don't have any marron flavoring," Angie said, "but I think we could try a simple mocha filling along with the chocolate. Sound okay to the two of you?"

They nodded. Stan licked his lips.

Angie mixed together the ingredients for the mocha cream filling and then decided on semisweet chocolate for the outside.

They plugged in the machine. It began making humming noises, punctuated with random metallic hic-cups.

The first test of the candy maker was to melt the semisweet chocolate at just the right temperature to temper it—to let it reach a shiny consistency without turning grainy—and then let it cool down enough to work with it.

The chocolate tempered beautifully, shiny and but-tery smooth. Angie beamed. Connie was impressed. Stan kept making taste tests.

When the chocolate thickened to a consistency that was moldable, Angie pressed a button and the candy maker burped a dollop of semisweet chocolate into each little chestnut-shaped cup. To her amazement, the molds began to spin, causing the chocolate to creep up the sides and cover them evenly.

Next a blob of mocha cream was dropped into each mold, then the left and right molds smacked together, sealing the mocha inside. The mold was thrust into the chiller, where it remained for five minutes. When it slid back out, the two halves opened up, and out dropped a piece of candy. It looked perfect.

Stan said it tasted delicious.

Angie pushed the button and the process began again. Five minutes later, a second piece of chocolate dropped from the mold.

"These chocolates take too long to make," Stan said. "You'll be here forever just filling a one-pound box."

"The instructions say this lever will make it run a little faster," Connie said, reading the manual. "Should we try?"

"I don't know if that's a good idea," Angie said. "The chocolates are coming out well at this speed. I doubt it can work much faster."

"But Stan's right about its being way too slow. We might try moving it just a little," Connie suggested. Angie gave the okay. Four minutes later, a third piece of chocolate dropped out.

Since Stan had eaten the first two pieces, they couldn't be sure the third piece was as well formed as the others were. It looked a little runny.

"Nobody invents a machine that runs so slow," Stan said, his hand on the lever. "Let's give it some juice."

"Stan, no," Angie said, but too late. He had pushed the lever forward to the fastest speed.

Two squirts of chocolate gushed into the molds, which whirled at warp speed, causing a funnel cloud of chocolate to fly up the sides of the mold, off the top, and out over Angie's kitchen, splattering all three of them. The machine chugged on.

Mocha cream plummeted into the molds. In a blur, the molds hammered together, lurched into the chiller, and exploded back out. Then the molds burst open and catapulted the still-sticky chocolate across the room to land on a cabinet door.

Angie, Connie, and Stan stared, slack-jawed, at the blob on the door.

"I'll slow it down," Stan said, and grabbed the speed lever. It came off in his hand. "Uh-oh."

The machine wobbled and shook with newfound freedom, the molds started spinning, and then the whole contraption began to bounce like a helicopter ready for takeoff. When it banged against the wall, Angie and Connie grabbed it, but they couldn't stop it from bouncing.

A torrent of chocolate shot into the molds, but now they were spinning so fast, the chocolate sprayed into the air. Angie shrieked and jumped back. Connie whirled around, trying to cover her hair with her arms.

The harder Stan worked to fix the machine, the faster the chocolate squirted out of it, showering them like a burst water main. Every so often it pitched a chocolate-covered wad of mocha cream with the speed of Greg Maddox.

"Unplug it!" Angie yelled over the noise of the machine banging against the wall and bounding off the floor, along with the whistle of mocha cream sailing by her ears.

"I can fix it," Stan cried.

"No, you can't! Unplug it, now!"

"I'll fix it. Trust me!" He shoved the lever onto the machine. "Success!"

A stream of chocolate sprayed Angie in the face like water from a hose. She shut her eyes and waved her hands in front of her, trying to stop the attack. "Unplug—*ulp*!" A glob of chocolate shot into her mouth.

"If that's success," Connie shrieked, "I'd hate to see failure!"

Stan flexed his chocolate-smeared muscles. "No machine's ever gotten the best of Stan the Man," he cried, pulling a butter knife out of a drawer to attack the appliance, since Angie didn't have any screwdrivers in the kitchen.

"I'm not taking a minute more of this just so you can play Mr. Macho," Connie announced, marching defiantly toward the machine. Her shoe landed on a thick lump of wet chocolate and her foot slid out from under her. She ended up sitting on the floor right beside the rocking monstrosity. Chocolate dribbled off the sides of the machine, plastering her blond hair down as though she were getting a dye job from a demented hairdresser.

Stan pointed at her and laughed uproariously, grabbing his stomach and rocking back and forth. She stood up, balanced precariously on the chocolate-covered soles of her shoes, grabbed a wad of gooey chocolate off the floor, and smacked Stan square in the face with it. He tumbled over, grabbing Connie for support, and they both landed in a heap.

Angie scrambled under the table, reached up, and pulled the plug. The machine shuddered and died to the sound of grave internal disorder.

Angie, Connie, and Stan sat on the floor facing each other, with chocolate dripping from their hair and smeared over their faces and clothes.

"Well, if I can't come up with an angelina that people want to eat," Angie said, looking at her friends, "I can think about developing a chocolate-flavored facial mud pack."

CHAPTER

TWENTY-TWO

Paavo and Yosh parked across from the Random Acts of Kindness Mission and watched to see who went in or out. They'd taken to doing that every so often, but despite Angie's fear that numbers running was going on there, the only people they ever saw—besides Hodge, Klaw, and Klaw's cohorts—were some society women showing up to do volunteer work. If Klaw was running numbers, the mission wasn't a drop site.

Paavo was glad to sit here and think about something other than the dead bookie and the grilling he'd gotten from IA. Finally, with no proof against him, they'd let him go.

"Hodge is driving me crazy," Paavo said. He pried the plastic lid off the Styrofoam cup of coffee. He hadn't been able to eat or sleep lately, his mind and emotions on overload, and had taken to living on coffee. "I can't find a single thing on the guy. It's as if he dropped out of nowhere."

"It might not matter." Yosh added Coffee-mate and

three sugars to his coffee. "Even though we know Lili's an ex-hooker and Warren's a hired gun, with no charges against them we can't do a thing. So even if we knew about Hodge, it might not help."

"At least we'd know what we're dealing with," Paavo said. "Any luck with Klaw's mystery woman Gretchen?"

"Not yet. The reverse phone directory didn't list any Gretchen or *G* in that building, but lots of women living alone don't use their own names or initials in a listing. Wouldn't you know, the building's got about twenty apartments in it? I'll do a door-to-door soon as I get some time."

"I'll fit some time in, too. I'll take top down, you go bottom up."

"Got it." Yosh took a sip of his coffee. "Christ, still too hot. Did you ever think that this Gretchen might just be a nice girl Klaw likes to mess around with?"

"No." Paavo stared at the mission, lost in thought, before he said, "Klaw has a reason for every move he makes—money or power. I'll see him tonight at a supper club with Angie. It'll be interesting to see what he's up to."

"That might be dangerous. Maybe I should come along to watch your back, just in case?"

"Thanks, Yosh. I'm sure there's no need. When he and I do finally finish this thing, it'll be a well-planned encounter, not some chance meeting at a club. I'll be all right tonight."

That evening, Angie studied herself in the full-length mirror in her bedroom, carefully assessing whether she'd achieved the right effect. She'd always wanted to be a flapper. The Roaring Twenties seemed like a great time to have lived. The war to end all wars had been fought—and won. There was no Depression, no Cold

War, no atomic bomb, no terrorists blowing up planes, buildings, and buses for causes no one understood. People just had a good time.

Yesterday, after leaving the mission, she'd gone to a vintage clothing store and found a sheath dress completely covered with silver sequins. It was sleeveless and had a low-cut square neckline. She'd found pale shimmering gray hose, silver shoes, light gray over-the-elbow gloves, and a long, wide silver ribbon for her hair.

Now she arranged thick bangs across her forehead, pasted big round spit curls against each cheek, and plastered the whole thing in place with the ribbon, letting her bangs and curls peek provocatively beneath it. She crimped the rest of her hair into a frizz until she looked more like Clara Bow than herself, which wasn't too hard to do, since the hot water and harsh soap she had used to get the dried chocolate out of her hair left it a frizzy mess anyway.

A bright red Cupid's-bow mouth completed the picture.

She glanced at the clock. It was nearly eight o'clock.

The doorbell rang. Paavo was right on time.

She pulled the door open. He wore a dark gray suit—she hadn't asked him to wear a 1920s outfit, knowing what his answer would be. No matter. Whatever he wore, he'd always be Valentino to her. But a pale undercast to his skin and a pinched tenseness to his mouth told her something had happened. "Would you like to talk about it?" she asked.

"About what?" he asked. Then, gesturing at her clothes, he said, "Not bad." She took that as high praise and decided not to pursue whatever had made him so unhappy.

"Shall we go?" he asked.

She hung back. Ever since Lili had first mentioned the club, despite her bubbly nonsense, the fact remained that Klaw and Paavo would be face-to-face once again. Angie found it scary. "I don't know," she said.

"I do."

The supper club was above a nondescript American-style restaurant. Once inside, though, one flight up, nothing was the way it appeared from the street. Paavo showed the pass Lili had given them, and a door opened to another world.

A huge man wearing a wide-lapeled pinstriped suit, a white stand-up collar, and a bow tie stood at the door making sure only invited guests were allowed in. In his hand was a very realistic-looking tommy gun—so realistic, she caught Paavo frowning at it more than once.

Tables were beautifully set with white tablecloths and crystal glassware that sparkled under the bright lights. Other women were also dressed in waistless dresses, many with big bows tied at the crotch, topping short pleated skirts that flipped up as they danced. The "Varsity Rag" was blaring.

Angie was surprised at the guests in the room. Some of the big-name, big-money people from Pacific Heights, Sea Cliff, and Presidio Heights—the best addresses in the city—were there, as well as several from Marin and the South Bay. Not only that, but there were more men than women. In fact, almost half the tables were all male.

Paavo seemed to study everything, particularly the goonish-looking men standing near the doors and by the liquor tables. Angie didn't like the way their jackets bulged. "I don't know about this," she said.

"Strange, isn't it?" he replied. When the band began to play "Somebody Loves Me," he took her hand and led her to the dance floor.

• • •

The meal was one of the best Angie had ever had. The entire menu was flawless—braised sweetbreads in puff pastry with truffle sauce, accompanied by a beet-and-arugula salad and steamed vegetables, finished off with a lemon-almond meringue. Paavo, though, barely ate anything.

When the food was cleared, a bar was set up and the diners moved en masse toward it for after-dinner aperitifs, cigars, and cigarettes. "I guess we need to follow," Paavo said, leading Angie toward the others.

"I wonder what's going on," she murmured. They had barely gotten out of the way when the waiters began to cover the dining tables with an assortment of gaming paraphernalia—felt for blackjack, poker, baccarat, faro, roulette, and craps. In no time at all, the club had been transformed into a casino.

The man at the bar began selling tokens for the games. Mounted on the wall was a list of prizes, donated by wealthy patrons, that the winning tokens could buy. Clever, Paavo mused. By making its money through the sale of the tokens, the supper club could claim that, technically speaking, it was not profiting from illegal gambling.

Paavo had an idea, though, that if he scratched the surface, he'd easily find a different story. The people at this gathering weren't interested in winning a set of Tupperware or a VCR. They already had one. Or two or three. And they weren't intimidated by the law. They were the type who could make sure no one at the Hall of Justice would press charges, no matter how open or illegal the gambling. Another example of this being a city of laws—one set of laws for the politically powerful, another for everyone else.

While Angie went off to the women's room, Paavo

wandered over to the bar. He bought ten tokens—at five dollars a pop, this was not a poor man's club. Then he ordered a whiskey sour for Angie and a Scotch and water for himself. As he waited for the drinks he had a strange feeling of something happening behind him, something that gave him a chill. He turned around.

At almost the exact moment Axel Klaw also turned. Their eyes met. Klaw nodded and crossed the room. "So we meet again, Inspector Smith," Klaw said. "I'm surprised to find you here. But suddenly I think I know why Lili couldn't find her pass. Your sneaky girlfriend must have stolen it. I blamed poor Lili and made her stay home."

"When I heard you'd be here, Klaw, I just couldn't keep away," Paavo said, his gaze cold as ice.

"Let me get that for you," Klaw said abruptly. He pulled out a thick roll of money and peeled off a hundred-dollar bill. "Keep the change," he said to the barman as he tossed the money down.

"Why bother to gamble here, Klaw?" Paavo said. "Isn't the mission good enough for you?"

Klaw blinked rapidly, then his eyes narrowed. "You've got it wrong, Smith. The mission is exactly what it looks like, or will look like after the auction."

Klaw's mention of the auction was a surprise—Paavo hadn't thought it could matter enough for him to remember it. "It doesn't look like anything much to me."

Klaw smirked. "Very observant, Smith. It's a play-thing for wealthy men and women who don't have anything better to do than volunteer work. What makes it so appealing is that it's supposedly for a good cause but the volunteers don't have to get their hands dirty. You wouldn't want your little Angie to get her hands dirty, now would you?"

"You're there, Klaw. That pollutes it as far as I'm

concerned," Paavo said. "But you won't be there much longer."

"Don't threaten me, Smith." He chuckled. "Not with all the troubles of your own you've got to deal with. Murder charges against cops don't get swept under the rug in this town. They're taken seriously. Very seriously."

Klaw's statement confirmed Paavo's suspicion about his involvement. The events had happened so recently, Klaw couldn't have known about them otherwise. Paavo hadn't even mentioned it yet to Angie. He didn't want to spoil this evening for her. She loved to dress up and go dancing, and even though tonight's date was basically to see what Klaw was up to, he could still pretend, for her sake, that it was a special date.

"You're wondering how I found out, aren't you? I'll tell you, I know a lot. Enough to give you some advice. You should worry, Smith. Your whole career's going to hell. Soon, you'll be a nothing."

Paavo's voice turned low and deadly. "I'll still be enough to put you exactly where I want you, Klaw."

Klaw's cheek muscles twitched convulsively. Abruptly, he turned and walked toward the exit. Van Warren appeared from nowhere, joined him, and they left.

CHAPTER

TWENTY-THREE

Paavo rang the bell to Peewee's mother's flat. To his surprise, Peewee himself opened the door. He peered nervously past Paavo and Yosh toward the street, then met their eyes. "What do you two want?"

"We want to talk," Paavo said. He and Yosh still had a job to do: Sarah Ann Cribbs was still dead, and her killer walked around a free man. Despite IA's trying to implicate him in the bookie's murder, there was no evidence and he still had his badge.

"How many times I got to tell you?" Peewee whined. "I ain't got nothing to say."

"Can we come in?" Yosh asked. "Or do you want all your neighbors to see you talking to the police? Might ruin your reputation, Peewee."

They followed Peewee upstairs to the living room. The three sat and faced each other.

"I guess you've heard Dennis O'Leary was killed," Paavo began.

"What do I care?" Peewee asked.

"Three of his regular customers said you were another regular. Do you want their names?"

Peewee fidgeted. "No. I know who you mean. I know someone fingered him. Same with Haram Sayir, who owned a liquor store. He was a nice guy. Too bad somebody wanted him dead."

Paavo caught Yosh's eye. The last thing he'd ever expected was for Peewee to volunteer information. "Then you know Sayir was also in the numbers racket?"

"Yeah. So what?" Peewee said. "It used to be harmless. A few guys pooling their money, having a little fun. Nobody got hurt. Not the way they used to do it."

"You're saying things changed?" Yosh asked the question expectantly, as if anything Peewee might say would be the height of intelligence and foresight.

"Lots of guys are dead. Ain't that proof enough?"

"But why are they dead?" Yosh asked. "That's what we need to find out."

Peewee cast his small, piggy eyes on Yosh. "You should know. Look around you. Can't you see?"

Yosh glanced at Paavo, then back to Peewee. "There are new players in town, is that it?"

Peewee gave a humorless chuckle as he rubbed his palms against his jeans. "Yeah, man. You could say that." He stood up and glanced at the windows. "Lots of new players. Even cops."

"It's not going to play, Peewee," Paavo said. "I know what's being said on the street. We want the truth this time."

Peewee turned on him. "Sure you know. You know a lot more than anyone else here, don't you?" He kept fidgeting as if he was expecting someone, waiting for something to happen. "Why don't you tell your partner about it? Why keep him in the dark?"

"Sit down, Peewee," Paavo said, holding his growing

anger in check. "Who gave you this idea that I was involved? Where did you first hear it?"

"Dennis O'Leary told me. He said you were one of his biggest customers. That you needed the money because you were trying to impress some rich girl-friend. But when you kept losing, you got more and more angry. You threatened him. You wanted a cut of his numbers share, and if he didn't pay up, you'd have him killed. I guess he wouldn't give in to you, would he?"

"You piece of scum!" Paavo said, standing. Fury burned in him.

"Don't hit me!" Peewee yelled.

Paavo froze. He was about five feet from Peewee and had done nothing that should make Peewee cry out like that. Unless . . .

"Hit you, Peewee?" he said, walking over to the window, then standing against the wall beside it. "I wouldn't want to touch you. Might get some disease that'd make my hand fall off." He peeked out the window. A year-old blue Ford with a couple of men inside was parked halfway down the block. He gestured to Yosh to take a look.

"What are you looking at?" Peewee asked.

"Vermin," Paavo said, his cold eyes on the man. "I'm looking at something so small and so low it can be squashed without even messing up the sole of my shoe."

Yosh nodded.

"We'll be back, Peewee, when you're ready to tell the truth, not some lies someone told you to say."

The two left Peewee's flat and got into their car, Paavo at the wheel. He pulled out of the parking space, but instead of driving off, he spun the wheel into a tight U-turn and roared down the block, slamming on the brakes when he reached the blue Ford. Leaving his car in the middle of the street, he got out and in a cold rage walked up to the car.

The IA man at the wheel, LeRoy Davis, rolled down his window. "Hello, Smith."

Mitch Connors sat in the seat beside him.

"Get an earful?" Paavo asked.

"We got it all on tape," Davis answered. "Now we just need to get it verified."

"You won't. It's not true, and you know it."

"Sounded true to me."

"Peewee mouthed off everything you told him to say," Paavo said quietly, contemptuously.

"He spoke the truth, Smith. We'll get proof soon enough."

"You're getting in my way with these games," Paavo said.

Davis chuckled and looked at his partner, then turned back to Paavo. "Soon, you won't have a way, Smith. You'll be history."

"Stay clear, Davis." With the ice-laden warning hanging in the air, Paavo turned back to the car.

"What's the matter, Smith?" David taunted. "Can't take being watched? Too hot for you? Maybe Peewee was on to something there. We've all heard about your rich girlfriend. Wouldn't be the first time a woman's made a cop go bad."

Yosh spun around. "You son of a—"

Paavo touched his partner's arm. "They're doing it on purpose. They aren't worth it."

Paavo's gaze narrowed as he silently stared down at Davis, then he turned back to his car.

"I'm not going to do it!" Connie folded her arms.

"Push!" Angie cried. "I can't maneuver two at once."

"What if we get caught?"

"Connie, you've got to. No one will stop us. We have our dignity, you know."

"But Angie, it's a Safeway shopping cart. It says so in big letters on the front and on the handle. They aren't going to let us walk off the parking lot with them!"

"Look at us. Who would dare stop us?" Angie held out her arms for Connie to better see her. She was wearing oversized black trousers, holey black high-tops, and a dark blue sweatshirt that hung almost to her knees. Over all that was a brown moth-eaten cardigan; over the cardigan, a black coat. Around her neck was a grimy long red woolen scarf. She wore a wig of long, straight black hair, topped off by a ragged blue woolen cap with a big tassel on top.

Connie wore once-white sneakers with thick woolen socks; beige polyester tights; an enormous dark brown, heavy woolen skirt; a man's plaid cotton shirt; a man's plaid flannel shirt, unbuttoned; a filthy gray jacket; a wig of long brown hair pulled back in a bun; and over it, a grungy black beret.

They had smeared dirt on their faces and wore no makeup. Angie also wore a pair of granny sunglasses—the ultimate negative fashion statement.

"We've got to do it, Connie," Angie insisted. "We've got to do all we can to figure out what's going on with Klaw. I tell you, when I came out of the women's room and saw Paavo and Klaw facing each other last night, I thought my heart would stop."

"I don't know about this, Angie. We could end up in jail."

"Don't worry," Angie said. "If anyone tries to stop us, I'll start acting really crazy. They'll gladly let us go on our way. Trust me on that. I do good crazy."

"Why don't we just buy the carts?" Connie suggested.

"Buy them? Why? We only need to borrow them a

little while. They're our cover, that's all. Safeway won't even know they're gone. Now push."

Angie drove the U-Haul truck to within two blocks of the mission. She'd never driven a truck before, and only slightly mangled a side mirror on a car that had been parked a little too far from the curb. If the driver had done a better job of parking, nothing would have happened at all. She figured he'd probably never even notice, but she got out and left a card with her insurance company's name anyway. She got plenty of strange looks from pedestrians and other drivers, but she wasn't sure if it was because of her dress or her honesty. Sometimes honesty was a random act of stupidity these days.

She couldn't believe the difficulties involved in simply trying to look like a proper bag lady. She and Connie had planned to hang around outside the mission, but they wanted to look like everyone else in the neighborhood so that they wouldn't attract too much attention. That meant they needed carts. And because there was no supermarket within walking distance of the mission, *that* meant she'd had to rent a truck to transport the carts.

She parked the truck two blocks from the mission. She and Connie pushed the carts to within a few doors of their destination, then stopped and waited. And waited some more.

"You're sure she's going out today?" Connie asked, leaning on her cart. Luckily, it was a typically chilly San Francisco summer day, or the two of them would have been sweltering in their layered finery.

"That's what she told me yesterday," Angie said. She reached into the cart and pushed aside a pile of rags covering an ice chest. Opening it, she took out two bottles of Perrier, placed each in a paper bag, and gave one to Connie—Perrier disguised as muscatel.

"I hope we didn't miss Lili." Angie stared at the mission awhile. "She isn't too good about keeping her days straight."

"Great! Angie, if you expect me to get dressed up like this again—"

"Look!" Angie whispered, grabbing Connie's arm. "There she is! Action."

Lili had stepped out of the mission and turned toward Market Street, walking at a fast clip despite her high heels and tight skirt.

Angie and Connie trundled after her, holding their hats and wigs on with one hand, steering around potholes and negotiating curbs with the other. Their carts careened over the rough pavement with a deafening clatter—enough to have alerted anyone but Lili, who seemed totally out of it as she teetered along on her four-inch stilettos, hips swinging, humming a little tune.

They were a little way down Market when Lili turned into the Muni subway.

"Park the carts by this lamppost," Angie yelled. "We can't lose her."

"But what if somebody steals them?" Connie asked.

"Who'd want Safeway shopping carts? Come on!"

They ran down the stairs, paid the fare, and reached the platform just as Lili was stepping onto an N car, headed out toward Judah Street. They jumped on as well, immediately sending six people to the back of the street car, as far upwind from them as possible.

At Van Ness Street, Lili got off and, back on street level, transferred to a 49 Mission bus. So did Angie and Connie.

Lili still seemed to have no idea she was being followed, not even when they followed her off the bus at Twenty-second Street. She walked up a side street to a small older home and rang the bell. As she waited, she examined her face in a small hand mirror, turning her head this way and that while she chewed her gum.

Ducking into a doorway, Angie and Connie watched.

An old man answered. *Her father?* Angie wondered, but only for a second. He kissed her on the lips, and the way his fingers splayed across her behind as he pulled her into the house dismissed any thought of a family relationship.

"Sheesh," Connie wailed. "Does everyone at that mission have more than one lover? Maybe I should join. Heck, I'd be happy with one at this point in my life."

"Stan's sweet on you," Angie said.

"On the other hand, my goldfish is very nice company. Quiet, I'll admit, but nice."

They waited for nearly an hour before the door opened again and Lili came out. She gave the man a quick kiss and a good-bye waggle of her fingers, then sauntered back toward the bus stop.

She rode back to Market Street, but this time, instead of transferring to another bus or street car, she went to the BART station. If she'd had one ounce of street smarts, Angie thought, she'd have realized by now she was being followed. Two bag ladies taking all the same buses, getting off on the same streets, and now riding the same BART train? Where was her head? True, most people did all they could to avoid noticing bag ladies as individuals. But Lili certainly didn't pay any attention at all.

She kept an eye on her watch and let two trains go by, then boarded the third one, a Fremont-bound train. It was commute time, and the train was packed with people leaving the city to go home to the suburbs. Nevertheless, Angie and Connie pushed their way onto the same car as Lili, cutting a swath through an army of horrified commuters and managing to keep an eye on the quarry the whole time.

She didn't ride very far, just three stops to the Embarcadero Station. When she got off the train, she had a Macy's shopping bag in her hand.

"Where did she pick that up?" Angie cried as they hurried up the stairs to street level. "Did you notice who was holding the shopping bag before her?"

"A lot of people had shopping bags," Connie said. "Plus briefcases, backpacks, tote bags, paper bags. Who knows?"

"That's what I was afraid you'd say." They emerged on Market Street. Lili was making a beeline for the Embarcadero and the mission.

"We've got to find out what's inside that Macy's bag," Angie announced, hurrying after Lili as she sauntered down the street, the Macy's bag sagging heavily from one hand as if its contents were about to burst its bottom.

"*Oh, no!*" Connie cried.

Angie froze. "What is it?"

"Our shopping carts! Somebody stole them!"

Angie grabbed Connie's hand and pulled her gaze away from the lonely lamppost on the opposite side of the street. "Forget about them. She's getting away. I'll stop her; you grab the Macy's bag, then run like hell."

"Where to?" asked Connie, huffing and puffing as Angie dragged her along after Lili.

"How about the truck?"

"I don't think a U-Haul makes a good getaway car."

Angie handed her the truck keys. "If you get enough of a head start, climb into the passenger side and hide on the floor. No one will think to look for you there."

"What will you do?"

"Create a diversion. Then I'll work my way to you. If I don't, call Paavo to bail me out, okay?"

"Oh, God," Connie groaned.

"Don't worry about it. If we get caught, at least we'll get a great headline in the newspaper."

"Oh?"

Angie grinned whimsically. "Sure—'Bag Ladies Bagged Bagging Bag.'"

Connie covered her ears. "I'm not listening to any more of this."

"Okay. Ready?" Angie asked.

"Why me, Lord?" Connie took a deep breath. "All right."

Lili turned onto the Embarcadero.

"Now!" Angie yelled. The two of them ran toward Lili, who stopped walking and turned around to see what the commotion was about. Angie, her raggedy clothes flapping and looking like a nightmare bird of prey, made a kamikaze dive right at Lili's knees. The two of them went down with a thud.

Connie plucked the shopping bag from Lili's hand and started to run, swinging the bag by the handle in order to lift it up into her arms. Angie scrambled to her feet and was right behind her, picking up speed, when Connie abruptly stopped.

Van Warren had stepped out of a car parked directly in front of them, a cannon-sized gun in his hand. Angie slammed into Connie's back, causing the still-swinging shopping bag to fly from Connie's hand and right at Warren.

The gun went off, hitting the bag and blasting it open. Money exploded into the air, raining down on Angie and Connie as they grabbed each other's hands and ran as fast as they could, screaming and shrieking for all they were worth. The gunshot, the screams, and the sight of dollars floating to the sidewalk caused brakes to slam and people to disgorge from cars, frantically crawling about to snatch up the fluttering bills.

Angie and Connie, though, never looked back.

CHAPTER

T W E N T Y - F O U R

"Oh, my God! He's not here!" Angie cried. She and Connie screeched to a halt in the doorway of the Homicide Bureau's inner office, where the inspectors' desks were located.

"Where is he?" Connie wailed, shaking from fear and panting hard from their run from the parking lot to the Hall of Justice. "What if somebody followed us here? You said he'd take care of us!"

"Stop! You can't just barge in there!" Betty, the secretary, jumped up from her desk in the outer office.

Angie turned to Connie in horror. "He kept hinting that they might fire him," she gasped. "What if they have?"

"Oh, no! How could they do that to us?" Connie shrieked.

"Or to him?" Angie wailed.

"Ladies, please!" Betty said. "I must ask you to . . ." She stopped speaking, shocked, as one of the bag ladies took off her granny glasses and wiped the tears from her dirty face. "Angie?"

"That's Lieutenant Hollins's office, isn't it?" Angie asked, pointing to a side door.

"Yes, but you can't— Wait!"

Angie burst into the office. Hollins sat at his desk chewing his cigar and reading the sports page. At the sight of two wig-wearing bag ladies bursting into his office, his mouth dropped open and the cigar fell out.

"How'd you get in here?" he asked, jumping to his feet.

"What did you do with Paavo?" Angie demanded.

"Who will help us?" Connie cried.

"What do I care?" Hollins bellowed. "Get out!"

"You moron!" Angie yelled. "You did fire him, didn't you?"

Hollins's whole face, up to and including his high, balding forehead, turned purple. "What the hell are you talking about?" he thundered. "I'll have you arrested."

"Arrested? Who cares about arrested? We were nearly killed!" Angie slammed her hand on his desk. "Not that the police department gives a fig what happens to its citizens!"

"Not about *some* of its citizens, that's for sure! Betty!" he bellowed for the secretary.

Angie waggled her finger under his nose. "You had the best homicide inspector in the whole country and you let him go! Your brains should be sautéed and served with eggs for lunch!"

"Get out now or I'll have you fumigated!"

"You don't scare me! I just faced down a killer. You're a nothing. A wart on a pig's snout. A pickled herring among barracuda. A chicken gizzard in a filet mignon world!"

"Angie, uh . . . cute hat."

"Ducks' feet in . . ." She whirled around, and her jaw dropped. There was no mistaking it. There he was, standing tall in the doorway, a quizzical expression on his face. "Paavo! What are you doing here?"

"I was at the photocopy machine. Betty came and found me."

"Oh, God!" She rushed over and grabbed his lapels. "We were nearly killed! Van Warren shot at us but hit Lili's bag instead. Money flew all over and there was a near riot on the Embarcadero, and we were so scared and ran right over here and then we thought that you were . . ." She glanced back at Hollins and blanched in horror at the thought of what she'd just said to Paavo's boss. "I . . . I thought you'd been . . . fired."

His face was hard. "Van Warren shot at you? Are you sure?"

"Yes. Absolutely." Glancing at a very red-faced Lieutenant Hollins, still standing at his desk, she smiled nervously at him, put the granny glasses back on her smudged nose, and fluffed her wig.

"Somebody tried to kill me," she said sweetly, giving him a big smile. "I guess I wasn't thinking too clearly when I shouted at you like that."

Hollins glanced from her to Connie to Paavo, his face growing redder by the moment.

Paavo turned her toward the exit. "Sorry for the interruption, Chief. I'll explain it all later."

"In triplicate, Smith!"

Arms circling their waists, Paavo quickly ushered Angie and Connie down the hall, away from Hollins and the little knot of homicide inspectors crowded in the doorway gleefully taking in every word.

"Paavo," Angie said as they waited for a down elevator to arrive.

"Yes?" he asked.

"Do you really think this is a cute hat?"

•   •   •

After taking off their wigs, washing their faces in the ladies' room in the Hall, and making themselves look reasonably presentable again, Angie and Connie went into the coffee shop to join Paavo.

In a babbling, excited chorus they told him all about trailing Lili to the old man's house just off Twenty-second Street, the Macy's bag switch on the BART train, and finally Van Warren's sudden appearance, foiling their attempt to steal the bag from Lili.

Paavo was so furious with them for taking such a chance—not to mention a peccadillo like *mugging* Lili Charmaine—that he sent them home in squad cars.

He and Yosh retrieved the U-Haul and scouted around for the missing Safeway shopping carts. He felt the streets of San Francisco would be safer if Angie didn't try to return the truck by herself.

After returning the U-Haul, Paavo and Yosh went back to the part of the Embarcadero where Angie and Connie had told him Warren stood when he fired at them. Paavo was fiercely determined to find the bullet Warren fired. With ricochets, it could have ended up almost anywhere. But if it had hit a car or pedestrian, they would have heard, so chances were good that it was still somewhere on that particular city block.

Nearly two hours later, Paavo found the bullet about ten feet off the ground, lodged in the wall of a building. Yosh boosted him up while he played Spider Man, splayed against the side of the wall and digging the bullet out with a penknife.

Back at the Hall, Paavo gave the bullet to the crime lab to see if they could match it up with bullets found in the murdered numbers runners or the bookie Paavo had found murdered. Then he went to his desk and used the cross-directories to find out who lived in the house

Lili had visited. Fortunately, he had more luck than either he or Yosh were having trying to find the elusive Gretchen.

It was a rental. The renter's name wasn't given, but the owner's was.

He called the owner, stated who he was, and asked for the name of the renter. "Ruiz Buyat," he was told.

Buyat . . . the name sounded familiar.

He took out the file of the interviews he'd held since beginning the numbers cases and went back over them.

There it was. Ruiz Buyat, sixty-four years old, Filipino, an employee of the StayBrite Janitorial Service—the outfit that held the Hall of Justice contract. He'd worked for the company twenty-five years and been a supervisor for the past eight. Paavo had spoken with him briefly when he was investigating access to the Property Control Section and trial case evidence.

Buyat had insisted that the janitors were prohibited from entering secure rooms unless someone responsible was present and watching. On the other hand, the service apparently had master keys to all the rooms. It would have been easy for a trusted supervisor to get his hands on the set of master keys.

A longtime janitorial supervisor could have easily watched the Property Control Section staff to find out where keys and combinations to the storage cabinets and evidence lockers were kept. Someone might even have figured out how to sneak in and switch some evidence.

A break at last, Paavo thought, fighting to contain his excitement. It was all still conjecture. He needed answers to a few more questions, and so he went down to the basement. The janitors' central duty station was located there—the spot where they checked in to work and kept their cleaning supplies and the smocks they wore over their clothes.

"Is Ruiz Buyat working tonight?" he asked the man behind the sign-in booth.

"Not tonight, sir," the fellow said.

"By the way, do you have a key to room B-forty-eight?" That was where the Property Control Section's locker room was located.

"B-forty-eight. Let me see." The man rummaged through some keys and found it, but then put it back down. "I'm sorry, sir. I can't let you in there. It's a restricted area."

But the key was available to the janitors. Restricted, sure. Restricted to some, but perhaps not to a janitor who chose to sneak in.

"That's okay," Paavo said. "I understand. Oh, by the way, do you know if Mr. Buyat worked the fourth floor recently? Or, more specifically, room four-fifty, in Homicide?"

"Since he's a supervisor, he can check up on any crew he wants. Mostly his charges are in the basement, but he can go up to four anytime. There's no way to tell. Is there a problem?"

"No. None at all. Just wondering."

"Should I tell Buyat you were looking for him?" the man asked, suddenly uneasy at the pleased look on the big homicide inspector's face.

"No need," Paavo said. "I'll call him at home."

CHAPTER

T W E N T Y - F I V E

"The smell of your chocolate is filling my apartment," Stan said. "I couldn't stand it any longer. I had to come over and help."

"Help me cook it or help eat it?"

"Your wish is my command, Angie."

Angie leaned against her door, blocking his entrance. She really didn't want to deal with Stan. She didn't want to have anything to do with anyone ever again. Yesterday, between Van Warren's trying to kill her and then Paavo's sending her home like a naughty child, she was ready to give up on the human race. Humans were either too dangerous or too foul-tempered.

On top of that, she was so scared, her bed had shaken all night—and she'd been alone in it.

"Aren't you ever going back to work?" she asked.

"I've got a new problem." He lifted a limp wrist. "Carpal tunnel syndrome."

"Really? I didn't know you could get it from using a TV remote control."

"How'd you guess?" He peered past her into her apartment. "Where's your cohort in chocolate?" he asked.

"She had to work today. Listen, Stan, I'm really busy."

"I can imagine. Cooking chocolate all by yourself! Never fear, though. I'm here to help."

She gave up and stepped aside. He scooted into the living room. "I don't need help," she said, shutting the door. "What I've got to do is to figure out my angelina. Reverend Hodge will let me use it as a centerpiece during the auction. That would be great publicity—a big boost for my career as a chocolatier."

"A piece of chocolate candy?" Stan peered back over his shoulder at her. "What's it a centerpiece for? Ants?"

"That's the problem, exactly! I wanted my angelina to be something small, not huge. But I thought I might be able to come up with an oversized version of it ... whatever it is."

"Maybe that's too much to ask of a centerpiece?"

"I've been thinking the same thing, I'm afraid."

"On the other hand," Stan said, his voice annoyingly enthusiastic, "you haven't had the genius of Stan the Man at work on the problem. I even amaze myself sometimes with the remarkable ideas that pop into my head."

"Oh?"

"I might come up with something you never dreamed of," he said. "What have you thought of so far?"

"That's the trouble," Angie sighed. "Nothing. And I've got only today and tomorrow to come up with something. The auction's only two days away!" She turned and walked back toward the kitchen, Stan following close behind. Cookbooks and magazines were spread all over.

"Where's the candy machine?" he asked.

"I shipped it back."

"Really? I thought you had a good thing going."

"You're sick."

He walked over to the counter by the sink. "You think I'm sick? What about you? Look at all these cabbage leaves! You've painted them with chocolate. Really, Angie, I know you have a recipe for chocolate cake with sauerkraut, the thought of which gives me near-terminal shudders, but if you put raw cabbage in your angelinas, I really don't think anybody's going to want to buy them."

"The cabbage isn't to eat, silly. I'm using it to make molds."

"Molds or moldy?"

Angie rolled her eyes and grabbed a magazine off the counter. "Look at this picture," she said, thrusting the magazine at him. He stared at a photo of cabbage-leaf-shaped chocolate pieces put together in a large roselike design. "I'm trying to learn how to make it," Angie explained. "I used a pastry brush to spread the chocolate onto the backs of some leaves and the fronts of others, then I let the chocolate harden. The tough part is to leave all the ribbed markings of the cabbage on the chocolate when I pull off the leaf."

"And that's supposed to look good?" Stan said, holding the photo out at arm's length and shaking his head.

To demonstrate, Angie tried peeling off the cabbage for the first piece. The chocolate cracked into tiny pieces. "See what I mean?" she moaned.

She tried the second one, this time more carefully, and had better success. By the third piece, she was starting to get the hang of it. But on the fourth piece, the chocolate shattered again. "Guess I'd better not get too cocky," she said to Stan, who was hanging over her shoulder watching with growing fascination.

When she'd finished peeling off the cabbage leaves, she bunched the small molded chocolate pieces in the center, then added increasingly larger pieces around it, until the whole thing began to look like a rose. When she'd finished, she stepped back and admired her handiwork. "How's that for an angelina?"

"It's pretty," Stan admitted. "It'd look nice as a centerpiece. Except for one thing."

"What's that?" she asked.

"It's no *angel*-ina. It's a *cabbage*-ina!" He roared with laughter. Angie didn't find it funny in the least.

Angie took her cabbage rose centerpiece to the mission. She wanted reactions to it from Reverend Hodge and the other volunteers. It didn't grab her the way she'd hoped a centerpiece would, but on the other hand, with all the madness around her—especially her worry that Warren might realize she was the bag lady who had tried to mug Lili—it was amazing that she'd come up with any kind of centerpiece at all. If all else failed, she'd buy a big floral arrangement. Who'd know the difference?

"Miss Amalfi!" Reverend Hodge walked toward her with open arms. "Only two more days. Isn't it wonderful?"

"I'm glad you're feeling better about the auction," she said.

"Well, I don't know if I feel good because it's still to come or because it'll be over soon. But whichever, I'm a lot more relaxed. So, what's that you're carrying?"

"I thought it might be my centerpiece." She put the box on a table and lifted off the lid.

He peered in the box. There was a long pause. "Chocolate cabbage leaves?" he asked finally. "We were poor when I was a kid. We ate lots and lots of cabbage. I don't get it."

She put the lid back on the box. "You're right. I have to work on it a bit more."

He walked away scratching his head.

Maybe the problem was that he recognized the leaves, she thought. Perhaps if they didn't look so cabbagey . . .

"Hey, Angie." Lili bustled into the office. "I heard you brought a centerpiece, but it wasn't awesome. The Rev thought maybe you want help."

"News sure travels fast around here," Angie said.

"Yeah. 'Specially when it's bad."

Angie took the lid off. "I thought it was pretty," she said, a little apologetically.

Lili cocked her head. "Cabbage leaves? Hello-o-o. Who wants to look at cabbage?"

"Maybe you're right. I could make it look more like a floral sprig."

"Heck, no. You've got to do something that people way in the back can see. An idea is raging in my head! Tell you what—if you can't find anything else, I'll let you borrow something I've got. People will be, like, all amazed when they see it. I think it's a miracle. Axel said I'm all whacked-out about it, but still, he can't explain it either. I even told Reverend Hodge that I thought it was, like, a miracle, and he said if that's what I believed, he couldn't say I was wrong."

"What is it?"

"It's a big bottle, and inside it . . . you're going to think I'm lying, or I've been drinking or something . . . but inside is a great big ship. It's got all the sails and everything. I mean, like, the whole thing is in there. And the bottle has a little bitsy mouth. And no seams. I'm not talking no glued-back-together bottle. I checked it real good for that. And then I spent hours and hours trying to figure out how somebody built that big ship inside the bottle, but I can't."

"A ship in a bottle?" Angie couldn't believe Lili's enthusiasm about such a traditional item.

"It's way cool, Angie," Lili said, her eyes wide.

"Thanks for the offer," Angie said dismissively, but then something niggled in the back of her mind. Was it what Lili was talking about . . . or what Stan had said? *Forget it,* Angie told herself. The two of them didn't know much about centerpieces. "If I need it, I'll let you know."

Lili looked at the chocolate cabbage leaves again. "Well, you're going to need something."

Paavo and Yosh knocked on the door to Ruiz Buyat's house. Paavo had called and stopped by the house last evening, and called again this morning, but there had been no answer. He and Yosh thought it was worth another try this afternoon.

"He's not there!"

Paavo turned toward the sound of the voice. A paunchy man stood on the doorstep of the next house up the block. "Do you know when he'll be back?" Paavo called.

"No," the man said. "I saw him go out last night but didn't see him come home. He didn't even pick up his newspaper this morning."

"Does he go away overnight often?"

"He works nights. He almost never goes out in the day, though."

Paavo walked over to the neighbor and presented his badge. "I'm trying to find Buyat or the woman who visits him. Do you know her?"

"The blond bombshell? Wish I did. Ruiz is a nice old guy, but I don't know what a fox like her's doing with someone like him. She can't be after his money. He don't have any."

Paavo handed him a business card. "If you see Buyat, the woman, or anything out of the ordinary over here, will you give me a call?"

The neighbor's eyes widened at the word *Homicide* on the card. "Sure."

"He's not wanted for anything," Paavo said. "I just need to ask him a couple of questions."

"Whew! That's a relief! I'd hate to think I was living next door to the Hillside Strangler or something."

Paavo and Yosh got back into their unmarked car. "Where to, partner?" Yosh asked.

"Let's go see if Peewee's still wearing a wire," Paavo suggested.

"I thought Hollins told you to stay away from him while he's working with Internal Affairs," Yosh warned. "Hollins doesn't want Peewee spooked."

"Peewee's already spooked," Paavo said. "Didn't you notice how nervous he was? As bad-ass as our friends in IA think they are, they aren't tough enough to cause Peewee to break out in a cold sweat. There's something more going on. I want to find out what it is."

"You're asking for trouble, pal," Yosh warned.

"We can watch Peewee's place awhile. He might take another little BART ride, and if he does and Lili Charmaine gets on the same train, we'll nail them both."

"What charge?"

"Indecent exposure."

They drove over to Peewee's house. They had been parked only a couple of minutes when a young man in a black leather jacket with the word *Aces* across the back walked up to Peewee's front door and rang the bell. He waited awhile, then knocked. When nothing happened, he leaned for a long time on the bell and pounded hard on the door. Finally, he took some kind of metal pin out of his pocket. Glancing guiltily up and down the street, he pressed his shoulder to the door, worked the lock until it sprang open, then slipped inside.

"Breaking and entering," Yosh said joyfully. "We got him—whoever he is."

They got out of the car and cautiously approached the house. What did the kid want there? His illegal entry gave Paavo a good reason to find out.

Suddenly, the door burst open. The kid bounded out, turned onto the sidewalk, and ran straight at Yosh. Yosh stuck out his foot and the kid went sprawling. He was handcuffed before he could even think about trying to stand up and run off again.

"I didn't do it!" he yelled. "Not me. I don't know who."

"What are you talking about?" Paavo asked.

"You're not pinning this on me. I was just going to try to get the money Peewee owed me 'cause my numbers came up. That's all. I didn't do nothing!"

"Stop whining and tell us what you're talking about," Yosh yelled.

"In there. Peewee . . ."

Paavo and Yosh exchanged glances. Yosh took the young man to the car while Paavo went back to Peewee's house. The front door was still open.

Paavo pulled out his .38 and slowly walked up the dark, paneled staircase, listening for any noise or movement. The upstairs flat was quiet.

The small, shabby living room was empty. Next to it was the dining room. Also empty.

He stepped into the kitchen. Hardened though he was after years in Homicide, he couldn't help feeling disgust, anger, and then sorrow at the sight that met him. Peewee's mother lay in a pool of blood on the kitchen floor, gunshot wounds to the head and chest.

On the stove sat a red-hot pot, a lit flame under it, its contents cooked to a cinder.

He shut off the gas.

In the back of the house he found Peewee sprawled out on his bed, riddled with bullet holes. Peewee had probably been asleep when hit, but that didn't explain how his mother could have been killed in the kitchen. She wouldn't have stayed there cooking while bullets were flying in the back bedroom. Unless she'd been hit first with a silencer so as not to alert Peewee.

Of course, there could have been two or more gunmen hitting them at the same time. But considering that no one had called the police after hearing gunshots, the silencer theory made more sense. A lone gunman could have broken into the house as easily as that young man just had.

Paavo went back into the kitchen and looked at the pot again, then at the table. Oatmeal. So the hit had been made that morning.

He telephoned Homicide and called for the medical examiner, the crime scene investigators, and a couple of patrol officers to secure the area and convey the young man to city prison to book him. Yosh was needed to help with the homicide investigation.

Next, he phoned Lieutenant Hollins. "This is Smith. We're at Peewee Clayton's—"

"What! I told you—"

"He's dead. Shot. His mother was killed, too."

"Shit! Are any of the boys from IA around? Maybe they saw something."

"They aren't here. But Chief, there's something else you need to do. Somebody needs a warrant to check on a janitor who works at the Hall named Ruiz Buyat. He didn't show up for work last night, and his neighbor hasn't seen him since yesterday." He gave Hollins the address and more information about Buyat. "It's just a

hunch," Paavo said, "but somebody needs to get inside
that house. I hope I'm wrong, but I've got a bad feeling
about him."

It was late by the time Paavo arrived home. Exhausted,
he pulled his mail out of the box and unlocked the door
to his house. When he flicked on the lights, his big yellow tabby, Hercules, bounded off his usual spot on the
easy chair to follow Paavo into the kitchen, complaining
loudly the whole time.

"You think you've had a rough day?" Paavo said as
he wearily opened a can of Kitty Queen Liver Dinner.
Hercules had probably spent the day hunting vermin,
mice and miscellaneous rodents, in between torment-
ing the German shepherd that lived down the street.
As he dumped the liver into Hercules's bowl it
occurred to Paavo that, except for the German shepherd, their days were more similar than he had ever
realized.

It was odd how the two pieces of this puzzle had
finally come together in the guise of a Hall of Justice
janitor. From Buyat he could follow a squiggly trail
right back to Axel Klaw. Klaw, his nemesis. Klaw, the
man who, years ago, had first caused him to think about
joining the police department—to right the wrong done
to his family. As he got older Paavo had realized he'd
been wrong about the power of a policeman, yet the
interest in the job stayed with him, and eventually he
did join.

Now the revenge he'd yearned for years ago was
within reach. Now he had to find a way to bring Klaw
down. A way to rid the world of the cancer that was
Klaw. A cold, black rage burned in him, deadly as dry
ice. He would see this through and end it one way or
the other.

Curiosity about the charity auction had been growing within him ever since Klaw mentioned it at the supper club. Klaw never paid attention to anything unless there was a reason. Paavo wanted to know the reason, especially since Angie was planning to be there. He needed to talk to her about it soon—face-to-face.

He flipped through his mail and stopped at a large plain envelope—unaddressed. He put down the bills and advertisements and tore open the envelope.

Inside was a black-and-white photograph. As he pulled it out, time seemed to stand still. He knew he must have continued to breathe, his heart continued to beat, but he was aware of nothing but the slight quiver in his hands, the deadly silence of the room.

He sat down on the sofa, his gaze never leaving the picture. He'd never seen this particular one before. It reminded him once again of how beautiful she had been, and how full of life. Her mouth was full and smiling, her nose small and lightly rounded at the tip. Her eyes were heavily made up in the style of the times, but that made their color, almost the exact same shade of blue as his own, even more startling and vibrant against her flawless skin. Her brows were wide and winged, her cheekbones high—another family characteristic. Where that bone structure made him look stern, it gave her face an elegant beauty. But the resemblance was marked.

Her hair, though, was very different from his soft, wavy brown strands. Their hair was the most obvious evidence that different men had fathered them. Hers was black and thick. She used to spend hours with all kinds of conditioners and gels, trying to make it smooth and elegant.

There was only one person he could think of who might have sent this photo to him: Axel Klaw. He'd done it to torment him.

Paavo smiled coldly. Once again, Klaw had underestimated him. Instead of making him crumble, to Paavo the photo was a gift. Although it brought back the agony of his loss, it helped him target the full measure of his hatred and of his revenge.

CHAPTER

TWENTY-SIX

Angie was waiting outside Everyone's Fancy when
Connie arrived at work the next morning. Angie had no
time to waste—the auction was tomorrow. She bought a
statue of a winged angel in flowing robes, her hands
devoutly clasped and her head slightly tilted as if listening to people's prayers.

The day before, on the way home from the mission,
she had visited a party supply store, and they had put
her in contact with a manufacturer of Mylar balloons.

Now, using the statue as a model, she whipped up an
enormous batch of white chocolate fudge. Treating it
like clay, she sculpted it into the general form of the
statue, making her angel about a foot tall. Once the
fudge hardened, she carefully spread melted Lindt
Blancor white chocolate over it to give it a smooth,
almost translucent appearance. The angel blurred into a
soft, abstract shape, creamy and beautiful.

"Perfect," Angie said. But it wasn't unique yet, and
her angelina needed to be special.

She made a circular wooden "fence" of twenty-inch-tall shish kebab sticks loosely tied together and then dropped the high fence over the angel, being careful of the wings. While she was working on the chocolate angel, the balloon she had had custom-made had been delivered. The balloon was deflated when she received it. It had an enormous mouth that could stretch around the stick fence; when inflated, the balloon would be almost two feet in diameter. When she thought big, she thought *really* big.

Working carefully, she eased the Mylar balloon over the stick fence. Using an air pump, she filled the balloon until it was round and solid, then tied the mouth shut.

Next came the part she was worried about. She laid strips of white chocolate over the balloon in a lattice pattern, making the chocolate thick enough that it would stand on its own, yet thin enough that it looked delicate and not chunky. She waited until the chocolate was hard and then stuck a pin in the Mylar, making a small hole for the air to seep out.

As the air left, she practically held her breath as she watched the Mylar pull away from the chocolate, leaving the angel encased in a delicate lattice design. Lifting the chocolate ball just a bit off the table she was working on, she carefully slid her stick fence, stick by stick, out the bottom of the ball, and then used a razor to slash the Mylar so that it, too, came off the angel and out the bottom of the lattice ball.

As the finishing touch, she turned a wooden box upside-down, spread thick white chocolate fudge over it to form a base, then carefully placed the angel and the ball that surrounded it onto the base. As the chocolate on the base hardened, it looked like it all became one piece—a large winged angel inside a seamless ball sitting on a square pedestal. An angel in a globe instead of a ship in a bottle. *Thank you, Stan and Lili.* The whole thing was so clever, she did the macarena around the kitchen a couple of times.

It had been a hell of a way to spend a day, though.

Even though she was tired from doing the careful, detailed work with chocolate all day, she had to tell the reverend about her angelic centerpiece. If he didn't like it, he'd have to settle for a floral bouquet. There was no time for anything else.

She stuck her head into the mission. The last people she wanted to encounter were Klaw, Warren, and Lili. When she didn't see any of them, she ran down the hall to Reverend Hodge's office. "I've got it!" she cried, bursting in on him.

"You've got what?"

"The centerpiece. Klaw—I mean, Clausen—isn't around, is he? I don't want to see that man!"

He looked around his office. "No, I don't—"

"Anyway, it's a white chocolate angel inside a lattice-work ball. It's meaningful—angels being helpful, charitable, and all—and pretty, if I say so myself." She looked over her shoulder at the open office door. "What about Van Warren? Have you seen him?"

"The centerpiece sounds good. But why are you asking about those two?"

"Reverend Hodge." She dragged the spare chair to his side. "They aren't what they seem. You've got to get away from them. They're dangerous men."

"We've been through this before—" he began.

"Please listen to me."

"I won't. I can't." Hodge jumped up and moved away from her. "Mr. Clausen is the one paying for all this. I need him. The mission needs him. Maybe after the auction, things will change. But not before. Afterward, if he's gone ... if I'm gone ... I know that people like Sheila Chatsworth, Mary Ellen Hitchcock, and others will run the mission and make it prosper. Have no worries about that."

"What do you mean, if you're gone?"

"Nothing, Miss Amalfi. Nothing at all." He checked his watch. "Oh, dear, it's getting late. I've got to see about the movers who'll be packing all the goods to be auctioned off."

Angie stood up to leave. "And I want to get out of here before Clausen and his pals return. Since you like the chocolate angel centerpiece—my *angel*-ina, angelina, get it?—I think I'll hire someone to deliver the centerpiece to the Palace of the Legion of Honor for me. Maybe I can trust someone who usually transports nitroglycerine."

"I wouldn't want to be there if they dropped it," Hodge said.

"No one would," Angie agreed. "Anyway, I'm going to go over to the Palace to figure out exactly where I want it placed, along with all the catered food. I was told we could set up the tables this evening. That way it'll be easier tomorrow when the food starts arriving."

"Good, good. That's one less thing to worry about, at least. Maybe, somehow, this will all come together. If it does, it's going to be a big night for all of us. A very big night."

"I can hardly wait," she said. "See you tomorrow!"

"Good-bye," he said, then murmured to himself, "finally—the big night is almost here."

Paavo stood in Ruiz Buyat's kitchen. Mail, bills, and receipts were piled up on a counter. He slipped on gloves and began going through them, looking for material that might breathe any hint of a connection between Buyat and Klaw.

Paavo's bad feeling about Buyat's disappearance had proved prophetic. Not until that morning had the police reached Buyat's landlord and obtained entry to the house. They found him dead, shot once in the back of the head. Another professional-looking hit, just like the dead numbers runners, just like Peewee.

The on-call homicide team, Benson and Calderon, had contacted Hollins, who sent Paavo to the scene.

Paavo quickly explained to them the connection between Buyat and Lili Charmaine. Looking at Buyat's body, he remembered talking to the man while he was investigating the handling of evidence at the Hall of Justice. Buyat had been evasive, but then, a lot of people had that reaction to police questions.

Now, as he leafed through the papers, he found a deposit slip from the Bank of America branch near his home. He lifted it out and could scarcely believe what he saw. Dated the day after he and Angie went to the Isle of Capri restaurant, it showed a deposit of five thousand dollars into his account.

It made sense, he realized. No one would question Buyat's access to the fourth floor or to the Homicide Bureau. After all, he was the janitorial supervisor. Paavo, like a lot of others in the bureau, often brought personal paperwork into the office. He would read his mail there, and pay bills, especially during the on-call week, when he spent more time at work than at home. Buyat could have easily learned little details such as his bank account number just by going through the trash. Paavo had never thought about destroying the carbons from credit card charges and so on, in an office surrounded by cops.

There wasn't anything more for him to learn at Buyat's place. Leaving the homicide investigation in capable hands, he returned to the Hall and met with Yosh to fill him in on the situation. They each sat at their desks, across a narrow aisle from each other. Each sat on a swivel chair, tilted way back, and talked.

"We need evidence," Paavo said, "but I think I know what's happening."

"I'm glad somebody does." Yosh tapped his pencil against his desktop.

"Since Klaw's been here, everyone on the street's been talking about a new banker moving in, trying to take over the numbers racket in the city. I'm sure he's using his girlfriend to collect receipts from the runners, and I suspect the empty apartment is his counting house—his bank. But he's losing control."

"Talk to me," Yosh said.

Paavo thought a moment before putting his suspicions into words. "The first few men he killed—Devlin, O'Leary, probably even Sayir—wouldn't go along with him as banker. He got rid of them. Peewee worked for him as a runner. But then IA contacted Peewee, made him work for them. Peewee was scared, but I think it was because of Klaw and Warren, not IA. Peewee was afraid that once he wore a wire for IA, Klaw wouldn't trust him anymore. He was right."

"You think Klaw killed Peewee, or had him killed."

"Exactly. Same with Buyat. We were on to him. We asked questions at his house, at his job, so Klaw got rid of him, too."

"Makes sense."

Paavo pressed his fingertips together. "We can't give Klaw any more warning than he's already been given, though. We can't move in on Warren yet. Hit men are a dime a dozen anyway. We arrest Warren, and Klaw will have someone else working for him before the day's out. Instead, we've got to watch and wait. But not too long. Klaw's involved in the auction that Hodge is holding. I don't know how, or what it means, but it's got to be a key part of Klaw's scheme. At the same time, I don't want to tip our hand too early. I want to find out what Klaw is up to and stop him completely, not just postpone his plans."

Yosh took a deep breath as he pondered Paavo's words. "Okay, Paavo," he said finally. "So we've got to be ready to move on, or right after, the auction."

"That's right. Let's just hope we stop him before anybody else is killed."

Back at his desk, Paavo had a message on his answering machine. *"This is Angie. I finished my centerpiece. My angelina. Wait till you see it! I'm going to the mission—hope I don't run into Klaw, the creep. I'll be home tonight. Can you come over? If not, don't forget the auction tomorrow night. It starts at eight-thirty, food and cocktails at seven. Love you. Bye."*

Paavo couldn't help shaking his head at the message. He had asked her time and again to keep away from Klaw. Now he was going to have to find a way to talk her out of going to that auction. He knew he'd have to handle it in person, though. He'd visit her as soon as he checked out a loose end one more time.

He and Yosh had tried a number of times to reach Klaw's mysterious girlfriend, Gretchen, with no luck. There were four apartments in which no one ever answered the door or the phone. For all he knew the apartments were empty, or the renters were on vacation, or maybe they were occupied by paranoids who never faced the outside world. He decided to try one more time.

He knocked on the door of one of the apartments.

A young brown-haired woman looked at him, then her eyes went wide with recognition. "Inspector!" She tried to shut the door in his face.

"Gretchen, that's no way to act." He stuck out his arm, stopping the door from shutting.

"Get away from me!" She spun around, grabbed her coat and purse from a chair beside the door, and pushed past him, pulling the door shut as she left.

Much as he tried to remember who she was, he couldn't. He didn't think he'd ever seen her before. "Wait." He grabbed her arm. "How do you know me?"

"You can't touch me! I know my rights." She pulled free.

"You do?" He held his hands out to show he wasn't about to touch her or hurt her. "Good, then you know you need to answer when I tell you I want to question you about Axel Klaw."

She looked at his hands. She was tall, but he was taller, bigger, stronger. "Who?"

"Alex Clausen—Axel Klaw, whatever he calls himself around you."

She paled. "I don't have to answer."

"Maybe not now, but you will eventually." She stepped back. He didn't like strong-arming her, but that seemed to be the only way to get her to listen. "Let me see some ID," he said.

She stared a moment, but as his words penetrated, she quickly pulled out her wallet and badge identification from her purse and handed them to him. Gretchen Ballard, police dispatcher, SFPD, Richmond station.

He stared at the badge, then at the young woman, and the pieces quickly slipped into place. "You do regular dispatcher duties at the station, I take it?"

She lifted her chin. "Of course."

"You send officers out on calls, including Rosenberg and Kellogg."

Her hands tightened on the strap of her purse. "They're good men, good at their jobs. I don't see that this is your business."

He handed her wallet and badge back to her. "Sometimes you get a little help, don't you, Gretchen? You hear that something will happen at a certain time and that you need to make sure Rosenberg and Kellogg are there."

"It's not illegal." Her hands shook as she stuffed her belongings back into her purse. "I never did anything wrong."

"Didn't you, Gretchen?" he asked rhetorically. "And what about rumors—telling stories about things that happened, stories about the Isle of Capri? Do you like to spread rumors, Gretchen?"

"I never meant to hurt you, Inspector Smith." Crying, she covered her face with her hands. "I never meant to!"

Paavo returned to the Hall after calming Gretchen down and having a long talk with her. He'd get Yosh to go out and take a formal statement. Maybe she was right, and what she did wasn't actually illegal. But it was probably a job-ending offense.

She explained that Kellogg and Rosenberg had shown up like a pair of knights in shining armor, ready to clean up the world. Their sense of justice and honor made them especially horrified at what they saw as a rogue, crooked cop. They didn't say anything to others unless asked, but what they said then—and the way they looked when Paavo's name was mentioned—was enough to add a ton of coal to the hell Paavo's life had become.

"If nothing else, we can bring Klaw in for questioning on this if we don't learn what he's really up to," Paavo said. "Hit him with criminal conspiracy, bribery—if we have to, we can stretch it to obstruction of justice."

"It'll slow him down," Yosh said. "And that's what we want until we can hit him with a bigger crime—like murder."

"Tomorrow night, at about eleven, show up at the auction," Paavo said. "As soon as it's over, we'll nail him."

"You're on, partner," Yosh said.

"Good." Now he had another reason to make sure Angie stayed well away.

The phone rang.

He picked it up. "Smith here."

"Hey, man. Get over here quick. I'm hurt bad. . . ."

"Snake?"

The phone went dead.

CHAPTER

TWENTY-SEVEN

Fifteen minutes later Paavo was in the alley. He lit a cigarette and waited.

Snake carried a cell phone, so he could have called from almost anywhere. He wouldn't have called Paavo, though, if he didn't think Paavo could find him easily and quickly.

Paavo wasn't wearing his black outfit, but instead wore a white shirt, tie, gray plaid sports jacket, and gray slacks. It wasn't a smart way to dress around here. This was the kind of neighborhood where people got nervous seeing someone hanging around who didn't belong. And for the one doing the hanging, it could get dangerous fast.

A dark figure filled the mouth of the alley. Paavo put his hand to his revolver, just to feel its presence, nothing more. The stranger began to walk toward him. He stepped on his cigarette and moved silently back, deeper into the alley. The man might be a friend of Snake. Or not.

Paavo braced himself, ready for the slightest movement.

"What you doing here?" The tough guy, now that Paavo could see him up close, looked about sixteen. Not even old enough to shave.

"Having a cigarette." It might have been his nononsense tone, or the fact that he didn't back off or cower, or simply one street-smart guy meeting another, but the kid held out his hands and backed up.

"Hey, man, just asking. No sweat, okay?" He turned and ran out of the alley.

Paavo realized he was wasting time standing around waiting. He had to try to find Snake Belly.

Since the Snake had always shown up from the back of the alley, that was the place to begin the search. Five buildings had back doors that opened onto the dead-end alleyway. He tried the doors, but all were locked, as he would have expected them to be. A couple of the buildings looked as though they might have some small apartments or rooms in them.

He walked out of the alley and around the block, checking out the fronts of the buildings, trying to figure which might back onto the alley and, of those, which looked most likely to be a place Snake Belly might wait for him to show up. He stopped at an empty warehouse. The windows had been broken; some were boarded up, some not. He tried the side door. It was locked, so he stuck his arm through the broken window beside the door, found the inside doorknob, and turned. The door opened with a high-pitched squeal of its hinges. He stopped, listening, and was met with silence.

Cautiously, he crept inside.

With gun in one hand, high-powered pocket flashlight in the other, he walked, footsteps from his leather-soled Florsheims echoing through the building. The warehouse was thick with age-old dust. Spiderwebs hung from the ceiling and covered stacks of boxes long left behind.

Some sixth sense, some cop instinct, made him continue on, deeper into the warehouse. He'd gone only a few steps when he saw the reason he'd come here. Snake Belly lay facedown on the floor, blood spilling from his mouth.

"Damn." Paavo holstered his gun and knelt, touching Snake's neck, feeling for a pulse. It was there but weak. Snake Belly's face was battered, his eyes swollen shut, his cheeks raw. His clothes were torn, as if he'd been in a fight for his life. In his hand was his cell phone.

Paavo was reaching over to pick up the phone when he heard a noise behind him. He looked up. Four men rushed out from behind some nearby boxes. He landed an elbow in the groin of the first man before the second one jumped him, knocking him backward. The cell phone skittered across the concrete floor. All four men were on him before he could reach for the gun in his shoulder holster.

"Gun!" one man shouted. They fought hard to pin him down.

He knocked one man out with an uppercut to the jaw and almost broke free, but the others stopped him. Big and powerful, they grabbed his arms, taking his gun, two holding him while the third man pounded him mercilessly, using his ribs and stomach like a punching bag.

When they let go of him, he dropped to the floor, doubled over with pain, on his hands and knees looking down at his own blood and vomit.

"We knew you'd show up here, Smith." One of the attackers had pulled a handgun from his pocket. "We had a little pool going on how long it'd take you to find us. You were fast. I won."

He lashed out one more time, trying to stand, desperate to break free. But his legs, his body, felt too weak, too torn apart to move. Almost immediately, the man with the gun moved closer.

Everything seemed to go into slow motion. He felt sick at heart, not scared, but only infinitely sad that it might end here in an old warehouse, before he'd had a chance to settle his score with Klaw, and before he'd had a chance to tell Angie all she meant to him. That was the worst part. Leaving Angie.

"No," Paavo whispered.

Then everything went black.

Angie couldn't stand it any longer. It was nearly eleven at night. Where was Paavo?

She'd left the mission that afternoon filled with news for him, anxious to see him.

With the auction the following night, she was going to be busy, starting with supervising the move of her centerpiece at nine the next morning. She hadn't even had a chance to ask Paavo if he'd be going to the auction with her. Since he was so irritated at her bag lady plan—though why *he* should be irritated when *she* was the one shot at was a mystery—their conversation had consisted of her talking to his answering machine and him talking to hers.

She'd been sure Paavo would show up at her apartment eventually, but the night had grown late without his even calling her. Finally, at eleven o'clock she called Homicide. Laurie, the night dispatcher, was already on duty.

"This is Angie Amalfi. I'm trying to locate Inspector Smith. Is he still working?"

"I'm not sure, Angie. I just came on an hour ago. Let's see." Angie was put on hold. "He's not at his desk, but there was a homicide this afternoon and he got called to it. He might still be working on it."

"I see. Thanks." She hung up the phone.

A homicide. It was rare that an inspector who wasn't on call was given a homicide to investigate, but it was known to happen, particularly when the on-call team was overwhelmed with a rash of murders. Knowing Paavo, he'd work on this new homicide all night, get a couple hours' sleep around dawn, then get up and go back to work again.

It could be days before she'd see him. So much for their big night together.

But if she could reach him, maybe she could convince him to spend at least an hour or two at the auction. If nothing else, to eat dinner. Although billed as hors d'oeuvres, the food would be good and plentiful enough to make a satisfying meal. And she'd love to have him see her angelina. She was quite proud of it.

More than that, though, she was worried about him. She wanted to see him, talk to him about the constant craziness going on at his job, about Klaw. She didn't want him to have to deal with all that alone. He was used to being alone—she understood that—but she wanted *him* to understand that he didn't need to be anymore.

She had his key, just as he had hers, to use in case of emergency. Although they didn't feel they should barge into each other's homes unannounced, it felt good to have exchanged keys. Maybe it was only a quasi commitment, but it was a commitment nonetheless.

Looking at the key reminded her of how much she had wanted to talk to him about their plans for the future. That seemed like a lifetime ago. Reverend Hodge had told her she needed patience about their future, that someday, this time of waiting and anxiety would seem to have gone by quick as a wink. If that was the case, she must have the world's slowest eyelids.

Enough moping around. She would simply go to his house and wait for him there. Surely, he'd come home eventually. On the off chance he might still stop by her apartment on his way home, she wrote a note:

> *Paavo,*
>
> *You won t believe this, but I m at YOUR house right now!! Will we ever get our act together?!? I love you*
>
> *Angie*
> *xxxOOOxxx*

There, she thought. That should make her feelings clear enough. Only a two-by-four would be less subtle.

When she arrived, Paavo's bungalow was dark and his car wasn't parked in the usual spot out in front. He didn't have a driveway or a garage since the house had been built before cars were invented. She locked the Ferrari and went inside.

The house was empty. Not even Hercules was there. Aimlessly walking around, she ran her finger over the back of the sofa that faced the fireplace and perused the book he'd been reading, the latest Clancy. The silence was eerie.

Opening the front door, she stepped out into the night fog that had settled onto the streets, making the street lamps indistinct. She called several times for the cat, even got a can of 9-Lives and a can opener and rattled the two together—a combination usually guaranteed to bring him racing home. But not tonight.

"Just be safe, Hercules," she whispered into the darkness. "You and Paavo both."

CHAPTER

T W E N T Y - E I G H T

Angie switched on the radio as soon as she woke up the next morning. It was seven A.M., time for the hourly news. She'd sat up until nearly three waiting for Paavo. Finally, she'd put on a pair of his pajamas and gone to bed, hoping he'd come in and be pleasantly surprised to find her there.

Instead, when she awoke, Hercules was curled up at her feet, but Paavo hadn't come home. She'd grown used to his working all night when it was his week for being on call. Most homicides seemed to occur in the night and evening hours. But he should have gotten a little sleep, at least. She could imagine him trying to sleep with his head on his desk instead of being here with her.

The best-laid plans, she thought with a sigh.

Since the local radio news had no reports of accidents or shoot-outs involving the police, she was able to breathe a bit easier. After making some coffee, she sat in the easy chair and phoned Homicide again. Laurie was still there. She'd be going off duty at eight, when the day shift took over. "This is Angie again. Has Paavo come in yet?"

"He hasn't checked in with me if he is. Let me buzz Homicide."

In a while she came back on the line. "Seems no one's around yet. Give them another half hour or so."

"Thanks." She hung up. She had tried to sound cheerful and carefree talking to Laurie, but right now she could scarcely breathe. Her fingers gripped the arm of her chair so tightly they ached. *It's foolish to get so worked up. He's all right. Out investigating. That's what inspectors do. Investigate.*

She took a quick shower, put on yesterday's clothes, and hurried home to change and get ready for the men who would deliver her centerpiece.

About eight-thirty, back in her own apartment, she called Homicide again. This time she got Yosh.

"Hey, there, Angie, how ya doin'?" He sounded boisterous as always. Well, if he wasn't worried . . .

"Just trying to find Paavo," she said. "He didn't go home last night. Do you know where he is?"

"He didn't? Hmm." Was that concern she heard in his voice? She pressed the receiver tighter against her ear. Was Yosh worried? "He left here after he got a call from a guy who helps him out on some cases from time to time. The guy had been hurt. Maybe Paavo took him to the hospital, decided to stay with him. We'll check around, see what we find out."

"I'd like to do some checking, too," she said. "What's the guy's name?"

"You know what? I'm not so sure. I only hear what Paavo calls him."

"What's that?"

"Snake Belly."

"Oh, dear."

Angie hung up. The thought that Paavo had gone out in the middle of the night to care for someone called Snake Belly and hadn't yet returned was not reassuring. Paavo was no Dr. Kildare. He was the take-'em-to-the-emergency-room type.

She called around to the big hospitals and asked if Inspector Paavo Smith was in the vicinity of the emergency room or the waiting area. He wasn't.

She didn't know what else to do.

She pondered calling Homicide again. She knew she was making a royal pain of herself, but this was Paavo she was worried about. Still, Yosh hadn't sounded particularly upset; nor had Laurie. Maybe she was being too protective.

Just then she heard a heavy knock on her door.

Paavo?

Her heart pounding, relief filling her, she ran to the door and pulled it open.

A huge, hulking mass of over three hundred pounds stood before her. "You want something delicate delivered. Right, lady?"

"There's something really wrong here," Angie said to Reverend Hodge when she reached him by phone. It was two P.M., and they still hadn't heard from Paavo. "No one knows where Inspector Smith is. All of Homicide's looking for him, but we can't find him! Klaw's behind it. I know he is. You can't trust him."

"What does it matter if I can trust him or not, Miss Amalfi?" Hodge replied. "I'm running my auction. It has nothing to do with Mr. Clausen or Inspector Smith."

"I'm worried. Something's going to go wrong. I know it. I feel it."

"What do you expect of me?" he cried. "You're nervous,

that's all. Me too! I'm very nervous! I'll admit it, all right?
I'll be glad when this is over."

"Maybe we need to postpone the event." The words
gushed out of her, words that had played in her mind all
morning.

"Postpone it? Are you out of your mind? We've paid
the caterers, we've collected money from twelve hundred people—thank God! And we might easily get
another three hundred showing up at the door."

"Is money all you think about? I thought you were
interested in the word of God."

"God speaks in mysterious ways. To me, he speaks
about money." She could hear his fast breathing. He
was hyperventilating again.

"Reverend, calm yourself. Look at this in an objective light."

"Objective?" he screeched. "I'll tell you about objective. I've got two truckloads of merchandise that has
been donated. I can't return it, I don't want to pay to
store it. Plus food. All those prunes and other things I
can't remember and can't pronounce that you ordered.
Forget postponing anything. You're overreacting."

"Like hell I am!"

"I think your boyfriend's dislike of Mr. Clausen has
colored your opinion of him."

"No kidding! Listen, I could tell you things about
your Mr. Clausen, and Van Warren, and even Lili
Charmaine that would make your hair curl."

"Miss Amalfi, I'm sorry. I just don't have time for
your hysterics."

"Hysterics! What hysterics? I'm telling you the
truth!"

"Miss Amalfi—Angie—get ready for the auction.
We'll have to be down there in a couple of hours to
make sure everything is set up properly. I'm counting
on you, Miss Amalfi. Go there, look at how beautiful

everything is, and I'm sure you'll be convinced, as I am, what a gem Mr. Clausen is."

"Gem? He's fool's gold, pure and simple."

Paavo opened his eyes to daylight streaming in through the warehouse windows. He pushed himself to a sitting position and nearly passed out from the effort. Slowly, all that had happened the previous night came back to him with aching clarity. He touched a throbbing spot on his head where a lump the size of a baseball had formed. His ribs and stomach hurt with each breath he took.

He looked around. Snake Belly. Where was he?

There was no sign of Snake. Not even his cell phone. Paavo reached for his gun. What was going on? Why hadn't they killed him? They said they had known he would come. That they had waited for him.

Klaw. He had to be behind the attack; nothing else made sense. Klaw wouldn't want him killed in a place like this by strangers. Klaw would want to make sure Paavo knew that *he* had been the victor in their battle.

He sat still, his eyes half shut, trying to take breaths that weren't excruciatingly painful and to let his head clear. It was hard to clear it, though, when he kept wondering what Klaw's next move was.

He'd looked for Snake at night and now the sun was up, so it had to be the next day. There was something about today . . . something special. What?

Then he remembered. The auction. And he hadn't yet been able to talk to Angie about not going to it.

Angie didn't want to look too drab compared to the items being auctioned. She selected a short, sleeveless Gianni Versace silk dress in a lemon sherbet color.

Super-high-heeled matching shoes. A diamond neck-lace and long, dangling diamond earrings.

She looked at herself in a full-length mirror and sighed. Usually, she enjoyed dressing up this way. But not knowing where Paavo was made her feel as if she were trudging through a fog thick as pea soup. Over and over throughout the morning and afternoon, she'd called his home, his pager, and Homicide. She'd managed to make Yosh and the others as nervous as she was. It didn't help them find Paavo, though.

About four-thirty, she drove to the Palace of the Legion of Honor. Rodin's *The Thinker* greeted her on the center terrace. One arm of the U-shaped building would hold the auction. Across the terrace, in the opposite arm, would be the buffet. Throughout was housed a museum.

The two trucks with goods to be auctioned were being unloaded. Hodge was probably over there with them on the auction side of the Palace. She wondered how he was going to deliver all the expensive items he'd taken personal charge of, or if they had already arrived. She wanted to see the Picasso.

Crossing the terrace to the opposite arm of the hall, she stepped into the room where the catered food would be placed. She stopped, awestruck. On the center table, in the place of honor, stood her angelina. It looked so much better in this setting than in her kitchen that she could scarcely believe she'd created it. Although grand in scale, it still managed to possess a delicate beauty. She practically tiptoed as she approached it. The movers had left it on the thick traylike sheet of clear plastic she had given them to carry it on. It might have looked better without the tray there, but it wasn't worth taking the chance of lifting it off.

She wondered if Lili would consider the angel

encased in the seamless chocolate globe another miracle. The way the idea had come to her, and then actually proved doable, did seem a bit miraculous. She wished Paavo could see it, and the thought brought back the empty, fearful ache that had been with her since last evening.

She rubbed a chill from her arms and made a silent prayer that he was well and safe and that he had a very good reason why he hadn't called anyone. She walked to the window, taking deep breaths to calm herself.

Through the side window she noticed an old brown van pulling into the back of the building, down in a service area parking lot. Since the museum was closed today and only people involved with the auction were supposed to be here, she figured the van must belong to one of the volunteers, and stood watching to see who had arrived this early to help her.

To her amazement, Klaw and Warren got out. They hurried to a back door and entered the building.

What were the two of them doing here already? They weren't needed—or wanted. Her fear that they were up to no good came back to her. She had to find out what they were planning. Everyone had worked too hard for them to ruin the auction, and if she could stop them, she would.

She carefully worked her way toward the doorway from the service area parking lot, cautiously listening for footsteps and peering around corners. The last thing she wanted to do was to burst in on them.

Since they weren't in the halls and there were a couple of offices in the back, she thought they must have gone into one of them. But why? She listened at one door. Silence. She listened at the next.

The sound of low male voices met her ears.

"We've got about an hour to take care of everything before the caterers show up," Warren said. "It's set for

eight o'clock on the nose. We'd better leave about fifteen minutes early. You can't trust anyone these days."

What's at eight o'clock? she wondered. The auction
would begin at eight-thirty. And why would Warren
care about the caterers? She pressed her ear more firmly
against the door.

"You think their timer might be off?" Klaw sounded
nervous.

Why would he be nervous about a timer? Could Klaw
be talking about the caterer and his hot foods? Every so
often a plate might need to be microwaved if it turned
too cold, but why would Klaw care?

"It won't be off by more than a couple of minutes,"
Warren said. "Five at most. They really don't want to
blow up the people who pay them. That's very bad for
repeat business."

Blow up? She heard Klaw's laughter. No, it couldn't
possibly be what it sounded like. Still, with Klaw . . .
No, not even Klaw would do something as insane as
what had just occured to her. She shouldn't be here
eavesdropping on those two, especially not with the
overactive imagination she possessed.

She started to turn away but froze at the next words
she heard.

"I'll call Smith around six," Klaw said. "I'd better be
able to reach him by then. I wanted him out of the way
for twenty-four hours, not dead. You sure they didn't
kill him?"

She made a soft, involuntary cry.

"He's tough, he'll survive. Not that it'll matter for
very long, though."

"Did you hear something?" Klaw asked.

Angie tiptoed backward down the hall. She had to
get out of there, get away. Find Paavo. Those bastards!
God, what had they done to him?

The door to the office opened. She started running,

but Warren caught her easily. He grabbed her, pulling her back against his chest. She tried to scream, but he put his hand over her mouth and nose, cutting off her air, and dragged her back into the office.

"Mr. Warren! Miss Amalfi!" Reverend Hodge cried, running toward them down the long hallway. "Whatever is going on here?"

Warren flung Angie into the office. She gripped the edge of the desk, gasping for breath.

"Reverend Hodge," Klaw said, standing at the door, "won't you join us?"

"What's going on?" Hodge cried, running into the room. "You hurt her! What's wrong with you?"

"They've got a bomb!" Angie said, backing away from Klaw and Warren. "It's set to go off at eight tonight."

Hodge blanched, his gaze gripping Klaw. "She's joking, right?"

Klaw didn't reply.

Perspiration broke out on Hodge's forehead. Desperately, he looked from Angie to Warren to Klaw. "She has it wrong, doesn't she? I mean, nobody would want to blow up the auction."

"Wouldn't they?" Klaw smoothed his jacket, tugged at his shirt cuffs. "It would be a very neat way to kill yourself, you know."

"What?" Hodge looked at them as if they were all crazy. "Kill *yourself*?"

"Not literally, of course," Klaw explained. "But everyone will think poor Mr. Clausen had been standing right next to the bomb and that's why all they could find of him was the opal ring he always wore and some teeth." He opened his mouth, hooked his finger to the right side and pulled back, exposing his gums. All the back teeth were gone, and the gums looked raw and bloody. Angie's stomach flip-flopped.

Hodge backed away, his face etched with horror. He blinked rapidly, wringing his hands. "But . . . but *why?*"

"Axel Klaw—and Clausen—had too many debts. Too many people after him. Las Vegas types who wouldn't leave him alone. He needed to die. But I, like the phoenix, will rise from the ashes and build my own little gambling empire right here in San Francisco. What name should I use, Van?"

The accountant's usually limpid features grew sickly sinister as his face spread into a half grin. "Why not Paavo Smith? He'll be dead, too."

Klaw bellowed with laughter. "That's right. Coming here to save his fair damsel in distress. He's been a thorn in my side all my life, and the only one around who'd bother to investigate thoroughly to be sure I was really dead. Can't have that, now can I? He could ruin everything."

"You could just disappear," Hodge said. "I'll tell everyone that you were here one day, and then you were gone. No one knows where."

Klaw's mouth twisted in disgust. "You don't hide from the boys in Vegas. They'll find you. The only way to stop them is to die—or have them think you're dead. This will get big press, national press. A story like this, so many deaths, blowing up this museum—they might even write about it in London. When the *New York Times* says I'm dead, everyone will believe it."

"But all those innocent people!" Angie cried.

Klaw gave her a penetrating stare. "To put it in terms you'd understand best, dear Angelina, you've got to break eggs to make an omelet." He laughed again.

"Do something, Reverend!" Angie demanded.

"Me?" Hodge squeaked.

"Him?" Klaw snorted. "He's nothing but a con man himself. I met him in Las Vegas, where he was selling retirees burial plots that had been filled for twenty years."

Angie didn't speak. She just turned to Hodge, waiting, hoping to hear him deny the accusation. She couldn't have been that wrong about everything, could she? Not Hodge, too.

"Tell her about the money from ticket sales, Hodge. How you moved it to another account. How you planned to make off with the Picasso and other valuables you were supposed to be keeping 'safe.' If you weren't so greedy and hadn't come here for last-minute ticket sales and anything else you chose to pocket, you could be in another state by now."

"Reverend Hodge?" she whispered, waiting for his denial.

"No one was supposed to get hurt, Clausen," Hodge said. "You promised."

"I lied," Klaw said briskly. "Now, although I'm finding this conversation incredibly amusing, I must get busy. We've got a lot to do. It's really too bad you showed up so early, Angie. You caused a slight wrinkle in our plans. But we've risen to the challenge. I guess Lili will have to oversee the caterers."

"I can still do that," Angie volunteered.

He grimaced. "I'm not a fool, Angelina." He aimed his gun at her. She shrank back, her hands against her mouth. "We're going to go for a little walk. If you scream, I doubt anyone will hear you since the only other people here are the men unloading the auction goods, and they're on the opposite side of the building. But if they hear you and come to investigate, I'll shoot you, and then I'll have to shoot them as well. So I suggest you keep your mouth shut."

Warren's gun was on the reverend. "Go," the accountant ordered, opening the door.

Angie and Hodge walked to the back of the hallway and down the stairs to the basement. "Right this way," Klaw said, leading them to the boiler room. It was hot and noisy, filled with steaming pipes. He glanced upward, then around the basement.

"This looks about right," he said.

Angie and Hodge glanced at each other nervously. Right for what? She didn't want to know the answer.

"First, Hodge, the key to the storage locker where the goods and money are hidden. It's at the airport, I assume?"

Hodge handed it over. "Damn you, Klaw."

"Now, Angie," Klaw said. "Your diamonds."

Her hand covered her necklace. "What about them?"

"Hand them over."

"You're going to steal my diamonds? You're a cheap thief on top of everything else?"

"Shut up and give them to me. Now!"

She unfastened her necklace and earrings. "You should be ashamed," she muttered.

Klaw's scowl deepened. After snatching the jewels from her hand, he nodded at Warren. They backed Angie and Hodge up against a cold-water pipe. Pulling their arms back around the pipe, they tied their wrists together with strong rope, binding them tightly to each other in such a way that they couldn't reach any of the knots.

"When the bomb goes off," Klaw said, "right above this spot, it'll act as a trigger. The sparks it causes will hit the gas that runs these boilers, and the whole place will blow sky-high."

He started to leave, then paused at the stairs and turned around. "I almost forgot." He took off his watch and placed it on the floor near them both. "That way you can see how much time you have left. Have a nice day!"

Paavo practically fell into his car and somehow found his way home. His vision was blurry, and what little he did see was double. The trick was to figure out which was the real lane of traffic and which was the illusion. Once home, he dialed Angie's number. When she didn't answer, he stumbled into the bathroom and took a hot shower, letting the water soothe the aches in his bones and muscles. His chest and abdomen were covered with ugly purple splotches. His jaw was bruised and puffy, and a cut over his left eye made it hard to see. Overall, though, his face wasn't nearly as bad as it could have been. He wondered if that was part of Klaw's plan, too. But why? What the hell would Klaw care about how pretty he looked before Klaw tried to kill him?

He touched his ribs gingerly and wondered if one or two were cracked. Even if they were, there wasn't anything to be done about them. He wasn't big on body casts. He leaned back against the wall of the shower, waiting until his head cleared. Finally, he got out, took a fistful of Tylenol for the pain, then called Angie again. She still wasn't home. Where was she? He should know, but he couldn't seem to think. It was too early for the auction, wasn't it? He wished his brain were working better—his head felt as fuzzy as his vision.

He called Yosh.

"Paavo, what the hell happened to you, buddy? Angie's been calling us all day, and we've been phoning all over creation!"

"I found Snake Belly, but then some guys jumped me. They did quite a number. When I woke up, the Snake was gone."

"You okay? You home or at the hospital?"

"I'm home. I'll be okay."

"You sound a little funny."

"A concussion will do that to you."

"You need a doctor."

"I'm okay, Yosh. What's going on?"

He could almost hear Yosh smile before speaking. "Listen, two pieces of good news. When the nosy neighbor we met the other day—Ruiz Buyat's neighbor—found out Buyat had been killed, he said he saw someone besides us near Buyat's house. He made a tentative ID of Van Warren."

"Great! That might be enough to scare Warren into talking about Klaw."

"Not only that. The ballistics report came in from the bullet you pulled out of the wall near the mission—the bullet from the gun Warren fired at Angie."

"And?"

"It matches the gun used to kill Patrick Devlin."

"Bingo! We can move on Warren tonight, right along with Klaw."

"Eleven o'clock, right?"

"Be there—with backups."

Whether it was Yosh's good news or time, his head was clearing rapidly. Suddenly, he remembered what had been in the back of his mind about Angie's not being home. She was overseeing the caterers—that meant she'd be going to the auction an hour or two before it started. She might already be there.

"Liar! Cheat! Scum of the earth! Garbage!"

"Miss Amalfi, that isn't the way to talk to a man of the cloth."

"Man of the cloth, my eye! How could you do it? All those people who gave you donations! All those people counting on you! And you were going to cheat them!"

"The rich ones won't care. They've got their tax deductions."

Angie tried and tried to loosen the ropes that bound her wrists, but nothing was working. Her wrists were raw, the boiler room was well over a hundred degrees, and she was steaming. In more ways than one. "Tax deductions! Is that all donations mean to you? Those people wanted something good to be done with their belongings. They gave them to *help* people. They trusted you and your worthy cause. Ha!"

"It *is* worthy!" The reverend was sobbing openly. "I wasn't going to take everything. Just the money and a few trinkets. Anyway, Mary Ellen and Sheila will be wonderful caretakers of the mission. They know what it's all about. They're organized. Besides, it keeps them off the streets."

"Just the money? I can't believe you! I can't believe any of this! I should be out looking for Paavo and instead I'm stuck here with a cheap fraud like you!"

"You're stuck with *me?* You're the one who doesn't have all her oars in the water. I don't want to be here!" He sniffled long and hard, then bawled, "I don't want to know you!"

"How dare you! None of this is my fault!"

"No? If you hadn't gone sticking your nose in places it didn't belong, we wouldn't be in this mess now."

"Right, we'd be upstairs, with no idea we were going to turn into confetti at the stroke of eight!"

"At least our last hours would have been happy ones!"

"You wretched man!" She kicked him in the leg with her very high heel.

"You struck me! If I were a Catholic priest, I could excommunicate you for that."

"It'd be worth it." She tried to kick him again, but he somehow managed to swing his leg out of her way.

"Ha! You missed!" he cried.

The next time she didn't.

•   •   •

Paavo slowly dressed to go to the auction and find Angie. Twisting, turning, and bending to put his clothes on was agony. He wrapped a bandage around his ribs, but it didn't help the pain and seemed to do little more than restrict his breathing. Earlier, when he stepped into his bedroom, he'd seen that his bed had been made and his pajamas neatly folded. When he picked up the pajamas, the scent of Fleur wafted over him, and he'd realized that she'd been here waiting for him last night. Yosh had said she'd been calling Homicide. She must have been really worried. He breathed in her perfume once more, shutting his eyes a moment. He would go to her as quickly as he could. Right now, she was probably running around with the caterers making sure everything was perfect. He smiled at the image. He knew she was going to be madder than a hornet with a smashed nest when he insisted she leave, but it couldn't be helped. A cornered Klaw could be very dangerous. He wanted her well away and safe.

The ringing of the phone interrupted his reverie.

"How are you feeling, Inspector?"

He recognized the voice. "I expect that was your little welcoming party, Klaw. Where's Snake Belly?"

"Tsk, tsk. Such a shame. Mr. Belly expired shortly after you arrived."

"Damn you, Klaw!"

"Don't damn me, I had nothing to do with it. By the way, I thought you might have missed seeing that little girlfriend of yours. She looks exceeding lovely tonight. Like an ice cream cone. Good enough to lick."

Goddamn the man! "Don't you touch her, Klaw. If you do anything to hurt her—"

"You have a completely wrong impression of me, Smith. I'm really a nice guy. I can be very nice to Angelina. I was always very nice to your sister, as she was to me. If she'd only cooperated with us, she wouldn't have died. Too bad. She was the best lay I ever had."

Paavo slammed the phone down so hard the receiver cracked in two.

CHAPTER

T W E N T Y - N I N E

Paavo threw the car into gear and roared out of the parking space in front of his house. He wanted nothing more than to get his hands around Klaw's neck and squeeze. He wouldn't let go until Klaw was not only dead, but stiff and rotting.

He turned onto California Street and blinked hard. His vision continued to fade in and out, sometimes clear, sometimes double. *Calm down,* he told himself. Angie is at the Palace of the Legion of Honor. Okay. Klaw was with her, but so were lots of other people. The caterers, the volunteers. They'd all be talking with her, watching her. Even the reverend would be there, which wasn't saying much. But Hodge wouldn't let anything happen to Angie.

As the city streets went by, though, Paavo had to wonder if Hodge or anyone else would be able to stop Klaw. He glanced at his watch. Seven-fifteen. The auction would be starting in a little more than an hour. The customers were probably already arriving. Angie would be busy greeting them, playing hostess, seeing that everyone had plenty to eat and drink so that they'd be in a good mood once the sale started.

He remembered how she'd worried and fussed about that centerpiece, about everything she was involved in for tonight's auction. He swore that if Klaw did anything to hurt her, he'd kill him, plain and simple.

He made a right turn onto Lincoln Drive. The road headed upward, first through a golf course, and then, as the hill became steeper, through groves of redwoods. At the very top of the hill was a large paved parking lot, and in the southern corner, backing into the trees, was the beautiful Palace.

He was only minutes away from it, minutes away from facing Klaw, from the confrontation the two had been heading toward for twenty years.

He pulled over to the side of the road. Since Klaw had returned to the city, he'd done nothing but taunt Paavo, with actions and accusations. And today he'd called about Angie and made threats against her, making sure Paavo would show up at the auction. Now he knew why those goons hadn't bruised his face. Klaw had planned this, too.

He started the engine again and continued the drive onto Lincoln Parkway. Cars filled most of the lot. He parked at the far edge and picked up his cellular phone.

"Help! Help!"

"I thought women knew how to scream."

"I *am* screaming, you two-bit charlatan! I'm hoarse from screaming, if you must know."

"We've got to get out of here," he cried.

"Don't start crying again. Tug at the ropes. They've got to loosen sometime."

"They're not! My wrists hurt. My arms hurt. My feet

hurt! Call for help, Miss Amalfi, please! I'm so tired of this."

"Help! Help!"

"It's not loud enough! Can't you do anything right?"

"I'll show you what I can do right!"

"Ouch!"

Paavo scanned the crowd of San Francisco's monied elite. Dresses that cost as much as a month or more of his salary, diamonds, and pearls adorned the assembled. He had spent some time quietly milling among the patrons, trying to find Angie or the reverend. To stand and walk without limping took concentration, and even then at times he needed to steady himself against a wall or chair when waves of pain struck.

Early on, he'd spotted Klaw huddled in a corner with Van Warren, and ducked out of their sight. A little later he found Lili and spoke with her.

He circled back to Klaw. As he approached, Klaw looked his way, as if each of them could sense the other's presence. "What did you do with her?" Paavo asked.

Klaw's gaze held his, each of them silently measuring the other. "The good inspector," Klaw said finally. "I didn't expect this. Come along. I'll take you to her." He left the great hall and headed down a long hallway. Paavo gave a little shake of his head, trying to will his sight to clear, the constant burning in his ribs to ease.

At the end of the hall, Klaw opened the door to an office and waited for Paavo to enter first.

The room was empty. Paavo turned a questioning look on Klaw.

"She's not far," Klaw said.

Warren stepped behind Paavo. "I'll take your gun now, Smith."

Paavo glanced over his shoulder at Warren. Warren was holding a .44 Magnum on him.

Klaw laughed. "I can't believe it was this easy. I thought you were a lot smarter, Smith."

"Do you plan to shoot me with all those people down the hall?"

"You think they're going to save you?" Klaw demanded.

"I don't know that it matters."

"Oh, ho, pretty cool, Smith." Klaw's face twisted into pure hate. "You won't be so cool when Warren pulls the trigger. Put the gun on the table."

Paavo removed it from his shoulder holster and set it down. "If you wanted to shoot me in the back, Klaw, you could have done it time and time again over these past few weeks," Paavo said. "You want more than that. A lot more, I think."

"Very insightful of you. Yes, one of the things I'm going to enjoy is for you to sweat out your death. Yours and that of the meddling little creature you screw around with. I'm going to enjoy watching you beg me for her life, if not for your own."

Paavo's gaze was hooded, his eyes cold, dark, detached. "Klaw," he said with an air of nonchalance, "you sound like a nineteen-forties B movie. All talk. Where's Angie?"

Klaw's face turned deep red, and the suave facade was gone. The hoodlum, the bully, the killer—they were all there in his mad, glowing eyes. "We'll see how long you're bored, Smith. We'll see how long before you come crying to me to spare you both. You said you wanted to see her? Right this way."

They led him down to the basement. Klaw opened the door, and Paavo walked into the sweltering heat of the boiler room.

"Paavo," Angie cried, her voice raw and desperate.

It took all his self-control not to lunge at Klaw's throat at the sight of her, her eyes wide and frightened, her arms pulled back and tied to a heavy pipe.

Hodge was with her, looking even more frightened, and tied the same way. He squeaked out in abject misery, "Oh, no! Not you, too!"

Klaw held the gun as Warren pulled Paavo's arms back around a pipe a few feet away from the other two. Warren tied his arms tightly, then, as he walked away, gave a sharp elbow jab to Paavo's ribs. Paavo bit down hard on his lip, doing his best not to show the pain he was in, not to black out from it. He saw Angie flinch, her tearful gaze meeting his with sympathy and love.

"This should give you something to talk about," Klaw said. "See the wristwatch on the floor? When it reaches eight o'clock, a bomb will go off. A bomb located right above this area. When it explodes, the floor will collapse on top of you. It may kill you immediately, but if not, when the fire hits the gas in the boiler, it'll blow up the building, and you right along with it."

"It's a coward's trick, Klaw." Paavo's head lolled back against the pipe, perspiration on his brow from the blow to his ribs, but his gaze was deadly, his eyes burning into Klaw. "Blowing up a building filled with innocent people. If you want to move against me, let's do it. Set the others free."

Klaw smirked. "You, my good inspector, are but an added highlight to my plan, not nearly the heart of it. I'll have to be content thinking about you watching the minutes tick by and knowing that no one can save you or your pretty girlfriend. I'll think of how you'll feel at that last moment when the bomb goes off, before the shock wave and fire hit." He smiled malevolently. "It's a thought that will warm my heart for years to come. It's been a pleasure, Smith."

Smiling cheerfully, Klaw and Warren left the room.

"Paavo," Angie cried, "what did they do to you? You're hurt."

"Who cares if he's hurt?" Hodge shouted. "I was counting on him to get us out of here!"

Paavo glared at the door, his hatred pulsating in his ears, throughout his very being. It took him a moment before he even heard Angie's question. "I'm fine. It's you—"

"I looked all over for you," she said. "God, I should have warned you not to come here! I should have stayed away! I should have listened to you! I'm such an idiot!"

"That's no news bulletin," Hodge muttered.

"Do I have to listen to your insults at a time like this?" Angie said through gritted teeth.

"*He's* the one you should yell at, not me! He knew Klaw was no good." Hodge turned to Paavo. "How could you let him lead you down here?"

"Paavo knew it was a trap," Angie said, her gaze never leaving Paavo's face. Her next words were for him. "But you had to find us, didn't you? You let him take you. . . ." Tears filled her eyes and she couldn't say any more.

"Fat lot of good that does us," Hodge muttered. "Now three of us get blown to smithereens, instead of only two!"

"I didn't know what he'd done to you," Paavo said. His eyes caressed her, and she would never again doubt his feelings for her. "Did he hurt you?"

"No. He took my necklace and earrings. Nothing more," she said. "I love you so much, Paavo."

"Stop with the mush already!" Hodge yelled. "Who gives a flying you-know-what, which I'd say if I weren't a man of God. I want out of here." He wriggled and squirmed against his bonds.

"You shut your mouth!" Angie ordered. "This so-called reverend, Paavo, is nothing but a snake in the grass. A cheap con man. He was going to steal the auction's money."

"There would still be enough left for Mary Ellen and Sheila to do good deeds."

"So you're only a bit of a thief? That's sort of like being just a little bit pregnant. You ... you cut-rate Billy Sunday!"

"Look who's talking. A worker at McDonald's knows more about cooking than you do!"

"Fred Flintstone could give a better sermon than you!"

"You sausage-stuffing succotash slinger!"

"You prayer-plying prig poacher!"

"Stop it, both of you!" Paavo commanded. "Now!"

Angie and Hodge clamped their mouths shut and gawked at him.

"We'll figure out how to get ourselves and everyone else out of here," he said quietly. "But you both need to calm down."

"How can I be calm when you're in danger because of me?" Angie said.

"It's not your fault, Angie. I knew exactly what I was doing."

She began to cry in earnest.

He hated seeing her cry. "Don't, Angie, please."

"For once the cop's right!" Hodge said petulantly. "First I'm in danger of being blown up, now I'm in danger of drowning."

At that moment they heard the click of the basement door. Then it slowly began to open.

"Ladies and gentlemen." Axel Klaw jumped onto the platform and took the microphone, his coloring high. "Last call for hors d'oeuvres. The big auction starts in about forty-five minutes. It'll be all you ever hoped for—and more! Fireworks! Action!" He held his arms upward. "Eat, drink, and be merry," he shouted, "for tomorrow you might be dead!"

Everyone laughed. Klaw stepped off the platform and whirled around until he spotted Van Warren in the corner. Warren gave him a thumbs-up. Klaw punched the sky.

Too bad he hadn't gone into acting—or politics. He sure could work a room. He was a regular David Letterman.

He looked at his watch. Too bad there was so little time left. If there'd been more, he might have tried a routine or two.

CHAPTER

T H I R T Y

Klaw stood with Warren beside a pillar. "It's almost seven-forty," Klaw said. "We'll say we're going backstage now to get ready for the auction. People are asking where Hodge is, damn it. I'm telling them he was delayed trying to find shelter for a widow and her three kids. These Goody Two-shoes eat up that kind of crap."

"We need to get out in five minutes or less," Warren reminded him.

"Don't you think I know that? Where's Lili, anyway?"

"Last time I saw her, she was talking to some rich guy from Silicon Valley. Maybe she wants a job in high tech."

Klaw frowned. "Or maybe she thought he said silicone. She's starting to sag."

"Did you tell her to meet us out by your van?"

"Hell, no. She's more trouble than she's worth. It's you and me, Warren."

"Oh, Mr. Clausen." Mary Ellen Hitchcock hurried up to him and placed her hand on his arm, smiling prettily. "Isn't this a lovely turnout? Everything looks so beautiful. I can't understand where Reverend Hodge is, though."

Klaw stepped back from her. He never could stand the cherubic, chatty type. "The reverend was delayed, Mary Ellen. He'll make the start, though, don't worry."

"But even Angie Amalfi is late," Mary Ellen continued, puzzled. "I thought for sure she'd be here to listen to people ooh and aah over her centerpiece. It's simply exquisite! Everybody's talking about it, trying to figure out how she got that big angel inside the lattice ball. They're trying to find seams, or spots where she tried to fudge—so to speak—by melting chocolate back together, and they can't."

Klaw glanced furiously at Warren.

"Excuse me, Mary Ellen," Warren said, taking her arm and turning her quickly from Klaw's side. "Why don't you and I check on the caterers, since Miss Amalfi isn't here?"

"Why, I didn't know you were interested in food, Mr. Warren."

"I'm interested in a lot of things, Mary Ellen. Call me Van."

"You're, like, all tied up!" Lili cried. "This is totally mind-blowing."

"Untie me, quick!" Angie screeched.

"Thank God! A miracle!" Reverend Hodge cried.

"Lili, you're wonderful," Paavo said calmly. "You did everything exactly right."

"I watched and waited, just like you said." She ran over to him. Then she smiled. "Wait till you see. This is too unreal." Pulling a switchblade out of her purse, she

cut the ropes binding his hands. "A girl's got to protect
herself. Some guys are such retards. Show them this
knife, though, their behavior turns all sublime fast."

"I'll bet it does," Paavo said. He took the knife and
freed Angie and Hodge.

"We've got to get out of here," Angie cried. "That
bomb will go off in about fifteen minutes."

"As if!" Lili said, looking from one to the other. "No
joke?"

"Lili, there's one more thing I need you to do for
me," Paavo said. "Will you do it?" He took the notebook that he used to take notes at crime scenes from his
breast pocket, ripped off a sheet, and started writing.

"Name it." Lili leaned close to him as he wrote.
"Just like this time. I waited until it was all clear, then
came in. I was way good, right?"

"Totally good, Lili. Now, out at the gate is a police
inspector named Yosh. Take this note to Yosh—it tells
him there's a bomb set for eight o'clock. He's got to
clear the place right now."

"Yosh." She nodded. "Got it."

He took hold of her arms and looked her straight in
the eye. "After that, get far from the building and hide
until it's safe to come out. And keep away from Klaw.
He wasn't going to warn you about the bomb."

Her fury grew slowly, filling her face, as his words
penetrated. "My God! That dirtbag! After all I've done,
riding goddamn smelly buses and crowded BART
trains. I am so totally pissed—"

"Take the back exit," Paavo interrupted. "Now go!"

She ran like a woman possessed.

Paavo, Hodge, and Angie took a deep breath, then
ran up to the main hall. Klaw stared in shock as the
three of them burst into the room. Hodge grabbed the
microphone.

"Ladies and gentlemen, may I have your attention?

We've just received word that someone may have planted a bomb in this hall. We need to clear the premises right now. Proceed out to the far end of the parking lot." People began screaming. "Stay calm, and walk!" Hodge ordered. "There's no immediate danger. We simply need to ask all of you to leave quickly."

Ignoring him, the crowd pushed and shoved, rushing toward the exit. Almost immediately, uniformed policemen appeared and began shepherding people out of the hall.

"Hurry, Angie!" Paavo turned her toward the door. She started to run along with everyone else. Paavo didn't follow. He scanned the crowd for Klaw, spotting him finally on the opposite side of the room, heading for the east exit. He started after him.

"Hold it right there, Smith." Van Warren stepped up behind him, his gun steady on Paavo's back. Klaw reached the back of the crowd that was squeezing through the side exit and began to knock people out of the way to get through. He was about to escape. Paavo whirled on Warren and jammed his elbow into the arm that held the gun. Then grabbing the arm, he raised his own knee and slammed the arm down on it with all the force he could manage. The bone cracked.

Warren shrieked and dropped to his knees. Paavo hit him in the jaw, stepping into the punch with all his strength. Warren skidded across the highly waxed floor, out cold.

Paavo clutched his side, trying to breathe and focus despite the pain, and hurried as best he could toward the door Klaw had used. But Klaw was no longer in sight.

"Hold it!" Angie grabbed Hodge's arm just as he made it out the doorway. "We've got to try to find the bomb.

There are people all over the building. They'll be killed."

"That's their tough luck!" Hodge tried to pull his arm free.

"We can try to find it," she said, "and get it out of here."

"You can, maybe. I don't even know what a bomb looks like."

"I do. I once had one in my dishwasher."

"Why doesn't that surprise me?"

"Anyway, I was in the room before the caterers set it up. I know what they brought with them. Anything else has to be the bomb."

"That's why I'm out of here!" He slipped away from her hold.

"Reverend!" She caught his coattails. "Stop! It's thirteen minutes to eight. We can spend five minutes searching and still get out in plenty of time. We've got to try."

"What if it's with the donations? We'll never find it."

"The donations are all the way across the terrace. Klaw put us under *this* hall, saying the floor would come down on us. The bomb's got to be here."

"Maybe. But Klaw's insane. Who can trust an insane man?"

"There's no insanity in his self-preservation," Angie said. "We can do it, Reverend."

Hodge's shoulders slumped. "You're right. People will die and it'll be all my fault." Hodge straightened his jacket with dignity. "Let's search."

"I'll check around the food and under the tables," Angie said. "You look in garbage cans, in corners, under chairs. Whatever." She ran over to where the food had been set up. There were a number of chafing dishes for the hot hors d'oeuvres, with stands rigged to pump gas to the flames under the dishes. She was almost positive that she'd find the bomb in that area. An explosive side by side with canisters of gas—that was a great way to create maximum damage.

But she didn't see a single object that seemed out of place or even resembled a bomb. Not that she was sure what a bomb would look like, despite what had happened to her dishwasher, but it was most likely bulky with lots of wires and some tubes or pipes or dynamite—in other words, weird and dangerous-looking.

She hurried over to the long table where her angelina sat and lifted the skirt. She saw another tablecloth. Lifting it slightly, she saw that it covered a huge wooden box—over six feet long.

"Reverend! What's this?"

He ran to her side. She tried to pull the box out into the open, but it was too heavy. She motioned to Hodge to take the far end of the table. They easily slid it out of the way.

Angie lifted the tablecloth off the box, fully expecting to see something that looked like a bomb inside.

Instead, she screamed.

So did Hodge.

The two clutched each other and looked down at a young, very dead African-American man. On his finger was Axel Klaw's opal ring. Against her will, Angie's gaze lifted to his mouth. It was puckered and shrunken as if he had no teeth.

Except, maybe, Axel Klaw's.

"Oh, God!" Angie spun around, and the world kept spinning. Bile rose in her throat.

"Let's get out of here!" Hodge cried.

"Right." She took a deep breath, then stumbled toward the centerpiece. "I'm taking my angelina with me." She tried to pick up the plastic tray. It was heavy. Very heavy. *Too* heavy.

"Reverend!" she cried. "My angelina!"

"Let's go."

"I think the bomb is in it. It wasn't this heavy before."

"Isn't it solid chocolate?"

"It's light, airy fudge. And the base is a wooden box I turned upside down. A bomb could fit in there—I think."

"Lift off the chocolate and let's see. *Wait!* On second thought, what if that triggers the bomb?"

"Let's carry the whole thing out of the building," Angie said. "We can take it out back by the trees."

"There's no time!"

She checked her watch. "Eight minutes. We've got to."

He gritted his teeth. "You just won't listen, will you? Grab one end. We haven't got all day!"

They each picked up a corner of the plastic the angelina sat on, and they started running out of the building. They went out the back, away from the parking lot and the public. Reverend Hodge's face turned red, and he was breathing hard.

Angie urged him on. They were outside the building. The hillside fell away, and off in the distance was the ocean. A narrow walkway with some stairs led to a service area with a small parking facility. Beyond was Lincoln Park. "To the trees," Angie said. Hodge was wheezing, perspiration dripping from his forehead. When they reached the few steps that led down from the outside walkway to the service area, he was trying to blink away the perspiration and hold on to the angelina with sweaty palms. He tripped.

"Don't!" Angie screamed. She held the board tight, afraid that if it fell and hit the ground, that might trigger the bomb. She locked her knees, trying to hold the whole thing up herself and somehow steady the reverend, who was wobbling wildly. He, too, was afraid to let go of the angelina. As he gyrated, trying not to fall,

he pulled her forward. She stepped down hard, still trying to brace herself, and stepped right off the walkway
and onto the hillside, about twelve inches below the
pavement. Her high heel hit, then broke off, her foot
twisting in one direction while the rest of her twisted in
the other. The pain that shot through her ankle was so
great that for a moment she thought the bomb had
exploded.

She cried out as she went down, the reverend right
behind her, but somehow they managed to keep
the chocolate from bouncing onto the ground. The
globe cracked but didn't shatter. The angel remained
intact.

"Oh, God, Angie," Hodge said, "are you all right?"

"I don't know," she replied, her voice small and
shaky.

"We've got to get up." He was panting hard, almost
wheezing. "It's three minutes before eight. Come on,
Angie. We've got to get this thing away from us."

She tried to stand, to put some weight on her foot,
but the pain made the world sway.

Paavo searched the crowd for Klaw. It was pandemo-
nium. After Paavo had called for immediate backup,
Yosh had brought the detail they'd planned to bring
later that night, at eleven o'clock. Paavo hadn't been
sure exactly what might happen, but he'd been certain
something was going to—and well before eleven
o'clock. He'd been right. Now patrol cars and officers
swarmed over the grounds. Some people had gotten
into their cars and pulled out of the parking spaces into
the driving lanes. Everyone wanted to go in different
directions, and the result was gridlock. Horns honked
and tempers flared.

The pedestrians weren't any better. They shoved

each other, fists swinging, as they all tried to run as far from the Palace of the Legion of Honor as they could.

Paavo wiped his forehead, blinking hard, searching among the blurry figures for Klaw or his black Lincoln. He scanned the crowd for Angie and couldn't find her either. Nor did he see the reverend. But Angie was small; she could easily have been swallowed up by the huge crowd. She must have gotten out. He'd seen her and the reverend heading toward the exit when he went after Van Warren. There was no need to worry.

He spotted Lili having an animated conversation with a young policeman. She looked fine, but where were the others?

At the edge of the lot, in the distance, he saw a light blur—a *blond* blur—down the hill among the trees on the ocean side of the grounds. Could it be Klaw? He peered hard, desperately. The stature, the stance. It was him.

Klaw must have circled around, trying to stay out of sight, and was now heading through the trees to the back side of the Palace of the Legion of Honor.

Paavo ducked to the side of the Palace. From there, he could see a van parked in a small area probably used by janitors, gardeners, and other service people. The van must be Klaw's. That was probably why he didn't see Klaw's black Lincoln in the regular parking lot. He and Klaw were about equally distant from the van, but he could go downhill to reach it, while Klaw had to go up. He had the advantage.

If he could somehow keep himself hidden until the last minute, he'd reach Klaw, face him, and—if their struggle came to that—gladly kill him. Kill him for what he'd planned to do to Angie, to all the innocent people here. For Snake Belly, for Jessica . . . for himself.

He was only minutes away from it, minutes from the

confrontation he and Klaw had been hurtling toward ever since Klaw returned to the city.

Klaw had played him like a fish on a line, purposely baiting him with one incident after the other, watching him twist and fight, trying to break free but, with each new yank on the hook, finding the point deeper and tighter. He'd watched his job, his life, grow more precarious with each day.

He loathed Klaw and wanted nothing but revenge against him. He'd lived with rage against Klaw for twenty years, thinking he'd buried it deep, when all that had happened was that he'd grown a thick skin over it, while inside the rage festered, wanting to erupt.

He darted to a huge Grecian-looking pillar and ducked behind it. From there, he ran to the next pillar. That was when he saw Angie sitting on the ground, holding her foot and rocking in pain. The reverend was staggering toward a Dumpster at the back of the service area, carrying Angie's chocolate angel. *What the hell?*

The centerpiece. A thought struck him.

They couldn't have found the bomb. They wouldn't have tried ... but why else would they be here? Why else ...

On his left were Angie and Hodge. On his right, Klaw was climbing the hill, every moment closer to the truck, to his escape. He had to stop him! To avenge so many ...

Once, Angie had told him he was obsessed with Klaw, that he was too personally involved, too emotional about the man, and that he couldn't see past his need for revenge. He had tried to deny it, but had she been right?

His hatred had swathed him like a heavy mist, coating and blurring everything around him. Suddenly, that mist seemed to shift, then lift. For the first time since this madness began with the phone number in the dead man's mouth, he saw all that was going on with clear eyes.

"Put it down, Reverend," Angie cried, tears of worry but also admiration filling her eyes. "You're not supposed to be a brave man! Come back here. There's not enough time!"

But Reverend Hodge tottered slowly toward the Dumpster, carrying the big angel alone.

Suddenly a figure sped toward him. Paavo grabbed the angelina from Hodge's hands. Hodge spun around, faced her, and winked.

"No!" she screamed as she took in the full horror of the scene. "Paavo! No! It's too late. Get away from it!"

She hobbled up on one foot, scarcely feeling the pain as she watched in horrified silence. From the corner of her eye she noticed Klaw reach the service lot, racing toward his van.

Paavo eased the angelina into the Dumpster and lifted the heavy lid shut. He doubled over, holding his ribs, his face etched in pain.

"Run, please!" she cried. "Paavo!"

He got up and reeled, swaying, in her direction. "Go on!" he called.

Doing as ordered, she stumbled, hopped, and crawled in her panicky effort to get as far from the bomb as possible.

Paavo would help her. He'd reach her soon and they'd be safe. Her tears fell from the pain and worry, her heart pounding. Where was Paavo? She wasn't moving that fast. Where—

Just then, the bomb exploded.

•   •   •

When the roaring sound died down, Angie was lying facedown in the dirt, not even sure how she had gotten there. Her whole body ached and she had the feeling she was not where she'd stood a moment ago. Silence met her. She lifted her head and looked at the debris around her, the burned-out metal from the Dumpster.

Paavo!

She turned quickly, and relief washed over her. Only a couple of feet away, he was struggling to sit up, holding his sore ribs, but otherwise he seemed to be all right. *Thank God*, she whispered.

She glanced over at Klaw.

He lay on the ground, his eyes open, his head twisted at an unnatural angle. Beside him lay the Dumpster's heavy metal lid.

CHAPTER

THIRTY-ONE

Angie and Paavo sat on a bench along the walkway that ran to the service area where Axel Klaw had come to his eternal reward.

Blobs of melted and incinerated chocolate, ash, grass stains, mud, and bits of garbage that Angie didn't even want to think about were splattered all over her. One shoe was in her lap, and her face was streaked with mud and chocolate. She had Paavo's jacket over her shoulders and sat huddled in it, trying not to think about the ugly scene that had just played out before her, or the horror that might have been. She shivered.

Paavo sat beside her. He too was sprinkled with chocolate, food remnants, ash, and mud. His hair stood straight up and was a little singed on the ends from the blast, and his face was covered with dirt. He put his arm around her and she laid her head on his shoulder.

Policemen, firemen, and paramedics covered the grounds. A paramedic came by to check on Angie's ankle, but she shooed him away. It was already a little better, but more important, she didn't want to do anything but sit beside Paavo and enjoy the fact that he was with her and he was safe.

Yosh came by and stood in front of the two of them. "Hey there, Angie," he said. "Boy, when you throw a party, it's a real blast."

"Send him home, Paavo," she said.

"Do you need me down there?" Paavo asked, gesturing to the area where Klaw's body was being examined by someone from the coroner's office.

"Heck, no. You shouldn't be anywhere but in the hospital. You're a mess, partner."

"Thanks loads."

"Angie, too." He studied her. "Say, I see you aren't wearing earrings. Klaw didn't take your jewelry by any chance, did he?"

"He did." Angie covered her earlobes. She hated going around with the holes showing; it was so tacky. "They were diamonds. A necklace, too."

"We found them on Klaw. I'll see that they're returned."

"Good." Paavo glanced at her with a nod, then back at Yosh. "What else is going on?"

"The coroner says it's the damnedest thing he's ever seen," Yosh said.

"What is?"

"The explosion. The Dumpster. He said he can't understand how the explosion caused the lid to fly *sideways* and all the way over to where Klaw was standing. He said if it had flown anywhere at all, it should have flown backward."

Paavo glanced at the dead man and frowned. "Divine justice?"

"Works for me," Yosh said.

"Whatever caused it," Angie said, giving Paavo's hand a squeeze, "I'm glad it happened." Despite being bruised and battered, he looked at peace for the first time in weeks.

"I'll go see if Sergeant Meade needs any more help." Yosh scanned the area as he spoke. "We found Warren inside and arrested him. Also found Snake Belly's body. If you see the reverend, let me know. No one has any idea where he is."

"Sure," Paavo said.

Yosh wandered away.

"How could the reverend have gotten away so fast?" Angie asked. "I thought he was lying on the ground right after the bomb blast. Wasn't he?"

"I thought so, too," Paavo said. "But when I looked up, he had gone. There was something on the ground. I guess he dropped it."

He reached into his coat pocket, the coat she had around her shoulders. From it he pulled the very old angel she had seen in Hodge's office. The one given to him by the holy man in Galilee.

Reverently, she took the angel. Memories of some of the talks in Hodge's office came back to her, especially his advice about her future with Paavo, about patience and believing in oneself—advice she hoped to follow. As she held the ancient carving in her hand, its paint worn and rubbed away in part, she remembered the strange wink he'd given her—the wink after Paavo had put aside his need for revenge and helped them instead. By doing that, Paavo had been spared an encounter with Klaw.

Yet Klaw was dead.

The lid had flown off the Dumpster sideways.

Could the reverend . . . ? Naw.

Hodge was just a con man. Wasn't he?

"We'll find Hodge," Paavo said, "and get back the goods and money he took from the mission."

She looked up at him and realized that if he and

Klaw had fought, even if Paavo had won, his life would have been changed forever. And if he'd lost ... The thought made her blood cold. "Klaw took the reverend's key to a locker at the airport," she said softly. "I'm sure Reverend Hodge put everything there for no reason other than to keep it safe. I imagine the other volunteers would tell you that as well."

His gaze captured hers and held it a long moment. "Is that how all of you feel about the reverend?"

"He helped everyone, Paavo. And carrying the bomb toward the Dumpster ... that was very brave."

"It was."

"He was a help to many of us," she said softly.

"True. He inspired you to come up with a terrific angelina," Paavo said. "I heard people talking about it. You'll be able to get your business up and running in no time."

She shook her head. "Forget it."

"What?"

"This is the second time in a week I've been covered with chocolate. I never want to see the wretched stuff again as long as I live."

"You've changed your mind about becoming a chocolatier?"

"Fat-free is the new craze. Maybe I need to think along those lines." She looked at her ruined clothes, the chocolate and mud all over her. "It couldn't be any worse to deal with."

Paavo lifted a glob of chocolate off his sleeve and shook it off his fingers onto the ground. "That's for sure."

She smiled. "Look at us. The chocolate couple."

"It gives a whole new meaning to the line 'You are what you eat,'" he said.

She laughed. "We could be escapees from an Easter basket ... or maybe a wedding cake."

Silence.

She chuckled at his sudden awkwardness.

He cleared his throat. "Time to get that ankle some attention," he said, taking her shoe from her lap and helping her up. She wrapped her arm around him, taking care not to hurt his ribs, just as he tried to give her enough support to walk. "Let's go home, Cinderella."

She held Hodge's angel out to him. "I want you to take this, Paavo. It's very old and very special. Keep it as a reminder of Reverend Hodge, of whoever or whatever he was, and of the divine justice that helped end this horrible episode in your life. He'll always be dear to me for that."

As he took the angel his eye caught the bottom of the carving and the words that were written there. He looked at the glow in her eyes, the wonder on her face, and quickly put the angel in his pocket.

"If that's what you believe, Angie, then nothing else matters."

She lifted her chin and smiled up at him. "I do."

Supporting each other, they hobbled toward his car. As they went, his lips curved ever so slightly upward with secret knowledge of the words on the underside of the angel. A secret he'd never reveal.

MADE IN TAIWAN.

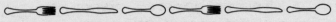

With a pinch of pernicious and a dash of dastardly,

JOANNE PENCE

**cooks up a scrumptious banquet of murderous fun
in the Angie Amalfi mysteries**

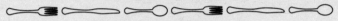

RED HOT MURDER

0-06-075805-8/$6.99 US/$9.99 Can

Suddenly Angie's tasty getaway to Arizona with her fiance is
starting to look more and more like her last meal.

COURTING DISASTER

0-06-050291-6/$6.99 US/$9.99 Can

There's already too much on the
bride-to-be's plate . . .
and much of it is murderous.

TWO COOKS A-KILLING

0-06-009216-5/$6.99 US/$9.99 Can

Nothing could drag Angie away from San Francisco—except
for a job preparing the banquet for her all-time favorite soap
opera characters during a Christmas Reunion Special.

IF COOKS COULD KILL

0-06-054821-5/$6.99 US/$9.99 Can

When Angie's friend Connie Rogers' would-be boyfriend
is sought by the police in connection with a brutal
robbery/homicide, the two friends set out to find the real killer.

BELL, COOK, AND CANDLE

0-06-103084-8/$6.99 US/$9.99 Can

When Angie is called upon to deliver a humorous confection
to an after-hours goth club, she finds herself
up to her neck in the demonic business.